The Medici Diamonds-Book One

Diamonds for the Devil

Nickie Fleming

ISBN: 978-1-936403-31-8

Credits

Cover Artist: Genene Valleau

Editor: Ashley Young

Printed in the United States of America

Dedication

In loving memory of my parents and grandparents, who passed their passion for books on to me.

1703
One-Faubourg St. Germain, Paris

Late at night, on a deserted street, animals and people were deep asleep. Nothing moved--or almost nothing.

The mansion stood somewhat apart from the others and had a big, surrounding garden. The building looked deserted, which made it an ideal place for a break-in.

Jaquot dropped the piece of metal he used to pry open a lock. "*Merde!*" he hissed, because the metal made a clanging noise as it landed on the cobbles.

"Don't get nervous, *mon ami*," said Louison, his companion.

Jaquot picked up the metal and continued on the lock. This one soon opened, and the two men slid inside the hall of the house. They were members of a gang of thieves who operated out of the Quartier Saint-Denis. They had received a tip that this house was well worth their visit.

"Where to?" whispered Louison, as Jaquot was the one who took the decisions.

"Nothing down here," answered Jaquot in equally hushed tones. "All the valuables are upstairs." He lit his lantern. Its narrow beam was just enough light to see where they were going.

The two men sneaked up the stairs and soon found themselves on the first floor. There they opened each door they passed. A few valuables, like an expensive clock and some silver candlesticks, disappeared in the leather bag they had brought along.

Next they entered a bedroom. A whiff of perfume filled the air, as if the room had been occupied not long before.

"Thought no-one lived here," said Louison.

Jaquot's light beam wandered through the room. All of a sudden, the ray reflected on something. Louison advanced to have a better look and soon held up a diamond necklace, which even in this dark room sparkled. "Our boss will be pleased," he said to his mate. At the exact moment he turned to inspect other parts of the room, he stumbled.

"You're getting older, *mon ami*," chuckled Jaquot. "Your eyes are not sharp anymore."

Louison did not answer--which was unusual for him. He kept staring at the ground.

Growing a bit worried, Jaquot hastened to his side. "What's the matter?"

His mate did not answer, only pointed to what was lying before him-- the stiffened body of a young woman.

In life, this woman had been a beauty. The silk nightgown she wore did little to conceal the luscious curves of her body. Now the face was distorted in pain and the open eyes reflected some of the agony the woman had suffered before death released her.

Jaquot moved the beam of his lantern a little. Next to the woman's outstretched arm lay a broken wineglass. He kneeled down and held his nose to the remainder of the liquid it had held. "Poison!" was his verdict. "Come on, *mon ami*, we're out of here!"

"Do you know who she is?" whispered Louison.

"No, and I don't care. I just know we have to be gone--I don't want anything to do with filthy murder!"

The two thieves hastened down the stairs without further notice to the other valuables in the house. Soon they disappeared in the blackness of the night.

Two
Same Location

Exactly one hour after the burglars left, other men entered the house. These were not so careful. They lighted dozens of candles and began a search of the premises. Every nook and corner was looked at, and one of the men explored the corpse with rough hands.

"Nothing," he reported to the one who was their commander.

"*Merde,*" was this one's reaction. "You'll hear the master. He was already in a foul mood and now…"

He slammed the door of the bedroom behind him and went in search of the man who paid them. Their master waited in the drawing-room. He held a riding crop in his hand and ticked the sides of his boots impatiently. His entire posture and attitude told that he was an aristocrat.

"Anything to report?" he asked, his voice sharp and cold.

"It is gone, Monsieur."

"What?"

Lesser men than Gaillard would have shrunk at this icy question. Gaillard knew the man and was not afraid of him.

"We searched everywhere, Monsieur. It has truly disappeared."

The whip lashed out and a china vase fell into pieces.

"The bitch! I've underestimated her."

"Monsieur, perhaps all is not lost," Gaillard dared to remark. "We shall return tomorrow and look for it once more."

"Good," the nobleman agreed. "Let's continue with the plan as it is. One day, I know I'll have that necklace back--no matter the means I'll have to use."

"It must be here in the house," said Gaillard. "We had her watched, as you ordered. She went out yesterday but still wore the necklace when she returned."

"Do as is said. I gave you instructions as how to dispose of the body, right?"

"You did, Monsieur."

"Then I bid you farewell. I've accepted the Regent's invitation for the hunt in Versailles."

Three
Quartier Saint-Denis, Paris

Le Chat Gris--an obscure inn in a shadowy street, not far away from the Pont Neuf. Here all the members of Scarron's gang came together to hand over their loot and get their reward in return.

Finally, Jaquot and Louison appeared before the table on which all the valuables were placed. Louison put down the necklace while Jaquot handed over the clock and the silverware.

Scarron--a big fellow who was the undisputed leader because he was the toughest of all the men--picked up the necklace. His eyes began to gleam.

"Beautiful stones, *mon ami*," he said. "Marcel, give these two fellows the purse Alain brought in."

"I don't want the money," Louison said.

Scarron's interest in the necklace grew by the minute. His speculative glance shot from Louison to Jaquot. He could see they were not quite themselves. What was the matter?

"And you," he asked Jaquot. "Will you accept the reward?"

"No."

"Why?"

"We have a bad feeling about these diamonds," Jaquot explained.

Scarron's hand came down on the table and he gave way to a roar of laughter, which was joined in by all the others. "That's a new one," he hiccupped. "Well, as you wish. I think I'm going to hang on to these stones for a while."

"Can I have them, *chéri?*"

The little gypsy girl, sensually balancing on the armrest of his chair, put out her brown hand to caress the diamonds.

Scarron rudely pushed her hand away. "No. I'll keep them for myself."

"Oh please," she begged. She gave him another tempting glance, which was ignored. Her lover could not be tempted this time.

Scarron's mind was busy for the remainder of the evening. He would keep his eyes and ears open and find out where the necklace came from. For that reason he would send for Rosenthal. That old Jew knew plenty about diamonds and could tell him how much they were worth.

Four
Place Royale, Paris

A young maid came up from the kitchen with the intention of making fire in the drawing-room. She was the one to discover the body at the foot of the stairs. Screaming her heart out, she ran out of the house and fainted in the street.

The news spread around town like wildfire. The ravishing Isabelle de Saint-Laurent was found poisoned in her uncle's house.

The motive? Jealousy, most likely. The girl had been something of a flirt, had she not? And had the servants not overheard the young master, her husband, saying he was going to kill her?

Three days later, the guards arrested Monsieur de Saint-Laurent, *au nom du Roi*.

Five
Quartier Saint-Denis, Paris

Scarron did not live long enough to enjoy being a rich man. The morning after he received the diamonds, Marcel found him with his throat cut. The diamond necklace could not be found--it had disappeared, along with the gipsy girl.

Later that morning, a young lad loitered in the Rue Quincampoix. He took pleasure bumping into non-suspecting passers-by who later on found their purse gone. All of a sudden, Mira the gipsy brushed past him. He felt something in her pocket and skillfully made it move places.

Dominique ran off to a street where he felt safe and only then examined his catch. He grinned widely as he put the necklace between the leather of his belt--a place he often used to keep things hidden from Scarron.

He started a naughty song and walked away.

1711
A convent in Dijon, Burgundy

Sister Marie-Ange walked into the infirmary. She directed her first glance towards the bed in the corner of the room. That space was occupied by a young woman who lay motionless. Her once beautiful black hair lacked luster and framed a face so pale the skin looked almost translucent. The eyes were closed, the lips bloodless. If it was not for the faint breathing, one could easily assume the woman had just died.

"Poor creature," the sister whispered. Each time she entered this room, she felt a deep pity for the deplorable state in which the young woman found herself.

"God have mercy on her," answered her companion, sister Béatrice, in a hushed voice.

The two nuns first cared for the other patients then finally turned to the cot in the farthest corner. They washed the woman's face and hands and sister Marie-Ange tried in vain to pull up the thin blanket to better cover the highly pregnant body against the freezing draught which entered through the chinks in the old windows.

Sister Béatrice, an older nun who ran the training of the young novices to turn them into accomplished nurses, remained a moment at the bedside of the pregnant woman. Being a healthy, weather-beaten and strong woman herself, she too felt pity and compassion she could not fully express. "I pray the Lord daily for a miracle," she whispered into the ear of Marie-Ange. "Really, I have tried everything I know to get her out of this state of oblivion. I tried herbal concoctions, a shock therapy with cold and hot water… Honestly, I don't know how to go on anymore and must confess I've come to the end of my knowledge."

Lost in thoughts, the two nuns left the infirmary when the bell for Vespers chimed. They walked at a checked pace to the chapel, crossing the closed cloister that offered an outlook over the well-kept garden.

"*Soeur* Béatrice…" Marie-Ange was still a novice and had problems in curbing her curiosity. Only two days ago she was appointed to help the older nun and she wondered about the woman who remained so silent. "*Ma soeur*, has that woman been like this for long?" she blurted out. The reprimand she expected did not come.

The older nun stared at the beads of her rosary and bowed her head to hide her feelings. "She was already in this condition when her family brought her here," she answered as silently as possible. "Her brother told our Reverend Mother she experienced a nasty shock and lost consciousness. Later on I discovered the poor thing was with child. Dear Lord, I honestly don't know what to do!"

"She might get better," the novice expressed her hope.

"The unconsciousness has lasted for months already," Béatrice said in a doubtful tone. "This can only mean something is extremely wrong. Luckily her bodily condition doesn't seem to get worse."

"We have to put our trust in the Lord," Marie-Ange repeated. "And in you, sister. You are the best nurse I have ever met."

Béatrice found comfort in this optimistic attitude. "The Lord will do whatever he finds right," she uttered and let it follow by a short prayer.

~ * ~

The reverend mother received the visitor in the sober reception room of the convent with its polished paneling and whitewashed walls. She kindly invited Count Armand de Vallencieux to take a seat. "How can we help you this time, *Monsieur le Comte?*" she asked.

Armand gave her an apologetic smile. His whole attitude suggested humility and sincere concern. "The matter is somewhat delicate, *Ma Mère*," he said hesitatingly. "Not so long ago, I received a message from your nursing sister. She thinks there exists a chance my sister's child could be born safely. Can you imagine in what an awkward situation this would bring us?" When he had brought Marguerite to the convent all these months ago, he had put up a story that sounded convincing enough for the innocent nuns. "When the baby lives, I thought it would be better he or she was taken to an orphanage where decent people can adopt the child."

The abbess folded her fine aristocratic hands and studied him pensively. "To my opinion, *Monsieur*, she finally answered, "it is wrong to separate a mother and her child, assuming both will live."

Armand immediately lowered his head in repentance. "Forgive me, Reverend Mother. Pity for my dear sister makes me speak like this. You see, there is a chance--although faint--that Marguerite will gain back her health and will remember... I've brought her home and made sure this bastard--excuse me--won't harm her a second time. Without the child she'll be able to forget this terrible episode. It will only resemble a bad dream, *non*? She will be permitted to start a new, Christian life."

Against her better judgment, the abbess had to recognize the truth in the words of the count, who appeared so sincere and so concerned about his poor sister. "So you want to bring the child to an orphanage? Yes, you may be right. We shall see."

Armand counted himself lucky with this answer. He knew he had almost persuaded the nun; she would do as he demanded. *Wish it had been that easy with*

René, he mused. *Who suspected our little brother could put up such resistance? He was dead set against my plans. 'You don't have the right to decide in Marguerite's place," he'd said. Of course I answered that I only want the best for our sister. 'The best for her?" he shouted. 'You only think of yourself!" Of course I do, and why not? We simply can't keep that baby. Even a fool like Laneuil would decline, if he learned about it.*

~ * ~

"Sister Béatrice! Sister, you have to come to the infirmary at once!"

The older nun was not pleased with this interruption of her sleep. She needed rest after a day spent in the herbal garden, tending to the plants and preparing her medicines. She opened her eyes, noticed the look of worry on Marie-Ange's face and sighed. "What's wrong, girl?" she asked.

"Sister, you have to come at once. The young woman who is unconscious... I think she is going to give birth!"

As soon as she heard these words, sister Béatrice's attitude changed. Gone was the tiredness. She jumped to her feet and hurried to the infirmary, followed by the young novice, to watch the miracle with her own eyes.

Once arrived there, she had to admit the novice was right in her assumptions. Labor had set in and the previously serene face of the young woman showed signs of pain. Her reddened lips moved and produced a soft moan every now and then. The nun sank to her knees and thanked the Blessed Lady in all humility. When she finished her prayer, she called sister Marie-Ange to her assistance and together they set to deliver the baby.

"Bring me lots of hot water and clean linen," she ordered.

She set to light a glaring fire in the hearth of the smaller room to where they had brought the woman. Once the fire was going, she set to work.

It was another small miracle the labor did not last very long. Slightly more than two hours later, the oldest nun held up a tiny boy child who cried out his lungs at this rough treatment. Both nuns could not withhold tears of relief.

"This is certainly a healthy boy," sister Marie-Ange laughed. She was shaking on her legs, not with fatigue but because she had never been so close to the mystery of life. "Such a pity the mother can't see him!"

Sister Béatrice cautiously carried the child to a table where she began to wash it. That done, she swaddled the baby in a soft cloth of flannel. She too sighed deeply, only for another reason. "This child will be sent to our sister-convent in Beaune," she told Marie-Ange. "I must admit I find it hard to see the wisdom of this decision, but this is as our Reverend Mother wants it."

"How cruel," the young novice cried out, forgetting her place. "Who says the mother will not recover as well? If that happens, she'll want to see her child."

Sister Béatrice shrugged her shoulders. "Nothing can be done about it. It is in the Lord's hands. Besides…" She neared Marie-Ange and whispered something in her ear.

The young novice's expression changed from astonishment to surprise, and her face turned red hot. "Yes, nothing can be done about it," she had to agree after these revelations.

"We can pray for the two of them," Béatrice offered.

The nuns sank to their knees and lowered their heads.

~ * ~

That same night, someone made sure everyone was sleeping before opening a window of the convent. A pigeon spread its wings and flew off.

The next day, the bird reached its destination where the message tied to one of its legs was read and understood. Some necessary preparations were taken. God's work was about to be interfered with.

1720
One

Traffic in Paris was in a mess once more. *Small wonder,* thought Marguerite, *with this nice spring weather everyone wants to go out.*

"*Madame la baronesse?*" A face popped up next to the window of the carriage. "The coachman says we're probably stuck here for an hour or more. Is there anything I can do for you in the meantime?"

"I'm in no hurry, Henri." She sighed nevertheless. One hour could be a long time, and the coach would get hotter as the sun reached its zenith. Could she? The new idea became more attractive by the second.

"As it is, I've changed my mind," she announced. "I want to go for a walk. We are not far from the Pont Neuf, are we? I'd like to have a look around there. You can come along to protect me. Come, help me out."

While he offered her his hand, she saw the servant frown.

"It is my duty to warn Madame that the bridge is an unsafe place for people of quality, especially when they are so richly dressed. You'll be an open invitation to every pickpocket present."

Marguerite could not prevent a light smile. Henri had served the De Laneuil family for ages and had grown very protective towards its members. "I'm sure you're exaggerating, Henri. Besides, you'll be there to watch over me. Don't I notice a big gun between your belt?"

"I'll keep my eyes open", he swore, cursing under his breath for the folly his mistress displayed.

~ * ~

If possible, the bridge was busier than the streets. Little shops were built on top of it, and these offered many different items for sale. Next to the shops, jugglers displayed their ability to tumble and swirl. High up in the air, a man walked over a rope that was fixed between two rooftops. A barber invited passers-by to take a seat and have a haircut or get rid of a bad tooth. Further away a quack was praising his potion that would cure all ailments. Throngs of people moved in all directions.

"Hold the thief!"

The cry came from a little woman who sold apples. To Marguerite's surprise two guardsmen showed up rather quickly and set in the pursuit of the pickpockets. People were brushed aside, stalls overturned, creating more hassle.

One of the thieves bumped into Marguerite. He was a boy, not older than ten. Without thinking, she got hold of his arm. "Keep still," she warned him, "unless you want the guards to arrest you."

A dirty face with dark and challenging eyes looked up to hers. Thick black hair curled over his ears and collar, the mouth was broad and ready to laugh. His bold stare told her something. She followed his gaze and noticed how she kept two fingers crossed-as an obvious sign the boy well understood.

A deep feeling of confusion took possession of her. What was she doing? What did this mean?

She had no time to think further. An officer of the guard approached her. The man bowed politely, but his face stood grim. "Madame?"

"*Monsieur l'officier?*" she responded with a friendly smile.

"I believe you are protecting a notorious thief and street robber," he stated in a cold voice. "The boy next to you is well known to us, and it is my duty to arrest him."

"I'm sure there is a mistake, officer," she corrected him swiftly. Her raised eyebrows indicated an air of mischief. "Jean," she added, "the boy you see here, is the nephew of my valet. Henri can testify to that."

The lawman frowned, especially when the servant replied.

"Indeed, I can vow to that," Henri said. He knew where his loyalty lay.

"I'm helping my uncle to carry Madame's purchases," the boy peeped up, unasked. His feeling of self-confidence returned after a brief moment of panic. He grinned.

The officer sighed, seeming to admit to his defeat. This time he had to leave without a prisoner. His opponent was a lady of quality, more precisely the wife of his highest chief, the Attorney General of Paris. Even though he knew she was lying, he could not question her.

"My apologies, Madame. I won't bother you any further."

"Don't worry, officer. I do admire the way in which you perform your task," she answered. "I shall recommend you to my husband."

As soon as the police officer moved out of sight, the boy tried the same. The game was over now. But before he could move, Henri's hand came down on his shoulder, pinning him. "You will thank the baroness properly for saving your miserable hide," he told him in a firm tone.

The boy wriggled but could not free himself. He looked around, hoping to see any of his mates. They were long gone. He would have to solve this problem alone.

"Thank you, Madame. And may I go now?"

"Why the hurry?"

"I have to catch up with my mates," he said. "They must wonder where I am."

"My guess is they've seen the officer right behind you, and now they think you're his prisoner. Did they come back for you?"

"My uncle will come for me!" he tried to reassure himself, rather than her. However, his tone seemed not all too convinced.

Marguerite gazed at him more carefully. She realized he was only a child--a child who was feeling afraid and insecure. The brutality he showed was a pose, a necessity in these environs. Right there, influenced by something she could not explain, she made a decision which would change her life.

"Granted that your uncle hasn't given up on you, he'd better try and find out where you are, because I'm taking you home with me," she said. "There's always room for a little page in a household as large as ours."

"Madame, you must be out of your wits!" Henri cried out, before he knew. This was going too far; he felt it his duty to protest in his master's name.

"I won't tolerate such behavior, Henri," she admonished him sharply.

"But Madame, don't you realize you're taking an enormous risk? This brat will steal everything that is not too big or too heavy and pass on information to all of his accomplices. One night they will come and cut our throats."

Marguerite burst out into laughter. She did not often do that, Henri knew. Ever since the day she became his master's wife, it seemed time she looked somewhat forlorn.

"Don't be so dramatic, Henri. Nothing will happen. I will personally see to that. The boy must promise me to be honest. If he should take something away, just like this…," she held up a pocket--watch on a golden chain and dangled it before Henri's nose, '…then I would feel obliged to notify the law!"

The astonished expression on both the valet's and the boy's faces was worth a lot. She kept on laughing until it slowly dawned on her she just gave a masterful demonstration on how to pick a man's pocket; another thing that totally perplexed her. What did this mean?

The problem was she had no recollections of the past. Her conscious life had only started nine years ago when she woke up from a coma in a Burgundy convent. Everything before that was a total blank.

The little rogue put a hand in his pocket and found nothing but a dirty handkerchief. Now he surely was at a loss, probably wondering how a noblewoman had mastered their own special skills?

Perhaps though he could find out more while he was living in her house and he was sure his uncle would find this intriguing.

"Good Madame, I'll stay with you," he said. "I think the streets will be a bit unsafe for me at the present anyway. And may I remark that you are very accomplished? I never felt a thing when you took that watch. Only my uncle can do better."

She nodded, not quite listening to his words. Where had she learned this? What had happened to her before she woke up in that convent?

On the drive back home her mind was occupied. Fact: she had suffered a bad accident--at least, this was what Armand, her eldest brother, claimed. Fact: she had been engaged to Etienne de Laneuil and so she had married him after her accident. Fact: all other memories were gone.

Etienne had taken her to a well-known physician because she suffered so many headaches in the years that followed. She remembered what the man told her: *Don't force anything, Madame. The brain cannot be urged, that is my strong opinion. My esteemed colleagues say I'm a fool to believe so, but I feel I'm right. Your mind has formed a natural blockade to protect you from things which were perhaps too horrible to bear. One day the reason for this will disappear and your memory will return.*

~ * ~

Darkness settled over the town. The big household of the De Laneuil's retired for the night--the fires were extinguished, the candles snuffed. The baron and baroness went to their individual chambers, so did the servants.

Not even the dogs sensed that someone climbed the garden wall, dropped over and crossed the deserted courtyard. With practiced skill the intruder climbed towards a certain window and easily gained access.

Pure instinct woke Marguerite. Immediately she noticed the dark figure near her bedside. She made an attempt to open her mouth for a loud scream, but a rough hand went over it.

"Not a sound, Madame," a not unfriendly voice whispered into her ear. "I mean you no harm, please believe me. This is the best way I can think of to get into speak with you."

She did not understand, yet she nodded slowly. At once the hand was lifted and she could breathe freely again. She tried to study the man's face more closely. "I have seen you before," she said, in equally hushed tones. "Your face looks familiar to me, but I haven't a clue as to whom you might be."

The intruder grinned and showed his strong white teeth. "You disappoint me, Madame! I thought everyone in Paris was familiar with the face of Cartouche."

Her eyes opened wide and her breath escaped with a hiss.

He clearly had pleasure in her astonishment. "Yes, I know I've got guts-- entering the house of the Attorney-General himself. I hope you are not going to give me away, *Madame la Baronesse*."

She shook her head, taken aback by his words. How unreal the situation looked. She, Marguerite de Laneuil, eye to eye with a dangerous criminal--and she did nothing.

"I am here because you rescued a little boy out of the jaws of justice this afternoon," he went on. "Jeanot is my nephew, you know."

"*Your* nephew?"

"I wanted to thank you personally for your noble gesture, Madame. As it is, I am very fond of that child."

Without asking for her permission he sat down on the bed, and she did not reproach him. The infamous criminal had a charm that most men lacked.

"I'm not for sending small children to prison," she declared.

"You have a kind heart," he answered. "I hear lots of good about you, baroness. That is why I dare make a request."

She frowned, and he smiled. "No, I don't want your jewelry or your virtue. My request concerns Jeanot."

"Oh!"

"You must know, Madame, I have tried to raise him as best as possible," he chuckled. "I taught him everything I know about survival. He can steal, fight, run… He's really intelligent and he could be a leader. But this is not what I want for my sister's only child. There is no future in our profession, baroness. You know that well enough. The law is constantly at our heels and one day we will get caught--*fini!*" His hand made a demonstrative gesture over his throat. "That's not what I want for Jeanot. I pray he receives the opportunity to become an honest citizen--and there you can help me, baroness."

He reached for her hand, which she did not pull back, and gently caressed her fingers. His strong hand felt warm and comforting. "Won't you give him a place in your household?" he went on.

"That was my intention when I brought him along," she said.

"And will you be his guardian, Madame? Will you take responsibility for him?"

Two

I must be crazy. What could have persuaded her to agree to what Cartouche asked? She had given in to the demands of a criminal, had made some sort of pact with the man her husband had sworn to convict.

She and the rest of her household would get immunity and protection on the streets of Paris in return for her taking care of a little boy.

And yet she felt no regret. *I like that man*, she confessed to herself. *I feel like I've known him most of my life.* She called for her maid.

"Good morning, Madame," Rosette greeted her. She came from Burgundy where Marguerite was born.

"Rosette, I want you to do something. Go back to the kitchen and tell the new boy he can bring me breakfast."

"Certainly, Madame."

Not much later Jeanot appeared with her breakfast tray. Marguerite noticed he had taken a bath. Someone had undertaken to comb his hair, but strands kept falling back into his face. His eyes stood bright and showed obvious pleasure.

"It's a beautiful morning, baroness."

"It certainly is, Jeanot," she agreed. "Put that tray down here." Her finger pointed.

He set it down on the table next to her bed and waited for further orders.

"Do you like it here?" she wanted to know.

"Oh, it's alright," he shrugged with studied nonchalance. "Cook is a sweet old lady; she gave me freshly baked croissants before she combed my hair!"

"So much the better. I intend to keep you here for some time, you know."

"My uncle told me," he said. "I saw him early this morning. He advised me to serve you well and to behave, or else..."

She laughed. "Or else? Will Cartouche dictate what happens in my house? The nerve! But honestly, I won't throw you out, not without a good reason anyway. I have given my word to your uncle."

She patted invitingly on the coverlet and the boy sat down on the edge of the mattress. He poured out a cup of cacao and offered it to her.

"So you're Cartouche's nephew," she remarked.

"*Oui*, Madame," he admitted without any shame. "Uncle Dominique looked after me ever since my mother died. I was still a baby at that time, and there was no father to care for me. A woman called Arlette fed me, and her friends took turns in watching over me while my uncle earned our living. Perhaps you can't imagine this, Madame, but we are actually one big family."

"Then you were luckier than I am." Her green eyes darkened at the thought. "I only have two brothers. One of them went to Canada before I married the baron and the other I only see occasionally."

Armand was not the kindest of people. His harsh expression told her he disapproved of her--for what, she did not know--and this was one of the reasons why she had agreed to marry Etienne so soon after her accident.

The boy nodded as if he could understand. "But now you are happy, right? Cook tells me that Monsieur Etienne adores you, and you are very lucky to have such a fine husband."

She smiled. The boy was right. Etienne was a godsend. Although much older than her, he was a good friend and they had a nice life.

"Have you any other skills than those you acquired on the streets?" she asked, changing the subject.

"I can count fluently, and I can write my name!"

"Who taught you that?"

"The dirt-writer at the Pont Neuf. He said I was a good pupil and promised me he'd teach me the entire alphabet. Alas, they hung him before he could keep his promise!"

"What was his crime?"

Jeanot grinned. "He wrote a naughty verse about the Regent. Actually it was very good--the verses didn't contain a single lie. We sold hundreds of copies."

"Hmm. What would you say if I offered to give you more lessons?" she proposed. "People who can read and write get good jobs."

"That would be great!" he cried out. "You are ever so kind, baroness!"

Before she could prevent it, he jumped up and gave her a big hug then quickly left the room.

~ * ~

Marguerite's latest pastime was welcomed in different ways.

Her husband, the Attorney-General, had nothing against it. "You should go ahead with the project, my dear," he advised her.

She has no children of her own, he meditated. *This parentless boy wakes up the motherly instinct in her. Should I punish her for that? It is my fault I couldn't give her a baby--I have known for a long time. Also my first wife Françoise could not get pregnant.*

Armand, her brother, displayed his scorn openly. "Foolishness!" he sneered.

Margot just could not be trusted, he knew for fact. *I'm ever so glad I'm no longer responsible for her thoughtless deeds! Etienne, the old fool, has what he deserved.*

Chantale d'Aubilly, her cousin and close friend, clearly had fun over the whole situation. "One can expect everything of you, my dear!"' she giggled. "You might as well start a new rage."

I just love my cousin, she thought. *At least she is friendly to me, what cannot be said of my own sisters…*

23

The major-domo formulated his complaints in the presence of the cook. "It is totally wrong! Who has ever heard of a simple servant receiving an education?"

Times were better before the baron married, he often mused. *Why could they not turn back the clock?*

The cook's reaction: "Ah well, he's such a cheerful child. Don't always be a pain in the ass, Julien!"

That crazy old fool! Her lips mimed a curse behind his back. *Madame would better to send him off and allow a younger man to do the job.*

Three

The carriage of the *Vicomte* d'Aubilly drove up to the main entrance of the Cours-la-Reine. This park was the favorite meeting ground of the Parisian beau monde and aristocracy because the etiquette was less formal there than in Versailles. One of the main advantages was that you could freely meet people, even if they were not formally introduced--and neglect them later on if you wished.

"I envy you, Marguerite," said Chantale, while her cousin's little page helped her out of the carriage. She was the third daughter of the Count de Salanges, an uncle of Marguerite, and since the spring of the previous year the wife of Philippe d'Aubilly, whose child she now expected.

"I really ought to be jealous of you," Chantale went on. "You're slender as a willow and you look gorgeous in your new dress, while I'm beginning to look like a fat cow!"

Marguerite indeed looked enchanting in a creation of pastel green silk which suited her complexion and her black hair. "Nonsense," she responded, trying to cheer up her cousin. The pregnancy sometimes depressed her a bit. "You look ravishing as well."

"Do you think it's pleasant to be pregnant on a warm day in May? I wish the baby was here already!"

"As soon as he or she arrives, all your sorrows will be forgotten," Marguerite knew. She was the jealous one. Ever since she married, she had hoped for a child.

They walked along the paths for a while until Chantale suddenly stopped dead in her footsteps. She opened her fan and whispered behind it. "Marguerite, look to your right, but carefully. You seem to make an impression on that man in the blue suit. His eyes keep following you. God, he's handsome!"

Marguerite turned her head and was met by the amused gaze of an elegant courtier who was dressed according to the latest fashion. The choice of the blue satin not only revealed his good taste and wealth, but the cut of the long coat and the tight knee-breeches accentuated his athletic figure in the best possible way. His face was beautiful without being feminine, with well-drawn eyebrows, a straight nose and slightly curved lips. His dark blue eyes met hers without shame.

"My compliments, Madame."

He came a bit closer, which made it impossible to walk away without being offensive. Marguerite did not particularly like to be manipulated in such situations.

"*Mesdames*, allow me to introduce myself. I am Marquis Hilaire d'Aubervilliers at your service."

The two women sank down in the prescribed curtsey. As the eldest, Marguerite took it upon her to make the introductions on their side. "I am Marguerite de Laneuil. And this is my cousin, *Vicomtesse* Chantale d'Aubilly," she said in a stiff tone, still not pleased at all.

The marquis kissed her hand first then that of Chantale. "*Enchanté.*" Then he continued: "I do know your husband, Madame d'Aubilly. When will we have the pleasure of welcoming you at the royal palace?"

"Philippe has told me there soon will be an open position in the household of the duchess of Orleans, but at the moment I prefer the peace of my own house. You will understand why."

"Of course," he nodded. "And Madame de Laneuil keeps you company?"

"She's my cousin and she lives in Paris." Chantale could always be persuaded to chat. "In the Quartier Marais, to be more exact."

The marquis noticed he had made a mistake and made the appropriate excuses. "Of course, now I remember! Monsieur de Laneuil is our Attorney-General. I did not know he had a wife."

"We married nine years ago," Marguerite informed him.

"It's a complete surprise to me. I was in the strong belief that I knew every beauty in the capital. Now it appears I missed out on one."

At last, a small smile appeared on her lips. "You're flattering me, Monsieur."

"No, I mean it when I say you are the most beautiful woman I've seen."

"I am going to blush if you don't stop this," she warned him. *He makes me feel like a schoolgirl.*

Chantale was watching them with obvious pleasure.

"My dear marquis," she hastened to intervene, "you force me to invite you to the banquet my husband and I are having next week. If you agree to come, you'll have a chance of getting to know Marguerite better."

"I'm sure you won't mind either," she then addressed her cousin. "Monsieur d'Aubervilliers will save you from boredom now that Etienne is so inattentive to go away and leave you on your own."

"My husband has to go to Dijon on urgent business," Marguerite explained, because she felt she had to apologize in Etienne's name. He did not often leave her alone. Right now he needed to see his solicitor to discuss estate matters.

"I'll do my best to entertain the ladies," the marquis promised. Then he took his leave.

The woman's gazes followed him for a while, and finally Chantale hugged her cousin.

"*Ma chère*, you've made a conquest! Oh, I'm sure he's smitten with you-- Marquis d'Aubervilliers in person! I've heard a lot about him… He's an intimate friend of the regent and he's very famous for his love-affairs."

"What's his reputation? I doubt it's a good one," said Marguerite. Her cousin giggled, the sad mood of before completely gone.

"Philippe says he's a heartbreaker. But you may never know... also for him there will be the true one, and you could be that woman, *chérie*."

"You forget that I'm already married. I won't be an easy prey to his lordship."

"Quite right, my dear. But that doesn't mean you can't have a good time with the marquis. You'll be the envy of every other woman."

~ * ~

"Madame, I'm trying to deal with a difficult problem."

D'Aubervilliers leant over to his table partner who, thanks to the excellent choice of food and drinks and to the animated conversation, did seem in the best of moods.

"And I can be of assistance to you," she teased him.

He nodded, hiding his smile. "As it is, only you know the answer. Pray tell me, Madame, how it is possible you have escaped my wandering eye for such a long time? Your cousin swears you have been living in Paris for two years now, and still we only met last week!"

Marguerite blushed but blamed it on the effect of the wine.

"That is correct," she answered. The first years of their marriage, Etienne and she had lived in Dijon where Etienne worked for a lesser court of justice. "I'm rather a housewife, I guess. And next is the fact that we move in different circles; my husband's friends all belong to the legal world. I'm afraid their conversation would not interest you."

"Would you not like to come to court? It is my honest belief you would be a success there."

She did not have to think over her answer. "No," she answered. "The court doesn't attract me. I'm quite satisfied with my actual life, and all I want is to be a good wife to my husband."

The marquis looked up, clearly surprised. "Is that all you want from life?"

She remained silent for a while. His question touched an area she was sensitive about.

"What more could I want?" she said at last, trying to avoid gloomy thoughts. "My husband has a high office and he possesses vast capital. According to my brother, I'm the most fortunate of women!"

Her attempt to ridicule the words did not quite work because the bitter undertone still emerged through it. The marquis took her hand and held it comfortingly to his lips. Yet his following remark indicated he did not understand the situation. "*Monsieur le procureur* is old, I understand. Don't you long for the love of a younger man?"

Her eyes shot fire and she tore her hand loose. "My husband gives me all the love and respect I could want, Monsieur," she said indignantly. "What makes you think I long for the embrace of a lover?"

D'Aubervilliers lowered his head in a sign of repentance. "Forgive me, my dearest. Faithfulness is a forgotten virtue these days, but one must have respect for it."

That brought a smile to her lips. "I don't blame you for your words, Marquis," she answered in a milder way. Why should she find fault with him for trying? She had heard such remarks before and should by now be used to them. She was old and wise enough to know how to deal with such situations. Why spoil this otherwise interesting acquaintance?

D'Aubervillier's face lit up. "Thank you, Madame. However, I must warn you that I don't give up my hopes. Your beauty has overwhelmed me, and I will do my utmost best to make you mine some day."

She nodded, taking up the challenge. "If you don't mind that I will say 'no' over and over again… and as long as you don't embarrass me."

"I don't tire easily, Marguerite. As from now you can count on me as your most persistent admirer."

~ * ~

"Nice chap, this d'Aubervilliers," Etienne de Laneuil declared after the last of their guests had taken his leave. This time, apart from the usual invitees, the marquis had been present at the *soirée* they had organized after his return from the countryside.

"Indeed, a man after my own heart," he continued. "Excellent manners, intelligent and witty, good-looking. What do you think of him, Marguerite?"

"He's charming," she admitted vaguely. She did not want to pursue this conversation with her husband.

"And completely infatuated with you," he added with a smile. "Oh yes, I am not blind! I think the two of you would make a beautiful couple. If he's patient enough to wait until I have gone, he can marry you."

His sense of humor made her totally uncomfortable. As much as she tried, she could not share his point of view. "I won't allow you to think even that!" came her sharp reply. "You are in the best of health, Etienne, and I don't think you'll leave me before your time."

He chuckled, obviously touched by her reaction. It showed she loved him after all--something he certainly had not been sure of for a long time. "I'll try my best, my dear." He put his arm around her waist and kissed her lips lightly.

"I don't wish for your death," she whispered.

He nodded. "I know. It's one of the things I admire in you. However, sometimes I wonder... I'm fifty-two, Marguerite and thus an old man. There must be things you miss..."

"I am happy," she told him, and hoped her voice was convincing enough to reassure him. Never, ever would she willingly hurt the man who had been so good to her.

"You're sweet, my love," he breathed into her ear. "It makes it so easy to love you. Come, let me take you to bed."

She kissed him and obliged.

~ * ~

That night the nightmare came to her once more. During the past nine years it haunted her dreams every now and then. Each time it seemed to become more real and new elements were added.

Right now, she was dancing with Hilaire d'Aubervilliers. He complimented her in a thousand and one ways. Then, all of a sudden she found herself in an empty room and was overcome by an inexplicable fear. The marquis called her name but she did not listen. She began to run--through dark corridors and dark passages where danger lurked in every corner.

Finally, she came to her destination. Here another man waited for her. She did not know him. He was wrapped in shadows and she could never see him clearly. But her heart told her not to be afraid of him. He opened his arms and swept her against his chest.

With a sigh of relief, she hid her face in his dark coat and enjoyed the firmness of his embrace. It felt so safe and familiar. When her eyes searched for his face, she looked into stark blackness.

The scream that left her mouth was so loud it woke her. She was in her bedroom bathing in sweat with Etienne sleeping next to her.

How strange! Why did she always have the feeling she knew the stranger from the dream? She sighed deeply and cuddled up closer against her husband's warm body. This was the only reality. Dreams were foolishness.

Four

"Bring this to my wife," Etienne gave his orderly a sealed message. He needed to work late and wanted to make sure Marguerite knew about it. "And please tell her not to wait dinner--I'll have something brought here."

He concentrated again on the case he was working on and time passed by. It was near ten o'clock when he finally put his pen down and blew out the candles which lighted his desk.

During the drive home, along the deserted streets, his mind was still occupied with the case and therefore he did not pay much attention to what was happening outside.

He never saw the men turn up, only heard a shout of warning from his coachman then a gunshot.

~ * ~

Marguerite began to feel worried. It was nothing for Etienne to stay that long at his office. At first, when she had received the message, she had sighed. She had retired to bed at eleven o'clock but had not been able to sleep. She felt something was wrong.

Where was Etienne? She called for her major-domo.

"Wake up the grooms," she ordered him. "They have to go out and search the streets the route the baron takes to come home."

"Are you afraid something happened, Madame?" Julien asked, not used to seeing the mistress so distressed.

"Yes," was the short answer.

Julien did not waste more time. His sharp commands rang through the hall and all of the youngsters among the servants got dressed in a hurry and armed themselves with sticks, knives and lanterns. They left the mansion in groups of four and swarmed out to check out the streets that lead to the *Palais de Justice*.

It did not take them long to find the coach bearing the crest of the baron. It stood deserted in the middle of the street. The horses snorted and moved impatiently, sensing something was out of place.

The major-domo was the first who dared to look into the interior of the coach after finding the bodies of the coacher and the groom. When his lantern shone into the carriage, he saw that the baron bore a deep wound, but also that his chest was still faintly moving.

"He's alive!" he shouted. "Quick, one of you take the place of the coacher and hurry to the Hôtel de Laneuil!"

Then he spoke to Bernard, the youngest of his lads. Bernard was speedy.

"And you run to Doctor Abbecourt. He's to come immediately to the baron's residence!"

"Yes, Monsieur," the young man said, while beginning to a sprint.

They did all they could, however help came too late. Etienne was still breathing when he was carried into his house, but not much later he drew his last breath in the presence of his wife.

"The bullet entered too close to the heart," explained the doctor, who came as soon as he got the message. "There was nothing I could have done, Madame, even if I arrived earlier."

Marguerite had to accept this. She also had to listen to the soothing words of the prefect of police who came to see her shortly afterwards.

"Your husband has become the victim of a street gang," he reported. "My officers say he got caught in a hold-up. Most likely, he refused to pay the money they demanded and had to pay with his life."

Marguerite just looked at him, her eyes vacant.

"Rest assured, Madame, we shall do everything in our power to arrest and convict these criminals."

This brought little solace to Marguerite. She missed Etienne more than she realized. His strength had been her support, and now she would have to fend for herself.

She went through the funeral ceremonies as it was her duty. She duly accepted the condolences of friends and family. She did not shed a single tear, but after the ordeal she announced she wanted to be alone. The only one who tried to change her mind was her brother Armand. His request to come and stay with him at the castle of Vallencieux was turned down

~ * ~

"Madame Marguerite?"

The soft voice of Jeanot disturbed her thoughts. With an angry look she raised her head. The boy did not go away.

"This message is meant for your eyes only," he said, handing her a piece of paper.

She accepted and opened it. The message was direct and brought her attention into focus. It read: '*Come to L'Ange Noir tonight. It is important. C*'

Her melancholic mood made way for other feelings. "C" meant Cartouche...

She had not wanted to think of him before. But now... She had to know the truth--and she would ask him in person if he had given orders to murder Etienne.

"Who brought this message?" she asked Jeanot.

"Philibert, my uncle's lieutenant. In person."

"Your uncle asks me to meet him in L'Ange Noir," she continued. "Do you know that place?"

"Of course. It's in the heart of Saint-Denis." He then put his hands on the desk she was sitting behind--staring at documents which she obviously had not touched--and his head came close to hers. "Uncle Dominique wouldn't ask if it wasn't extremely important. He would also not ask you to come to Saint-Denis if he saw a chance of coming here. Alas, the police patrols have doubled and the streets are not safe for us. He advises you to wear a disguise, Madame. We can't run the risk of leading the guards to our lair. Perhaps you can ask Rosette to bring you a set of maid's clothes."

~ * ~

Late that evening, an unimportant chambermaid and a little pageboy left the *Hôtel de Laneuil* through the backdoor. Nobody took much notice of them. A passing guard asked the girl if she had a date, but she quickly hurried by.

With a safe distance between them and the house, Jeanot at last hailed a cab. This carried them as far as the Pont Neuf. There the driver refused to take them any further, because of the district's bad reputation.

"It doesn't matter. We'll continue our way on foot," Marguerite decided.

She did not wait for Jeanot's indications, but moved through the tangle of alleys as if she visited this neighborhood on daily basis.

The boy followed her, totally at a loss. "Why did you ask me where L'Ange Noir is, if you know the way yourself?" he panted. Then he wished he had kept his tongue.

His mistress's face got a worried look. "I don't know," she admitted hesitatingly. "The name didn't mean anything, and yet I seem to be familiar with these streets. Oh, Jeanot, I often feel so confused!"

"Why, Madame?"

His dark eyes studied her with interest and compassion at the same time. He still had not completely figured her out. Of course he knew about her accident--but could that account for all of her strange actions?

35

Impulsively she opened her arms and pulled him close to her breast, which seemed to comfort her in some way. "I don't remember anything of what happened before nine years ago," she explained. "I only remember that I woke up in a bare room somewhere in a convent in Burgundy. The nuns told me I had suffered an accident. Then my brother came, who told the same. And yet...I don't know what to believe. Ever since that moment I have terrible headaches and sometimes these nightmares..."

"You'll get your memory back," the boy said.

At last she smiled. "That's what the doctor said as well." Then she shrugged, banning all negative thoughts for the time being. "Right, no use worrying over things we can't change. So come on, your uncle is waiting."

They entered the inn and were welcomed by its owner, a fellow named Ronchard. For Jeanot he had a friendly greeting; for Marguerite a wondering glance. Then he asked her to follow him. He guided her to a backroom and left her alone with Cartouche.

They faced each other.

Cartouche broke the silence first. "I know what you must be thinking, Madame. That's why I feel it's important to have a word."

"I will listen," she said in a weary voice. Facing him, she now lacked the guts to ask him if he was a murderer.

Apparently, he could read her mind. "Your husband was killed on his way home, and now you are wondering whether my men were involved in that hold-up or not. Let me assure you, Madame, we had nothing to do with it. In Saint-Denis a given word is sacred."

Her gaze pierced his, but he did not shy away from her stare. She could only admit that he told the truth. "I believe you," she finally said. ""I had no reason to doubt your word, but..."

"Once a villain, always a villain?" he smiled. "No, Madame, you have done me a great service, and I would never wish you any harm. We too have a code of honor, you know."

"I realize you are trustworthy," she repeated, while she felt he needed some assurance from her. She held out her hand. "Let's seal our agreement once more, Monsieur Cartouche. And thank you for your concern. It proves you have a kind heart."

He laughed. "A lot of people wouldn't agree with you, Madame!"

"I don't care what others think," she replied. She began to smile as well and felt more and more at ease with Jeanot's uncle. The only regret she felt, was that this man was hunted down by the law and that she was partly responsible for it.

"You better go into hiding," she advised him. "I talked to the prefect only yesterday, and he complained about the brutality of the street gangs. It would be a blessing for Paris, he said, if his men finally caught Cartouche and his gang."

He shrugged. "We know what lies ahead of us but thank you anyway. Cheer up, they still haven't got me! Moreover, as long as the police keep patrolling the streets, you have nothing to fear. The murderers will keep a low profile."

She stared at him. "You *know* who killed my husband?"

"Of course," he answered. "I know most of what goes on in Paris. In this case I feel somewhat embarrassed, though. We had word a robbery was planned, but unfortunately we arrived too late to undo the harm."

"Who has done it?" she demanded, not listening to his excuses.

"A gang of ruffians of Florentine origin. Their leader is a man called Rufio. They'll do anything for money. I believe Rufio would cut his mother's throat if the price was right! They don't have their headquarters in Paris because we don't tolerate them on our territory. So when Philibert reported he saw Rufio on the Pont Neuf, it was almost certain he was hired to commit evil."

His words made her think. She now knew the name of the murderer. Would the prefect be able to track him down?

"You have done all that can be expected," she finally said to Cartouche. She wanted to say more, but something withheld her just in time. It did not seem very logical to ask one criminal for assistance in hunting down another. "But I must return home now."

"Jeanot and Philibert will see to your safety," Cartouche said. "And if you'll allow me, I want to give you some word of advice."

"Yes?"

"I wouldn't stay alone in that big house of yours. Can't you ask any of your relatives to come and live with you for some time?"

She shook her head. "Of course I can invite people. But I don't want that. I can deal with my grief on my own. Are you afraid I'll do something dramatic when I remain alone?"

His eyes looked straight into hers and she shrunk back for the truth she read in them. "I'm afraid not, Madame. I think there's a strong possibility you have a powerful enemy."

Her eyes opened wide. He waited a moment to give her time to grasp the impact of his words. "Haven't you understood, Madame," he said, "the Florentines are mercenaries? They receive money to carry out plans. They don't make the plans themselves!"

"You think that..." she stammered, "...that someone paid to kill Etienne? But who would do such a thing? He had no enemies, as far as I know."

"*You* have an enemy, Madame. Someone who has a strong motive to remove your husband. Someone who wants to do the same with you."

She stood, completely stunned. "I know of none such person. I don't think I've ever done anything to harm another being, and as for Etienne, I'm sure of it. He was always very strict but fair. Who, in heaven's name, would want his death?"

She paused, held back by a fleeting thought. Unconsciously she spoke the words aloud. "No, that can't be. I have an admirer, a marquis. He would never go as far."

Cartouche smiled, glad she did not ask him how he knew the enemy was hers. It would be so difficult to explain... "Of course not. As long as society accepts the fact that men and women have lovers, no *amant* will seek to kill his mistress's husband--probably because they are the best of friends themselves."

She wanted to say that Hilaire d'Aubervilliers was not her lover, but she kept her tongue. A vague feeling of uneasiness took command over her senses.

She realized it had become extremely urgent to find out more about her past. She *had to know* what happened before the accident.

Because she was so wrapped up in thought, she was not aware of the fact that Cartouche gently guided her outside and now carefully wrapped a cloak around her shoulders. Doing this, he held her in his arms for just the briefest of moments. His touch was warm and comforting. "Perhaps you want to reconsider, Madame. Please go somewhere else! Can't you go and visit that cousin of yours?"

How did he know about Chantale, Marguerite wondered. Does he know everything? But then she nodded. It was not such a bad idea. The Aubilly's were spending the summer in the Vendéé, where Chantale awaited the birth of her child. She could certainly use someone to cheer her up.

"Yes, I'll do that," she promised.

He seemed satisfied, and he let go of her. "Take good care of yourself, Madame!"

Five

The sun stood high in the sky when Marguerite walked down the narrow path leading to the river. There, near the bank, was a white painted bench on which she sank down with a sigh of relief.

She leaned back and rested her head against the low brick wall of Chantale's herbal garden. Already on a first exploration, this secluded spot on the estate of the Aubilly's had attracted her. The smell of the herbs reminded her of the convent in Dijon and *Soeur* Beatrice--the atmosphere was almost identical. In this hideaway she found the necessary rest after a tiring day's work-- she took care of the household while Chantale rested--and had the opportunity to order her thoughts.

The warmth of the September sun caressed her skin. It was so peaceful here! It did not take long for her eyes to close and soon she was fast asleep.

~ * ~

"Aha, at long last I've discovered where you always disappear to."

The mocking words woke her up. It did not surprise her to see the face of Marquis d'Aubervilliers.

After Chantale had given birth to a fine baby boy, her husband had given a big baptism party for the neighborhood and friends--and of course the marquis could not be left out.

Most of the guests left when the celebrations were over, but Hilaire stayed on at Philippe's request. He also spoke to Marguerite and pointed out the advantages of a union with the marquis. She would get higher social standing by marrying him, and the bringing together of two separate fortunes would make them almost the wealthiest people in France.

She did not quite know what to do. Etienne had encouraged this union as well, but all she wanted was to be loved. She needed someone who would take care of her, who would love and respect her. Someone she could equally love and admire and feel safe with. Someone who would give her children. She had not been able to conceive with Etienne, but she was still young enough.

"Marquis d'Aubervilliers."

She gave him her hands and allowed him to pull her off the bench. But instead of releasing her after that, his arms held her fast against his chest. She could smell the perfume of his shaving-lotion and the strength of his muscles. Then his mouth came down on hers.

It was a pleasant kiss. She had not felt a man's desire for a while now and thoroughly enjoyed the pleasure.

"My sweetheart," he moaned. "I want you so much. Please say you'll be my wife!"

She made an instant decision. What good was it to linger in the past? Perhaps this man could give her all she wanted. He was certainly ardent enough.

"Yes, Hilaire," she whispered back.

From then onward she was caught in a maelstrom of events. They would be married out of the Parisian home of her uncle De Salanges but she did not want her aunt to make all the arrangements. She needed a wedding dress. She had to draw up a list of *invitees*. She had to see an attorney--because Hilaire insisted on the fact that her properties should not become his but remain all hers.

In the meantime, she returned to her house in Marais. She became more and more certain she had made the right choice and often she was singing aloud. The staff rejoiced with her, only Jeanot appeared to be somewhat distressed. He tried to avoid being in the same room with her--until even Marguerite noticed something was wrong.

"What is the matter with you, Jeanot?" she stopped him one day. "You look as if you have lost your most valued possession."

'I'm fine, Madame," he said grudgingly. He stared at his feet.

Marguerite was not fooled by his denial. She took him by the arm and dragged him along to the dressing-room. "I want to have a word with you."

She pointed to a sofa and sat down, determined to find out what was wrong with the boy. "I can't understand your attitude, Jeanot," she told him in a friendly manner. "You seemed happy enough at first. Do you perhaps miss the adventurous life with your uncle and his friends?"

He shook his head. Then he changed his mind and admitted silently: "Yes, I do--who wouldn't? But I enjoy being with you, Madame Marguerite," he added quickly. "I wouldn't want to go back. I only wish that..."

She frowned. He broke off his sentence and blushed, very much confused. "What do you wish for?" she tried to help him, although it came out rather sharp. "No, don't turn your head away from me!"

Two dark eyes looked straight into hers. They were radiant with hidden emotion.

"Speak up, or I'll lose my patience," she repeated.

"You asked for it!" he exploded. "All right, I'll tell you what's on my mind. I think it is a mistake to marry the marquis--pure and simple."

Slowly, Marguerite's cheeks showed two spots of flaming red. Before she knew it, her hand shot out and lashed the boy's face. "Imprudent brat!" she cried out, deeply hurt by his words. "How dare you speak like that!"

Jeanot jumped to his feet, ready to defend himself. It was a reflex he remembered too well. His fists clenched and the knuckles turned white. "You asked for it," he said. "You better believe me. This marriage will make you unhappy. You don't know the true character of the man you are engaged to. He's malicious!"

42

Marguerite's anger now reached the point of boiling. "Your insinuations are out of place!" she hissed. "Leave this room before I give you a whipping you won't forget!"

"I'm staying, "he stated, just as determined and holding his ground. His dark eyes challenged her to hit him again. The tension rose.

"I'm not through, Madame!" he then said. "You must know that the marquis behaves in an entirely different way when he is not with you. I watched him cripple a dog, just because the animal ran before his feet. And he enjoyed it."

"The dog perhaps bit him," she replied.

"The animal made him stumble, and his nice satin breeches got muddied. But what is worse, he became even angrier when one of the maids laughed at the incident!"

His words did not make an impact. He did not mention what happened to the maid later on, how she now did her work with a swollen face and bruises on her skin--apparently the result of a tiff with her lover.

"The marquis has a reputation in Saint-Denis," he popped up. Now he was rewarded by a sharp intake of breath.

Marguerite's anger slowly ebbed away. Could the boy be right? Was there any truth in his accusations? Was she so wrong about the man she had begun to love?

"He's a gambler of the worst sort," Jeanot went on. "He enters houses of ill repute. He's after your money, Madame!"

She smiled, relieved to hear only that. The child showed concern, how sweet! "He barely needs my money, "she said. "Hilaire is a wealthy man in his own right. And what of his gambling. Well, that's not a crime. Every gentleman takes a gamble every now and then."

"You have nothing against it?" he asked, clearly shaken.

"As long as it remains a pass-time," she acknowledged. "And to wipe away your fears, I can assure you that the estates and the money Etienne left me will remain under my control, however unusual this may be. Hilaire suggested it himself and the solicitor drew up a contract in that sense."

"How clever!" he exclaimed. "Can't you see he wants to throw sand into your eyes, Madame? He pretends to be a saint."

Her angry mood had long ebbed away. She thought she could detect the cause of the boy's antipathy against the marquis. "I won't send you back to your uncle's," she laughed. "You will be my page boy in the new household, and nobody will learn about your past."

"I can take care of myself," he grumbled. "It's you I worry about, Madame. Uncle Dominique has especially asked me to keep an eye on you."

"I know," she admitted, endeared by his attitude. "But I think he hinted to possible 'accidents' and to threats to my safety. He would certainly find it a good idea that I take a new husband."

He shrugged his shoulders and left the room. There was no talking to Madame. She was blinded by her affection and could not be persuaded to listen.

~ * ~

On October 17th, 1720, Marguerite de Vallencieux, widowed Baroness de Laneuil, became the wife of Hilaire Louis Charles d'Aubervilliers, and hence she would carry the title of marchioness. The ceremony, only witnessed by the close family, was short and intimate. A warm glow went through her body when Hilaire slid his ring over her finger. Her cheeks blushed in the same shade as the roses on her white satin dress and her green eyes sparkled like emeralds.

Her new husband smiled at her when the priest took their hands and blessed them. She offered him her lips for a sweet kiss.

Six

As soon as the last dish of the extensive celebration meal was cleared away and the dancing begun, Marguerite decided it was time to retire to her room. She wished her guests a pleasant evening and, accompanied by a couple of giggling cousins, mounted the steps. In her bedroom, Rosette was already waiting. The cousins helped her undress and put on a flimsy nightgown, exclaiming their admiration. When they finally left, Rosette brushed her mistress's hair until it shone like the wing of a raven. Then she invited her to step into bed and wished her a pleasant night.

An Italian clock ticked away the seconds. The candlesticks became smaller and smaller and the room became darker. Marguerite began to feel the unease.

What was keeping Hilaire? Had he not promised to join her as soon as possible? At long last, she fell asleep.

~ * ~

She woke up when Hilaire entered the room at last. She had no idea of the time, but it had to be very late--or early in the morning. He threw his coat aside and took off his wig. The rest of his clothing followed. He did not say anything, but got into bed and took possession of her body.

Even with her modest experience--Etienne being the only man she had slept with--Marguerite realized this was not an act of love. It was done in an automated way, without feelings. Once he was satisfied, he turned over and fell asleep. Already she knew she had made a big mistake in marrying him.

The next morning, she found him at the breakfast table, dressed in a travelling outfit.

"Are you going away?"

"My dear, I've received an invitation for the hunt at Fontainbleau, so I'll be gone for a couple of days."

"I thought..." She hesitated, not sure she wanted to air what was on her mind. "We were just married..."

"Nothing much in that," he laughed. "You're not a commoner's wife anymore, my dear. You must learn how people in our circles behave."

"So you leave me?"

"You're free to do whatever you want," he said. "If you want to come hunting too, just say so."

She shook her head. "No, I don't want that."

"Then I must bid you farewell for the time being," he replied. "Oh, and by the way, do you know you resemble a woman I once knew? A Margot de Bassy? You two could be twin sisters."

With those words he left her to her ponderings. What could she do? She had exchanged vows which were holy to her. She was the wife of Hilaire now, however she regretted it. She had to live with that and make the best of it.

~ * ~

On the fourth day of her new married life she had a visitor.

"*Monsieur le Comte de Vallencieux* has just arrived," a groom announced. She followed him down to the drawing-room where her brother Armand was seated before the fire.

As soon as he saw her, he jumped to his feet. "Let me congratulate you on your recent marriage, *petite soeur*," he said, while kissing her cheeks. "I would have liked to witness it personally, but alas, my regiment was on autumn maneuvers. I do hope you received my good wishes in time, and of course I came as soon as I could."

"Why, thank you Armand," she replied, full of surprise. Normally her brother did not display such amicable manners. "But please sit down. Can I pour you a glass of wine?"

"Yes, I'm hard up for a drink," he laughed. "My throat has never been drier--I've come straight from Compiegne."

"Are you staying for a couple of days?" she asked, while she called for Jeanot. When her brother acted this friendly, she did not want to do less.

"I have to return to Vallencieux tomorrow, so don't make any special arrangements for me. I'll only stay this one night. I suppose I've only come because you ought to know I'm extremely pleased with this marriage."

"That's the first time you approve of something I do," she said without thinking. She could not hide her sarcasm. This show of brotherly love made her suspicious.

Armand shook his head, for once honest in his feelings. "You and I haven't always been on good terms, sister," he said. "Can you believe however that I always acted in your best interest? Grandfather wasted the entire family fortune and there was no money for your dowry. You can't imagine how worried father and I were when we considered your future! A girl without money has no chances, even if one of her ancestors is Henri the Fourth. So when Etienne asked for your hand, it came to us as a blessing from above. He fell in love with you at first sight and would have taken you if you were a beggar. And as it happened--you have to admit this--you were happy with him, weren't you?"

"Yes," she answered, impressed by his speech. "It was a good marriage, after all. I was… satisfied. Etienne was a good husband to me."

"He made you a wealthy woman," Armand stated. "And now you are the Marchioness of d'Aubervilliers."

"Yes."

If this dry answer made him wonder, Armand did not show. Marguerite often had such moods. "I have good news for you," he changed the subject.

"I'm thinking of an engagement myself. I became thirty this year and I think it's time to sire a son and heir."

She was at once interested. "Who is she? Do I know her?"

"I don't think so. Denise is the widow of general Gontrand. She's still a young woman, twenty-four, and very docile. She may not be a beauty like our mother or you, but I think she'll be a perfect wife to me. The general left her some money, which we can use well on the estate. The roof needs fixing badly, remember?"

"You have my blessing," Marguerite toasted and her lips curled into a smile. She wanted to say more, but abruptly shut her mouth when the tall figure of her husband showed up in her eyesight. She had not heard him enter.

"Marguerite, *ma chère*," he smiled, "where are your manners? Aren't you going to introduce me to our guest?"

"My brother, Count de Vallencieux. Armand, this is my husband, Hilaire d'Aubervilliers," she gestured, following up his order.

The men made each other's acquaintance and soon were involved in an animated conversation. Marguerite asked to be excused and went to her private rooms where she thought about what she was going to ask Hilaire later on.

She warned Madame Villard, the housekeeper, the table had to be set for three then slowly dressed for dinner.

~ * ~

Not long after Armand retired to bed, Marguerite joined her husband in the library, where he was looking at some documents. She handed him another glass of wine.

"I wanted to ask you something," she began. Ever since he mentioned the other girl, she had been wondering... A twin sister? She had none. Two girls who looked almost identical--a coincidence?

"You said you knew a Margot de Bassy," she continued.

48

He smiled, but it was not a very pleasant sight. *Perhaps I'm overacting*, she thought, *but do I see cruelness on his face?*

"Certainly, a long time ago," he answered.

"Who was she, then?"

"No one important, my dear. Just a *courtisane* whom I met when I was younger. She thought she was clever, that one, and she played a dirty trick on me."

"And what did you do?"

He shrugged. "Nothing, I'm afraid. She disappeared. But should I ever meet her again, she won't escape my punishment."

A cold shiver ran over her spine. "You said I look like her."

"Yes, that is true. But you come from a noble family, she was just trash from the street."

"I suppose everyone has a look-alike somewhere."

"That's what they say anyway.'"

Not much later she went to her rooms and hoped he would not come to join her. She was lucky in that aspect, but she did not sleep well. Her mind was too busy with the new information. She realized she had to find out what happened in the past, and if the Margot her husband had mentioned and she were the same person.

Seven

Rain fell down in streams and a southwestern wind tormented the trees and the undergrowth. It was a chilly night in November, with an atmosphere fitting the spirit of All Saints.

The streets lay deserted. This weather compelled the citizens to stay indoors behind their warm fires. The unfortunate guards sought shelter at an inn and warmed their bones with brandy.

The horseman could not wish for better circumstances. Nobody witnessed his approach to a desolate house where he jumped out of the saddle. Nobody saw how he opened the gate with a big iron key. Nobody asked what he was doing.

The mysterious stranger obviously knew his way around. He led his horse to the stables, lit a lantern and walked along the empty boxes--cold and hollow--to the door that connected the stables with the kitchen. His footsteps echoed on the broken flagstones.

He paused for a moment and listened. Then he cursed. Gaillard had not yet arrived!

If possible, the kitchen was colder than the stables and a shiver ran down his spine. Still cursing, he set himself to the task of lightning a fire. It was not easy, as he was not used to such chores. The wood left beside the fireplace was damp and would not burn immediately. At long last, a flame caught on. He undid his cloak which was soaking wet, hung it over a chair and placed it before the fire. Then he descended into the cellar and returned with a bottle of brandy.

He wiped off the dust, opened it and gulped some fluid down to warm his blood.

Many more minutes passed before Gaillard finally showed up.

"You're late," his master chided.

"I come from Versailles," the man answered, shrugging. "In this weather it would be irresponsible to gallop down the lanes. Ah! I see you've got a nice fire going."

"Having servants is such a comfort," the nobleman sneered. "But let's come to business now. It appears that some people are nervous and a bit suspicious. I propose we do something about that."

"Yes, that would be best," Gaillard agreed, while he settled himself in front of the fire. "Will you pass the brandy to me?"

The other tossed the bottle. His movements showed his anger but Gaillard could not be bothered. In the course of the years he had lost the last bit of respect for his master and he refused to be intimidated by him--if he had ever been. He knew he was indispensable as a go-between and resolver of dark affairs. This knowledge gave him a certain power over the nobleman.

"Did you find out what I need to know?"

"Yes, I checked the antecedents of the woman," Gaillard started, completely at ease and not wanting to be hurried. "Marguerite de Vallencieux. Sole daughter of Jaques Armand Philippe, Count de Vallencieux., and of Anne de Salanges. Almost twenty-seven years old by now. The lady has two brothers, Armand and René. The eldest is in the king's service and the youngest immigrated to Canada. Nothing peculiar about the brothers. Marguerite was engaged to Etienne de Laneuil, a widower, in 1710. However, before the wedding could take place, the young lady disappeared--off to some adventures?--and it took her brother a year to find her. Apparently she suffered an accident and was brought to a convent in Burgundy to recover. The marriage went ahead a couple of months later. First they spent some years in Dijon, and later Monsieur and Madame de Laneuil set up house in Paris. After the deadly accident of the Attorney-General, the merry widow became the wife of the noble Marquis d'Aubervilliers."

The nobleman grabbed the bottle out of Gaillard's hands and swallowed through a large gulp. "Do we know what happened during her disappearance?"

"No--at least not yet. I discovered the name of a man who supposedly spent time with her in the summer of 1710, somewhere near Auxerre. But we haven't been able to locate him."

"Good. Continue the search. And what about Margot de Bassy?"

"Nothing," Gaillard said. "Ever tried to ask questions in Saint-Denis? Lucky for us, though, we have an advantage: we know that sweet little Margot became Duchesse, the hostess of the Domino club. And one night she showed off your diamond necklace..."

"Damn her!" his master cursed. "How I regret showing it to Isabelle in the first place! I believe the devil himself is playing around with it. How did it come into the possession of a hooker?"

"We're trying to find out."

"But not fast enough. And I can't afford to be linked to murder, don't forget that."

"The two women?"

"Yes--if there really are two different ones--I have my doubts on that matter. To start with, we must get rid of Margot de Bassy. I am sure she recognized me that night in the club."

"How should it be done?"

"Poison. It's clean and easy."

"It worked well on the other woman," Gaillard nodded.

His master cursed again. "We haven't been careful enough with her. See the mess she got us in."

"It was that foolish maid's fault. Why couldn't she take away the necklace before she gave her the poisoned wine? No, she ran off, scared out of her wits."

"You ought to have seen to that," the nobleman reproached him. "Because of this mistake we haven't reached the end of this mess. There are still too many people around who could bear witness."

"You can rely on me," Gaillard promised. "I won't screw up this time. I can't foresee any problems in disposing of Marguerite d'Aubervilliers. I'm rather friendly with one of her kitchen-maids. She told me they needed another valet at the house."

The nobleman took his cloak from the chair and flung it over his shoulders, ready to set off. "One more thing, Gaillard--take a fast-killing poison. I don't want her to suffer more than necessary."

He pressed his hat on his half-wet hair and disappeared without saying goodbye.

Eight

A thousand candles shed their light and lit up the d'Aubervilliers residence. Tonight, the birthday of the marchioness was celebrated and the marquis had spared no costs to make this an event that would be mentioned for days to come.

At the first floor, the marquis and his lady welcomed their guests. Marguerite wore a regal gown of yellow brocade, trimmed with lace and tiny sparkling stones. Despite the current fashion, she refused to cover her shiny black hair with powder or a wig and instead wore it pinned up high and woven through with emeralds--the same jewels that adorned her ears and neck. To make her beauty stand out even more, the marquis dressed in a simple outfit, although the lace of his tie and cuffs was of the most exquisite quality and his tie-pin consisted of a priceless and brilliantly sparkling jewel.

"His Royal Highness, the Regent. The Princess of Orleans. The Duke of..."

Excitement spread through the wide room. Marguerite straightened her shoulders and held her head upright. The prince and his train walked up the stairs. As soon as they entered, she sank down in the deep *reverence* demanded at the court, her chin almost on her knees.

Philippe d'Orleans immediately extended his hand to her, which was adorned with many priceless rings. He helped her up. A charmed smile appeared on his somewhat fleshy face. "*Je suis enchanté, Madame*. Really, it pleases me to meet you at last."

Then he addressed himself to Hilaire, and went on in a familiar way: "I must compliment you on your choice of bride, *mon ami*. You may well be trusted to select the most beautiful of women for your personal use."

He started laughing, and after a while Hilaire joined in with him. It became apparent to all present that both men were on intimate terms, and many envied the marquis for this show of privilege.

"My dear chap, I insist that you'll soon introduce your lovely marchioness to our court. We shall be looking out for that." The regent patted Hilaire on the shoulder then set off to taste the wine in the adjoining drawing-room.

Now the introduction of the less important people began.

"*Madame la Duchesse de Berry.*"

"*Monsieur le Duc de Saint-Simon.*"

"*Monsieur le Marquis de Villeneuve.*"

"*Le Maréchal Gontré.*"

"*Lord Newton.*"

Marguerite was busy exchanging words with the field-marshal and hardy noticed how a man dressed in black bowed over her hand. She only saw his powdered wig.

"My respects, Madame."

The voice was hoarse and intriguing. Then the man raised himself--and she looked into his maimed face. An irregular scar, most likely caused by a sword thrust, ran from temple to jaw. It touched the right eyelid, which was constantly half-lowered, and twisted the mouth's corner--which gave the face an eternal sardonic expression.

For a moment, she did not move. Someone behind her tried to muffle a cry. It was enough to remind her of her duties as hostess. "We thank you for coming, Monsieur," she forced herself to say.

He nodded and she noticed the surprise in his gray eyes. No, it was more than surprise--it almost looked like anguish, as if he had suffered a terrible shock. How strange! She could understand her own reaction, but his was peculiar.

As if he sensed her thoughts, he thanked her abruptly and moved away with a haughty air.

"Marguerite, how could you!" Chantale whispered into her ear, her tone indignant. "How could you invite this degenerate? Has nobody told you he's an outcast? He's never invited to any party of importance."

Her chin pointed in the direction of Lord Newton. He stood somewhat apart from the others and looked bored.

"I did not know," Marguerite answered. "I suppose it was Hilaire who suggested we should invite Lord Newton. Apparently the Regent holds him in high esteem. What's wrong with him then?"

"Oh, I can't tell you precisely," Chantale admitted. "It has something to do with an old scandal. I believe something with his wife. I was only a child when the rumors spread around--too young to overhear the conversations of the elders. Anyway, I do know that old King Louis banished him from France. But Philippe d'Orleans pardoned him a couple of years later. He owns vast sums of money, which he apparently won by gambling."

Marguerite could not prevent a smile. "I wouldn't call that a crime! Is that the reason why he can't be received? In that case, we'd have to close our doors to many people."

"You are making fun of me," her cousin complained. "No, that is not the reason! I told you I don't know what he did, but it must have been something awful. Only the Regent accepts him, but he is friendly to everyone who fills his pockets."

The young woman became intrigued. She appeared to stumble into one mystery after the other. "What is an English earl doing at the French court?" she wondered aloud.

"He was raised here," Chantale said, glad to be of assistance. "He's the stepson of Monsieur de Montfort. He raised the boy as his own."

"His mother was English then?"

"I suppose so. Newton got his title when his uncle and two of his cousins died. Now he is the sole heir of the Duke of Shrevenport."

"I see."

"I get the cold shivers every time I see him--to say nothing of what I'd do when he laid hands on me. Do you think he'll find one single dancing partner?"

"You're exaggerating, cousin. I think he'd make an attractive man but for that ugly scar. Don't you see? But oh, I'm sorry… Hilaire beckons me. We'll continue our talk later."

She hurried over to her husband who told her that His Royal Highness wanted to open the ball with her. The man with the scar was instantly forgotten.

~ * ~

Many hours later the ballroom offered an abandoned sight. The masses moved to the dining room where a gigantic cold buffet was set up. Here and there some whispering and muffled laughter came out of a dark corner.

In the library, driven gamblers staked enormous amounts of money, their eyes greedy and calculating.

Marguerite watched Hilaire's doings with growing anguish. She never expected he would gamble so excessively! At first he was lucky and won fair amounts. But for some time now luck had left him. He wrote one *promesse* after the other, for thousands of *livres*. Yet he played on in such a reckless way that it brought her shivers and cold sweat. Why did he not put down his cards? Two more games and he would be ruined…

The Duke of Saint-Simon had the winning hand. With a sigh of relief she saw how Hilaire finally pushed back his chair. "Enough for tonight," he said with a faint smile. "Another round like this, and I would have to beg my wife for some pocket-money!"

"You can't have everything, d'Aubervilliers," Lord Newton remarked. "A beautiful wife and Fortune's favor? It's more than one man deserves."

"You seem to get away with it quite nicely, Newton," Hilaire answered, while throwing a meaningful look at Bénédicte de Condé, Duchess of Maine and a granddaughter of the great Condé. It was a public secret she was attracted to the scarred lord and would do almost anything to get him into her bed.

Newton leaned back in his chair to be more comfortable and took a draught of wine. "Ah, but then I'm after all *Monsieur le Diable*," he said ironically. "The women all tell me I'm horrible, but given a chance they are only too keen to get into bed with me--isn't that strange?"

Bénédicte de Condé looked insulted and Marguerite felt it her duty to do something to remove the tension. It did not only arise from this incident. It had mounted from the moment Newton joined the players and cast incongruous, secretive glances at her--perhaps he thought she did not notice them. "Please apologize for that remark, *Monsieur*," she reprimanded him.

"Your wish is my command, fair lady," he smiled. "I shall do as you ask, and hold my tongue for the rest of the evening. Do I regain your favor now?"

Marguerite did not answer. She sensed he made fun of her and she felt the anger rising. She had observed him as well and concluded the man was a sarcastic bastard after all.

~ * ~

Because Hilaire stopped playing, there was an open place at the table. It was late in the evening, and perhaps this was the reason why nobody seemed willing to take in the empty spot. As a last resort, the duke of Saint-Simon turned to Marguerite. "We'd like to play a final game, Madame. Can we persuade you to join us?"

She hid a sigh behind her fan. She had secretly hoped the guests would start to say their goodbyes. She felt tired after such a long night, as she was not used to staying up very late. However, she could not afford to offend the duke by a refusal. She had not picked up a single card throughout the evening and it could give the impression she was afraid to lose some money. "Of course," she stated courteously, "but you must forgive my inexperience and eventual mistakes. I don't play very often."

"You are too modest," the duke smiled.

Newton dealt the cards and the game commenced. To her big surprise, Marguerite was extremely fortunate and the handling of the cards looked much easier than she expected. She knew immediately which card to play and used the mistakes of others to her advantage. Soon she heaped up her winnings.

Madame du Maine lost and called out she was giving up. "I do say, you have a smooth routine, Madame--for a beginner," she added vehemently. It seemed to irritate her to be defeated by a woman she recognized as a rival. She too noticed the looks exchanged between Newton and the marchioness--and had an entirely other explanation for them. Yes, Marguerite d'Aubervilliers was a rival in gaining Newton's affection.

"My compliments, *Madame la Marquise*," Newton complimented her. Still, there was kind of laughter in his words, as if he doubted her status.

She decided to let it go. "I propose we all follow Madame du Maine's example," she said instead. "I can't ignore my duties any longer."

"It'll be dawn soon," de Saint-Simon agreed. "To be honest, I can't say I am sorry to stop. I have lost a year's rent to you and Lord Newton."

"I didn't think you cared for that, *mon vieux*," Newton drawled. "Come on, let's play another round."

The duke smiled, but shook his head determinedly. "You forget we are guests at a ball, Newton. It is very late already. I am going home."

"And you, Madame, can I tempt you?" the lord invited Marguerite. "We can play a game of hoca, forget about the rules and set our own stakes."

"No thank you, Monsieur. I suggest you find another partner."

She rose from the table, straightened her skirts and wanted to walk away. His following remark brought her to a standstill.

"I thought you had some nerve, Madame! This could well become an interesting game. You should really consider it."

She frowned, irritated by his attitude. He surely was a master in psychology. He knew she would respond when he dared her courage.

"Milord is referring to a certain situation in the game of hoca," de Saint-Simon came to her assistance. "When only two players remain, they may quit or decide to go on. Previous losses or winnings don't count anymore in that stage, and they can choose a stake of their own liking. Each one has to accept, of course."

"It demands nerves of steel and an iron determination," Newton added. "I challenge you to show your spirit, Madame."

"This is really going too far," the duke interrupted. "You shouldn't tease the marchioness, my dear man. Madame, don't pay any attention to what he's saying. I beg of you!"

"Marguerite is a grown woman. Let her make her own decisions," Hilaire put in. When he sensed the excitement, he had come back to the gambling table.

"What should I do?" she asked him.

He shrugged. "I don't know. I'd be tempted, of course. Perhaps... Yes, I think I'd do it."

The tension rose higher. Philippe d'Aubilly heard part of the conversation and walked over. "Don't do it, Marguerite," he advised. "Remember what happened to your grandfather de Vallencieux. He lost his entire fortune in a game of hoca."

More and more people gathered around the players and various remarks were heard. It became incredibly hot and crowded.

"Madame?" Newton urged her.

She realized a power game was being played. His whole attitude told her he underestimated her daring and he tried to make her look like a fool. Did he act this way because she rebuked him earlier, or was there a deeper reason? Well, it would not work. She would not give him the opportunity to spout further remarks.

Scarlet blushes appeared on her cheeks. "I'll play," she said loud and clear.

She did not hear the deep sigh that went through the assembled crowd. She only saw the green table and the amused smile of her opponent.

"Choose your stake, Madame."

She took a second to think. Then she turned to de Saint-Simon and asked him how she should phrase her words. He gladly told her all she needed to know.

"If I win," she said at last, "I demand of you that you'll leave Paris and rid us of your presence."

He kept a poker face. "Accepted, Madame. If I win, I demand of you that you'll share my bed for one night."

Her eyes opened wide, and she closed her fan rather brusquely. "Accepted," she answered with a tight throat. *I'm a fool to agree, but something makes me do this.*

The duke dealt the cards and acted as the banker. Gone was his desire to return home.

Marguerite concentrated on her hand of cards. She did not look around and did not notice how glances were exchanged around the table. Her self-confidence grew and she regained her composure. The cards were just right--if she could not win with these, she would probably never.

"Another card?"

For one last moment she studied the odds--then she denied. With a firm gesture she lowered her hand and spread the cards on the table.

As if on command all heads turned towards the Englishman. He relaxed in his chair and waited until he noticed the nervous trembling of her fingers. Finally he decided to put down his own hand, but left the cards covered. He stood up and took one of her hands into his.

"You have beautiful hands, Madame," he said slowly, while he brought her fingers to his lips. She felt a faint touch of his breath. "Elegant, and yet so strong--as is fitting for a lady of character."

She tore her hand loose, at which he laughed cordially. Then, acting very nonchalant, he turned over his cards one by one. "Shall we agree upon tomorrow evening, Madame? I'll send my carriage to pick you up around seven." He made a courtly bow in general, addressed one last glance at her then took his leave.

Speechless with anger and frustration, Marguerite stared at his set of winning cards. Fate had decided indeed. They were to become enemies.

Nine

"I won't go! I won't even think of it!"

Marguerite's hair swirled wildly around her face and her eyes shot fire. She looked bewildered. In the course of the day a nervous tension had built up which now discharged in a violent outburst.

Her grasping fingers sought and found an object, picked it up and threw it away. The vase shot through the room with force, missed Hilaire's head by an inch, and smashed into pieces against the wall.

Her husband considered this outburst with complacency, as he realized it was his casual remark that triggered this explosion.

"He set me up," she raged on. "I am sure of it. I don't know how he did it, but he cheated. All the time he's been out humiliating me. I hate that man!"

The marquis smiled wryly. Now she went too far. He could understand that she was angry for her loss--Marguerite was not the person to admit defeat--but when she began about foul play... Damn Newton! Did he always have to be so sure of himself? Why not be courteous and allow the hostess of the evening to win a game?

"Aren't you exaggerating?" he tried to calm her down. "As far as I could judge, it was a fair game and you lost. Debts of honor must be paid."

"Oh, you!" she hissed. How could she make him understand? How could she explain what she only understood vaguely herself? Lord Newton, her intuition told her, was a mighty threat to her peace of mind. "I won't allow that he touches me," she whispered.

"Don't act so childish, Marguerite," her husband admonished her, finally losing his temper. "Tonight you'll dress in your best attire and you'll meet Newton."

"How can you say that?" she cried out, deeply hurt by his attitude. "You are my husband!"

"You mustn't see it in that light. You are only paying back a debt-- nothing more, nothing less."

"Don't you care then?" Disappointment shone in her eyes and all of the fire left her. She shrugged helplessly and wiped some curls away that stuck against her hot cheeks. She allowed Hilaire to take her into his arms and rested her head against his shoulder.

He stroked her hair and tried to comfort her by just being there. "I do care, sweetheart," he said gently. "If it makes you any happier, I'll challenge Newton to a duel tomorrow."

She tore herself loose with an impatient gesture. "If it makes *me* happy?"

"Of course. It has nothing to do with me, after all," he remarked evenly.

She stared at him, trying to sense the thoughts behind that bored look. Once more she was faced with one of the less unpleasant angles of his character. He really did not care! "You want me to sleep with him?" she asked.

"I don't want that," he replied. "If you really were to be his mistress, if you desired to be with him and by doing that bring shame on my name--yes, then I would kill him and punish you as well. But the two things can hardly be compared. You'll only share his bed once--a thing you have to do. And for the good course of things, we'll settle the incident with a duel that will meet every question of honor."

"You don't love me," she phrased her thoughts.

"Who's looking for love in a marriage?" he said impatiently.

"I did," she admitted silently. They would never be close again; that dream had vanished. They would remain strangers, polite and courteous, who lived separate lives in the same house.

"You are too idealistic, Marguerite," Hilaire said. "We get along fine, don't you agree? We both have a fortune to spend, and our match was a most sensible thing. It consolidates our position in society. We are even happier than most couples, since you are very attractive. As long as you continue to seduce me, we'll be happy enough."

His words were the finishing stroke. They chased her out of the room and up to her bedroom where she cried hot tears over herself, over what could have been.

~ * ~

Marguerite stood in the hall of Newton's residence and waited. Her face was white and she felt chilled to the bone. She shivered, despite the welcoming fire in the hearth.

An elderly woman approached. The muscles around her mouth folded into a queer smile, as if she had fun over something Marguerite knew nothing about. "Madame la Marquise? I am Lord Newton's housekeeper. Will you please follow me? Milord is waiting for you in the blue room."

Marguerite nodded and followed the housekeeper, who showed her into a room further down the hall. She took a couple of steps forward and waited for Newton's move.

He immediately left the chair he was occupying and came forward to greet her. Gallantly he kissed her cold hand. "I am so glad you have come, Madame," he stated.

"Did you expect differently?" she asked. She walked down the room to the fireplace and stretched her hands out to the glow of the flames.

Newton threw her an askance look. "I don't know what I expected," he admitted. "A lot of things, I guess. Indignation, eyes like daggers, a raging fury, even a gun to punish me for cheating at cards."

He said it frankly, waiting for her reaction. Oddly enough, none followed. Marguerite did not even move--the terrible cold that made her freeze absorbed all her energy.

Something in the way she stared at the fire seemed to alarm Newton. He came closer and only then noticed the paleness of her skin, the blankness of expression and her shivering limbs. Gently he caught her by the shoulders and slowly turned her towards him. "But you are not well!" he exclaimed. "If I leave you like this, you'll faint any minute. I am an idiot for not noticing it before…"

She shook her head. She had not enough force to tear herself free from his touch--a sensation that somewhere deep down in her memory was recognized as firm and assuring. However, she was too far gone to register this notion. "I am not sick," she said silently. "It is cold outside. I'd feel better if I could drink something warm."

"I'll take care of that immediately. Please have a seat."

He drew a chair closer by the fire and made her sit down. He knelt down beside her, unwrapped her cloak and rubbed her frozen hands until the blood started to pulse again. In the meantime warm wine was brought to the room and the glowing heat of it finally drove the cold from her body.

"You're blushing again," her host noticed with satisfaction. "I like it better that way! I propose we'll have dinner now and afterwards, I'll see you home personally."

She did not give an answer.

"It is only fair I should do that. As I confessed to you, I used a trick to win the game. Against all my better instincts I wanted to see you lose...don't ask me why. You are a very good player, Madame, but for a very long time I earned my living with cards and picked up every trick in and out of the book. You simply could not win. Now I regret my action more than I can express."

Her lips opened and shut a couple of times before she decided on what to say. She was not surprised to find out he had cheated, more by the fact he admitted it openly. For heaven's sake, what kind of game did he play? "I did suspect you cheated," she finally said, but not with an angry voice. "So I am the winner of the game, after all."

"Do you insist I leave Paris, Madame?"

She hesitated shortly then shook her head. "No, I don't. We'd better forget that game. But as a sort of compensation I ask for your honesty. Why was my defeat so important to you?"

He looked irritated. "Didn't I state earlier that I rather not give explanations? You're much too curious, Madame!"

"You made that plain," she returned. "But allow me to speak my mind as well. The reason why I am curious--if you like to call it so--is that I have no memory of what went on before 1711. Recently things happened which make me want to find out how my life was before that date."

"I am sorry," he said. "But I suppose I knew. I...guessed it."

"You recognized me!" Suddenly she knew it with certainty. It partly explained his shocked expression when they were introduced. Yet there remained more to it--more than he was willing to admit. "Please, Monsieur, be frank with me," she pleaded against her better judgment. Please say when and where you first met me."

A light shortly flickered in his eyes then again it was impossible to read his glance. What did she see? Remorse, sorrow, passion?

"I am sorry, Madame. I really can't answer that question. Be assured that I only act in your best interest. Some things are better left alone..."

"But you know something about me," she insisted. Her voice rose to a higher pitch.

He made an impatient gesture with his hand. "Perhaps," he admitted, "perhaps not. I could be mistaken. I suggest you find your information elsewhere."

"You are not a gentleman," she concluded. She realized nothing would tempt him to say more.

He produced a wry smile. "You have already made that plain to me. You detest me, don't you? In fact, sometimes I feel you hate me. I can't blame you for it, but it would interest me to know what causes this aversion. Is it my looks or rather my behavior?"

He asked it casually, as if the answer did not matter. She felt, however, the undercurrent of tension that overwhelmed her once more. "Your appearance doesn't bother me, Monsieur. Your attitude is revolting, I admit, but

I am sure it is done on purpose, just to shock people. I can understand that in a way. You are shut out of society, you are probably hurt…"

"Thank you for your honesty, Madame. You are a rare specimen of the female race, I must say. You are the first woman I have met who is not afraid to speak frankly--and I do admire such qualities."

His gray eyes caught her gaze and focused her attention--suddenly the world around her disappeared into thin air. In her mind, a vague memory tried to wrestle itself free from the bondages of oblivion. It did not work out. The pain became intense, mentally as well as physically. Her mind gave up the fight and dragged her along in comforting darkness. She lost consciousness.

Newton immediately became a different person. His shoulders sank deeper and the lines around his mouth came to stand out more. The damaged eyelid trembled heavily. He bit his lips and stared, seemingly taken aback at the unconscious woman. Then finding his energy and instinct to act, he picked her up and carried her out of the room. Loudly, he shouted for assistance.

Blood…blood was everywhere. On her hands, on the ground, on Armand's clothes. The look on his face was demonical and Marguerite screamed her heart out. The piercing sound shook her from the nightmare, and she found herself in bed--in a strange bed for that matter, covered in sweat.

At once two strong arms closed around her and held her tight. She rested her head on a man's shoulder and closed her eyes again. He whispered soothing words of comfort into her ear. The rhythm of the low voice had a calming effect. Without great surprise, she identified the man as Lord Newton. She was afraid and Anthony was the only one who could protect her from the horrors of the dark. Each time she shut her eyes again she was back at this dreadful place and its cruel pain.

"I'm so scared," she whispered against his shoulder. ""I sit on the ground and my hands are covered in blood… And what is Armand doing there? Oh, it is just terrible!"

"You had a bad dream," Newton assured her. "You fainted some time ago, perhaps that was the reason? My housekeeper was rather worried because it took you so long to regain consciousness. She thought it better if one of us remained in the room with you."

"I don't think it's a nightmare," she said. "I believe this dream tries to tell me something--something which is important. If only I knew what it means. It's not the first time I've had such a strange dream."

"Better not think about it anymore," he advised. "If it is of real importance, it will come back to you, one day or another, then you'll understand. Now try to sleep a bit. The night is half gone and I won't allow you to try and return home at this time. Please accept my hospitality."

"No!" she cried. "I can't stand being alone right now. Stay with me, Anthony, please don't leave me!"

He raised his head with a shock to meet her gaze. In his eyes she read overwhelming joy.

"You remember my name..." he said, very softly.

She nodded vaguely. "Did I say Anthony? I guess I overheard Madame du Maine use your first name, yesterday evening. I am sorry for being so familiar."

The joy was wiped away and only seconds later it was as if it had never been. Lord Newton's face had its normal sardonic expression. "You're welcome to call me Anthony if you want to, *chère dame*."

Although she still quivered, she produced a faint smile. "Yes, I would like that. I wish we could become friends as well."

"Friends? You surely can't mean that, Madame. Do you forget I'm an outcast, that I am suspected of having done unspeakable things?"

"I don't care," she said, very certain of herself. "I believe I am allowed my own opinion. I don't think you will treat me unkindly anymore."

"I stand amazed at that certainty," he replied. He felt annoyed. She was a mighty threat to his piece of mind. How long would he manage to keep his true feelings hidden from her? *Margie my love,* he wanted to cry out, *I was so blind in the past. Blind, and ignorant. Rude and too damned proud. Will you ever forgive me?*

"I need a friend so much," she whispered, reaching out for him. "The only friend I now have is a child, however dear to me. Alas, a child can't fill the void left by my previous husband's death."

She did not look at him, and did not realize he knew nothing about her marriage to Etienne. He did not know she remembered her first husband as the best friend she ever had--and not so much as a lover. "As a friend, I'd like to ask you to stay here with me for the rest of the night. I have grown afraid of the dark."

He shrunk back from her, did not trust his reactions any more. He was not sure if she was really this innocent or just very calculated. Far too long he had distrusted women and their raving ways. The only weapon against it was sarcasm. "So you're not special after all. Let me assure you, Madame d'Aubervilliers, such tricks don't work on me. You are not going to tempt me into doing something I'll regret later. You are a married woman, and although adultery may be *en vogue* these days, I refuse to take part in it."

His raw attack upset her and brought tears to her eyes. "I don't ask you to make love to me," she stuttered. "My marriage vows are holy to me, even if my husband hasn't such high regards for them." She hesitated, not yet willing to talk about the failure of her marriage, especially not in front of the man who suddenly felt so important to her.

"You don't?" he said, friendlier now.

"No. It is just that your presence here in the room would reassure me. I know you will wake me up when I have another nightmare."

Her weakness endeared Newton. Now he did not refuse her hand. His thumb tenderly caressed her fingers. "Alright. In that case I'll have to stay. I'll rest on the sofa and wake you when necessary." He sighed lightly, because this promise cost him some trouble.

"Thank you," she breathed contently.

"It won't make a difference after all," he said. "Whether you spent the night in my house or in my bed, you were here, and I suppose your husband will challenge me to a duel, for the sake of honor."

She gave no answer. She slept already.

Ten

On a December morning, after a restless night, Marguerite felt the need to go riding. She jumped out of bed and opened the curtains to see how the weather looked, as the past weeks had been cursed with lots of rain and heavy gales. A big smile spread over her face when she saw evidence of a clear sky. Yes, she definitely wanted to be on a horse now.

Without hesitation she called for her maid.

Rosette discretely hid a yawn behind her hand. Her mistress was up early, and after spending a long night at the ball given by the baroness d'Allande. She had expected her to sleep until noon, at the least.

"My riding habit and my cape," Marguerite ordered cheerfully. "And please inform the stable lads I want my horse saddled as soon as possible."

"Don't you want any breakfast, Madame? Cook has made cacao for you today, and I brought it up already."

"No, I don't want anything yet. You drink it, Rosette, I know how you enjoy that."

"Yes, Madame."

The maid smiled and picked up her mistress's chamber-gown, which lay thrown on the floor. Then she hurried to the wardrobe.

When Marguerite reached the inner court some twenty minutes later, she noticed with satisfaction that a boy was steadying her mare Julietta, which was prancing nervously. She greeted the animal, an Arab thoroughbred, with a gentle stroke over the nose, and was then helped into the side-saddle. The mare obeyed the gentle pressure of her heel and immediately sped through the open gate.

Soon they left the city behind. They rode into the Bois de Boulogne, where the deserted lanes invited them to a gallop. She gave Julietta free rein and completely gave in to the joy this reckless speed provided. After a while, however, she shortened the reins and forced the mare into an easy canter. The cold air painted cherry blossoms on her cheeks, and her eyes shone with pleasure.

Riding was Marguerite's most loved pastime, and she was very good at it. When she sat atop a good horse, she could beat anyone in a race. With her hair blowing in the wind and the warm contact with the animal's hide, she forgot everything. Whenever she was troubled, she would go for a ride. The fresh breeze made the problems seem less relevant.

The whole of Paris buzzed with rumor after the famous game of hoca at her birthday ball. It was a source of fun to some; a reason to condemn her behavior for others. For the whole of two days Marguerite and Lord Newton were the talk of town. Then the Countess de Riconville ran off with her lover and the gossip focused on a new victim. Nobody showed any more interest in the duel between Newton and the Marquis d'Aubervilliers, which was fought at daybreak in the gardens of the Luxembourg. Both men considered the fight as a formality, and as soon as Newton ran into an innocent scratch on the left arm, they extended hands and parted as friends.

For Marguerite the incident was not so evident. She found it difficult to cope with the fact that her marriage was reduced to a mere '*marriage de raison*', and she doubted she could ever forgive Hilaire for bringing this into the open.

Their attitude towards each other changed in the days and weeks following the incident. They no longer lived as husband and wife. Marguerite shut her bedroom door behind her and subsequently the marquis began to spend his nights outdoors. Sometimes he stayed away for two or three days. She ignored this for convenience's sake and always showed him only the shallow respect she owed him.

Lord Newton had not tried to contact her anew. She understood he did not want to embarrass her any further. But at night, in her lonely bed, she often thought of the hours she spent in his presence. And finally she could no longer deny the apparent truth. She wished he had actually made love to her! She wanted to feel the heat of his lips, the burning of his skin against hers. She tried to fight this weakness but knew all her efforts would be in vain.

~ * ~

Before she realized it, it was near noon. With a sigh of regret, she turned the mare and rode back to Paris.

"Rub Julietta and give her an extra portion," she told the stable lad who came running as she trotted into the courtyard. She hopped out of the saddle without his help and entered the house. She threw aside her whip and riding gloves in the hall and hurried up the stairs to change clothes.

"Rosette, I need a bath!"

The maid did not immediately show up. Marguerite undid her cape and pulled her fingers through her tangled hair.

"Rosette?"

Where was that lazy girl? Patience was not Marguerite's first virtue, and when it became obvious Rosette would not show up, she lost her temper and began to shout the maid's name, her tone becoming angrier with the second.

"Can I help you, Madame?"

Jeanot happened to be around when his mistress came home and he came to see what was causing this tantrum.

"Oh, it's you." Marguerite calmed down a bit. "Try to find out what Rosette is doing for heaven's sake. I've called her a couple of times already. It's nothing for her to neglect her duties. She knows well enough she has to start packing for our trip to Vallencieux tomorrow."

"Yes, Madame."

The boy disappeared, but soon enough he returned to Marguerite's bedroom. "I don't understand," he reported. "Rosette is not in her room and one of the kitchen maids told me she hasn't been down since she came for some cacao."

"That would mean she has not left my rooms," Marguerite concluded, getting more worried by the minute. "I just hope she's fallen asleep. I admit I woke her rather early this morning."

Helped by Jeanot, they went through the apartments. They opened the doors to the wardrobe, to the adjoining rooms of Hilaire. Finally Marguerite went into the small room where her bathtub stood.

There she caught her breath. She tried to withhold the boy from looking but was too late. Jeanot pressed himself between her and the doorpost and also faced the same terrible sight. Next to the tub, the body of the blonde maid laid cramped and stiff.

Jeanot did not shrink back. In his short lifetime, passed in Saint-Denis, he had seen enough dead bodies. Without showing any emotion, he knelt down beside the corpse and began to examine it. He especially paid attention to the face. The blueness of the lips told him poison was used. To make sure, he put his face closer and sniffed. Then he looked around until he found what he was looking for: a used cup with a bottom of cacao in it. He held it carefully under his nose.

"Like I thought, poison!" his verdict came. "One of the fast-killing ones."

Marguerite stared at him. She began to shiver.

"That cacao was meant for me," she stammered. "I told Rosette I didn't want it so she could drink it up."

"For you, Madame?" Jeanot repeated. Then he nodded. "Yes, you may be right. It was against this that my uncle tried to warn you."

Marguerite pressed her hand against her mouth, completely overcome by despair. She could no longer deny the truth: her death was of major importance to someone.

"But why, Jeanot, why would someone want to kill me?" She had not asked Cartouche, who could have answered the question. The boy was just as ignorant of the facts as she was.

73

"Perhaps the reason is to be found in the past," he said at last. "You told me you do not remember what happened in your youth. I suppose all your recent troubles are related to something that happened then, before you married Monsieur Etienne."

His realism had a positive effect. The panic slowly ebbed away.

"Yes, I came to the same conclusion," she admitted. "Poor Rosette! I hope she did not suffer a lot. She was a good lass, and I'll miss her."

"This poison kills instantly," the boy said, "which is a blessing. But you, Madame, have to be extra careful from now on. There may be other attempts."

She shivered again. She was brave enough to cope with the fact that her life was threatened, but it frustrated her to be in the dark about the possible cause. She made a decision she had postponed for too long.

"As soon as we are back from my brother's engagement celebration, I'm going to make a start at finding out what exactly happened nine years ago."

She did have a name: Margot de Bassy. And she had Cartouche to ask around. Something should come out.

~ * ~

Later that day, Hilaire returned from a visit to his cousin. She realized she would not be able to keep the death of her maid a secret so she bade him to come to her rooms as soon as possible. When she related how she found Rosette's poisoned body, Hilaire showed genuine concern.

"But that's terrible, *ma chère*," he told her. "We must find out how and why this could take place, without respite!"

He immediately called together all the servants and told them about the murder. "If anyone knows more, let him or her speak up now," he ordered.

A young kitchen hand began to sob. Hilaire ordered her to tell what she knew.

"Rosette came down to the kitchen," she confessed. "Cook had made cacao for the mistress, but she was outside, dealing with the baker's boy. I was supposed to look after things in the kitchen."

"That's hardly a crime," Marguerite said. The maid sobbed even harder.

"Yes, but I was not alone in the kitchen. The new man, Gaillard, came to see me… He's been very friendly and I like him a lot. It was him that poured out the cacao for Rosette to take up."

It was at once clear to both Hilaire and Marguerite that this fellow Gaillard had put the poison into the drink and thus was to blame for Rosette's death. The marquis ordered that the man should be brought before him, but they found his room empty. The fellow had long been gone.

Because of their eminent departure to Burgundy, which could not be cancelled, they had to leave the case in the hands of the police prefect. He promised to do what he could and immediately set his investigators to work.

The next morning the couple left to attend the betrothal celebrations at Chateau Vallencieux. Hilaire saw to it their coach was accompanied by a group of armed riders to make sure nothing untoward could happen to them on their way.

Marguerite put on a brave face, as she realized she could not stay indoors forever. She would have to be very careful and could not trust anyone-- apart from the few people she instinctively knew would not betray her: Jeanot, Cartouche and Newton. It was the boy who brought her a set of dueling pistols provided by his uncle.

"For you to carry along when traveling, Madame," he said. "They are very easy to handle, my uncle says. See, you only have to aim then pull the trigger." He showed her how.

She thanked the boy and made sure she had one of the loaded pistols in her purse. She intended to carry it along everywhere she went.

~ * ~

Three days later, during the dinner and ball the betrothed couple at Vallencieux organized, Marguerite received an unexpected clue that could help her solve the mystery of her past.

The chateau was filled with neighbors, relatives and friends of the Vallencieux family. Armand clearly wanted to show the world they were not broke yet. Among these people was an older woman, and by chance Marguerite was dragged into a conversation with her.

"You will not remember me," the lady said. "I'm a relative of your first husband Etienne. My name is Solange de Bassy."

That name again! Marguerite's attention shot into focus. She smiled, to encourage the woman to share more confidentialities.

"No, I don't remember you," she said in a friendly voice. "But you must forgive me for that. I suffered an accident."

"Oh yes, I heard about this unfortunate affair," Madame de Bassy agreed. "So terrible! But your brother took good care of you, I know he did."

"Yes."

"And now you live in Paris I'm told. I've never been to the capital. One of my sons has, however. He's a good friend of your brother and they both went to seek their fortune in Paris. His name is Claude."

Marguerite got more and more intrigued. Claude de Bassy? Would he be related to Margot?

"Do you have daughters too?" she asked the woman.

"No, unfortunately not," Solange said.

More to think about--she only had to check one more thing.

"Did Claude de Bassy ever visit Vallencieux?" she asked Armand, when she found a chance.

His answer was more than pleasing: "Of course he did!" her brother answered. "He accompanied Etienne when he first came courting. A nice guy,

76

but he had no way of dealing with money. I saw him in Paris not long ago, and he's completely impoverished!"

Now she knew she had to find out about Margot de Bassy, but she also needed to talk to the man Claude as well.

~ * ~

She did not get an opportunity to do this straight away. When the celebrations at Vallencieux were over, Hilaire insisted they return to Paris immediately. The year was drawing to its end and he wanted to attend the grand ball and fireworks at the residence of the dukes d'Orleans--now the palace of the Regent. So the coach was loaded and the couple reached the capital on the thirtieth of December. The prefect of police came to see them that day, reporting how his men had been unable to find out the whereabouts of the man Gaillard.

"But we'll keep looking," he promised as he took his leave. "One day or other, we'll find a trace and will be able to arrest the fellow."

It was time for supper by then, and afterwards Marguerite went to bed as she felt pretty exhausted by the long trip.

The next day, after sleeping until noon, Marguerite went to see Chantale. She had promised this before she went to Vallencieux. Especially now she was glad to be able to spend a couple of hours at her cousin's because this one's endless chatter enabled her to forget her problems for a while.

Chantale was very enthusiastic about the gown she was going to wear for the ball. "Philippe spent a fortune on the silk!" she boasted. "And he bought me a fur coat to wear during the fireworks. Are you also going to wear your fur?"

"I think so," her cousin answered, trying to keep her tone lighthearted in an attempt at cheerfulness. "But I must go now. I need to get ready on time."

"Of course. I'll see you later on then."

She accompanied Marguerite to her coach and watched it drive off.

~ * ~

The coach came to a sudden standstill. The shock was so abrupt that Marguerite catapulted out of her seat and landed at the opposite one, bumping her head in the process.

While she rubbed her temple to ease the sore, a bullet smashed the glass of the rear window where she had sat and pierced itself in one of the cushions. Instinct told her to hide between the two rows of seats and to keep her head down. No more time to wipe away the blood on her forehead.

Then she heard footsteps coming closer and closer. The door of the carriage opened. Through half-closed eyelids she spotted a slightly built man with olive skin. She held her breath and kept completely still. She could feel his burning glance focus on her.

Perhaps he was not totally convinced by her stillness and the trace of blood on her temple. She felt him come closer, wanting to examine his victim. When the dark shadow fell over her, Marguerite got her chance.

In one swift movement she reached for the gun in the purse that had landed on the floor and was sitting beside her. She grabbed it, totally surprising the villain, and released the trigger. The bullet hit the man full in the chest, just like Jeanot had predicted. The killer collapsed, the eyes staring and the mouth half open. His dead body fell over hers.

Keeping her emotions in check, she breathed eagerly in order not to cry out and pushed the body aside. Then she crawled out of the carriage, picked up her skirts and began to run as fast as she could.

The second gunshot alarmed the Italian's accomplices. They stopped their skirmish with the coacher and the groom and concentrated on the pursuit. Marguerite heard their approach and knew she could not stay ahead of them much longer. She already gasped for breath and was at the end of her reserves.

Luck stayed on her side, however. Just as she was about to give up, her eyes caught sight of a narrow alley on her right--darker than the rest of the neighborhood. She flew into it and found shelter in the porch of a house, praying darkness would make her invisible to her pursuers. She still held the gun in her hand, but knew well enough it was worthless after firing the bullet.

The gang closed in on her and from the sounds, she deducted they were nearing the alley. But then, all of a sudden, she heard more running feet. These came from the opposite direction. Soon the neighborhood echoed with the sound of a turbulent fight.

She carefully left her hiding place, keeping close to the fronts of the houses, because she wanted to see what was going on.

On the street before her, shabbily dressed men, armed to their teeth, stood against the Florentines. These were soon outnumbered and the fight was over in a wink. The nightly peace of the street was restored.

~ * ~

"*Marquise*, you can come out now. You're safe with us."

With relief, she recognized Cartouche's voice. He and his men had come to her rescue! Her legs wobbly, she staggered into the light.

Cartouche immediately was beside her. His strong arm went around her middle and prevented her from tumbling to the ground. He laughed. "I always enjoy a good fight! As for you, you did not do bad either. Where did you learn to shoot, Madame? Your shot went straight through Rufio's heart!"

She trembled even more. He understood immediately she was at the end of her powers, so he held a flat bottle under her nose. "Here, have a drink. The brandy will do you good."

She obeyed him without dispute. The liquor had a sharp taste but warmed her body agreeably. Slowly her senses returned. "I must thank you for being here," she managed to say. "It must have been providence that sent you to this neighborhood."

"Providence has nothing to do with it," declared Cartouche. "Jeanot reported to me what happened to your maid. Since then we've been keeping an eye on you."

She nodded, accepting the facts. "So I thank you, Monsieur Cartouche."

He laughed once more. "Don't you think you'd better call me Dominique, Madame? That is my given name, after all."

At last she could smile. "Yes, that would please me. I think we can even become friends."

"I feel we already are, Marquise."

"Why do you call me so? You could call me Marguerite, which is my given name."

He shrugged. "Marquise suits you. After all, you are married to a marquis. I don't want to sound too presumptuous in calling you Marguerite."

"You have my permission," she answered. But then she became serious again. "You know, you were right. Now I know someone is out to kill me."

"That is correct," he agreed. "These were the same men who killed your previous husband. Luckily for us, their master will now have to look for others to do his dirty work."

"There's something I don't understand," she told him. "If they want my life, why in heaven's name did they kill Etienne?"

Cartouche could not--or did not want to--answer that question. "I don't know the answers, Marquise. Perhaps it was a mistake, perhaps not. From what Jeanot has been telling me, I gather we have to dig into the past. And don't you think we are better placed than you to gather information? I do have sources and I shall gladly be of assistance to you."

"I'd like that," she said. They exchanged a glance of mutual understanding.

Then he took her firmly by the arm. "Come, I'll escort you home now. We can't remain here forever, for the police will surely arrive soon."

"Is that safe for you?" she wanted to know, concerned about his safety. They walked in the direction of her coach. Cartouche kicked Rufio's body into the street and signaled her to get in. She tried not to look at the blood that stuck to the bottom of the vehicle and the cushions.

"It's dark enough to go unrecognized," Cartouche finally answered.

He did not give the blood a glance. She supposed he had grown accustomed to it.

"Are you going to the Regent's ball?" he wanted to know, as they were nearing her house.

"Yes, we received an invitation."

"Then I advise you not to go into the gardens on your own. Who knows where the murderer might strike again…or whom he proves to be?"

Eleven

All at once it became too much to bear. Marguerite could stand it no longer: the glamour and glitter of the highly decorated rooms in the palace, the expensive gowns and the fragrant perfumes, the false smiles and the continuous chatter about unimportant events.

She needed a change of scenery. She had to get out of here, find a place to come to her senses. The evening had not gone well for her. After the attack on her coach, Cartouche had escorted her home where Hilaire was waiting for her. The gang leader had the good sense to leave the coach before they arrived, so she need not explain who he was to her husband.

"What happened?" Hilaire asked. "I expected you home much earlier. You did visit your cousin, didn't you?"

"Yes," was her short answer. She really felt no need for his concern and had problems in remaining civil. She knew with certainty the sentiments he uttered were false, and that he really did not care what befell her. "We were attacked," she added, remembering she still owed him obedience. She could not keep the events to herself--the servants would certainly speak.

He frowned. "That is terrible, my dear! I won't let you out of my sight as from now--I care for your safety!"

"Thank you," she said evenly.

"I'll send a messenger to the Palais Royal. Of course we won't attend the ball tonight--His Royal Highness will understand our reasons."

82

She shook her head. She could not face spending the evening at home, with only Hilaire as company. "No, please don't do that. I know how you look forward to being there. I'll go as well. I don't think anything can happen there."

He smiled. "You are brave, my darling. Are you sure about this?"

She nodded. "I am. And now, if you allow me, I'll go to my room to dress for the occasion."

She had gone to the ball dressed in all her finery, had greeted the Regent and had done what was expected of her. But right now, she wanted to be on her own for a while. She thought for a moment, considering the risks then sent a lackey for her cape. Soon afterwards she left the interior of the palace. Outside, the cold was intense, but she did not feel it. At the deserted courtyard of the Palais Royal she found the peace she craved. She studied the twinkling stars in the firmament and wondered what the next year might bring to her. She did not startle at the sound of nearing footsteps--somehow, she had been expecting them.

"You seem to appreciate the festivities as much as I do, Madame," spoke Lord Newton.

She turned around to look at him. "I'll never feel at ease here," she answered. "I really don't belong at the court. My husband would not understand those sentiments. He wants me to shine on every occasion and win the Regent's favor. Yet I feel out of place in such a role. It just isn't me!"

She smiled apologetically. "Here I go again! I don't know what makes me say all those things to you--nor what you must be thinking of me now."

He avoided an answer by asking if she cared for a stroll. He offered her his arm and led her away from the courtyard into the surrounding gardens. For a long time the rustle of her satin dress was the only noise that could be heard.

At last Lord Newton broke the silence. "Someone told me what happened to you this afternoon. Nevertheless you came to the ball, looking better than ever and were able to face the curiosity. I admire your courage, Madame!"

It sounded like a compliment, and it meant more to her than the sympathy Hilaire had shown. "I'm not so brave," she however denied, sensing honesty was at its place here. "I came to the ball because I did not want to stay home with my husband."

He let the last remark go, although he seemed to register it. "You won't deny it was a scaring experience," he said instead. "There may be danger for you here. Perhaps you should have stayed home."

"That would not solve anything," she replied. "You know, fear is a fierce emotion. It reaches a point where you are so scared that nothing seems to bother anymore--and then you become half as careful as you ought to be."

He nodded to show he appreciated her sharp psychological insight. "I repeat, you are a brave woman. And know you are quite safe with me. Nobody will try to rob you of your jewels or money in my presence."

She snorted. "Those scoundrels were not out for my possessions. They meant to kill me."

He accepted her statement without apparent surprise, but because of the close contact of their arms, she sensed how his muscles tightened. Suddenly she felt a strong urge to take him further into her confidence.

"I need to talk to somebody," she addressed him frankly. "Please hear me out." She told him the entire story.

He listened without any comment. He kept walking until they reached a frozen fountain, where he let go of her arm. She should not feel how his hands trembled!

"Why me?" he wanted to know when she stopped speaking. "Why not share this with your husband? He's the one who ought to help you in your troubles."

She did not need to think. "I am not very close to him," she replied. "We only married because it was…convenient. I feel he's more of a stranger to me than you are."

He made an irritated movement which she did not catch immediately. Instead she went on. "I've had this feeling from the day we first met. Since then I became more and more convinced destiny brought us together."

"I'm afraid destiny had little to do with it," he said hoarsely. "I saw you and wanted to possess you. Sometimes I indulge in my evil ways."

84

"I don't believe you," she stated with inner certainty. "Not after last time. You said other things then. I thought we had become friends, so why can't you be straightforward too?"

"Enough, Madame!"

Now his tone was rude and had the intention to hurt. He succeeded easily in this. Marguerite came to an abrupt standstill and a look of profound pain manifested itself on her face.

"Is this the way you treat friends?" she cried out. "What are you trying to prove?"

"Nothing!" he responded. "Didn't they warn you about me, Madame? I am an outcast--and do you know why society shuns me? Because I was convicted for having murdered my wife."

His revelation shocked her but did not reach the objected goal. She did not turn away from him in horror.

She waved aside any possible doubt and said, "I can't believe you're capable of murder. There must have been a mistake."

When she tried to lay her hand on his arm, he shook it off with a violent gesture. "You're wrong!" he shouted, undergoing the old hurt once more. "I could easily have killed her! I used to imagine how I'd lay my hand around her slender neck and press…press… so that she could scorn me never again. Only-- I didn't. Someone crossed my plans and was clever enough to put the blame on me. I was condemned to be beheaded, but my stepfather used his influence with the old king and got me a pardon. The sentence was changed into lifelong banishment. I had to leave France, and I shall never forget those years. The humiliation, the anger, the pain…"

"It has passed now," she dared to remark.

He laughed unpleasantly. "Oh yes, it all turned out so nicely! My uncle, whom I never heard of since my father became estranged from his family, died of typhoid fever and shortly afterwards his two sons succumbed to the disease as well. Luck! Now I happen to be the sole heir of the Duke of Shrevenport…and because of that, the Regent restored me to my rights and allowed me to return to France. And what did I gain? Entrance to the court, and the openly displayed contempt of those who did not give me a chance to prove my innocence in the first place."

Now she was no longer offended by his harsh words. His outburst gave her the chance to better understand how bitterness had turned him into the person he was now, and why he found it so easy to use irony and sarcasm. She realized she gained field in winning his total confidence.

"I believe you are not guilty," she said. "Have you never tried to find out who killed your wife?"

He looked away and did not answer straight away. He appeared to be brooding over something.

"Can't you tell me?" she urged him.

He looked into those beautiful eyes and read the need in them. He bit his lip and pressed his nails deep into his skin until pearls of blood appeared. Still he did not speak.

"You shut yourself off from those who care for you," she concluded. "And I do care… You simply won't give me a chance."

"Marguerite, please!" It was a tortured man who spoke, a man who did not make it easy on himself. He was determined to continue on the path he had chosen. He did not want to burden her with his guilt. Why burden her with his guilt? "How can you understand?" he went on. "You don't know half of the truth!"

"Not when you keep throwing such high barriers," she stammered, losing courage at last. She swallowed through the tears that welled in her throat. Then she decided.

"I am sorry," she said. "I won't bother you any longer. I suppose I went too far with my curiosity. Goodbye."

Decidedly, she turned her back on him and headed back to the palace. One step, two steps …

He felt as if his heart was being ripped out. The pain became too severe, too unbearable.

"Marguerite, don't leave," he whispered, finally giving up the battle with his self-discipline and needing to give in to the overwhelming desire to take her into his arms.

She stiffened in her stride and looked behind. Then everything seemed like a dream come true. He swept her into his embrace and ravished her mouth with hungry kisses which she eagerly returned.

His heart lept. He felt how she completely surrendered to him, without the least bit of restraint. If it were not so deadly cold, he would have made love to her there and then. Now he lifted her into his arms and hastened to find his carriage.

~ * ~

As soon as daylight broke through the darkness of the room, he sat up in bed. Marguerite was still fast asleep, her lips curled into a sweet smile. He studied the soft lines of her face, her proudly shaped chin and her straight nose. Then his glance lingered on the delicacy of her breasts, the nipples still swollen as a result of their lovemaking. His gaze wandered along the slender waist and the full roundness of her hips, to remain focused on the creamy thighs and the beautiful long legs with their hidden treasure. Desire overtook him again.

The past night had been wild and passionate. They both gave everything, held nothing back--so different from the first time they shared a bed. Now she equaled him in ardor and daring, and although she had no memory of the past, she instinctively knew what gave him delight. He could feel no regret, and yet…

In the cold light of day he realized he had acted on emotion. There would be a price to pay for it.

He woke her up.

"How late is it?" she asked drowsily. "It looks early to me."

"It's time you returned home," he said.

"I don't want to," she murmured and crawled up close to him.

He did not give her a chance. He jumped out of bed, as if bitten. "Get dressed!" he ordered. "Perhaps you don't care for your reputation, but I do. If someone witnesses you leaving this house, they won't leave a shred of your good name. Moreover, I must say I'd rather avoid a fight of life or death with your husband."

She burst into laughter. "Don't worry about Hilaire! For all I know he's with his mistress, and he surely won't be home before dinner."

"That doesn't matter," he said, sounding rude once more. "What happened last night can't be repeated."

Her face clouded and the pain was visible in her eyes. He could not stand the sight, and hurried to take her into his arms. "Darling, I don't want to hurt you. Please, don't take it like that. I'll always remember this night, but I'm afraid to drag you along in my uncertain future. You'll come to regret this in the end."

Her arms slid around his neck and brought his face closer to hers. "Now you listen to me," she whispered, with strong determination. "My marriage to the marquis doesn't mean anything to me. I thought I was in love with him, but I was wrong. He is not the man I took him for. Until now I realize I have never loved a man. I didn't know the meaning of the word. I guess I was afraid to love, as you still are. Those attempts on my life, however, taught me one important lesson. I now know how important it is to live life to the full. And my life has meaning when I'm with you."

"Why do you say I'm afraid to love?" he breathed, caressing the velvet of her skin.

"Because you are, I feel that. You still don't trust me enough. Why?"

His gray eyes studied the depth of her green ones before he answered. Was she entitled to the truth? Should he forget his intentions? When she gave him her tender smile, the decision was made without further thought.

"You have the right to know this," he said. "There have been other women in my life, which is evident, but I have never given my love easily. When I was married to my wife, I loved her with all my youthful innocence. How she

88

took advantage of it! And later on, when my circumstances changed for the worst, I met this young girl and fell in love with her. My big mistake, however, was that I never admitted it to her. I let her think I was indifferent to the affection she showed me…and lost her that way. Since then I became afraid to love--and spoil things once more."

In the heat of the moment she did not think of asking him if she was that girl--and he felt glad for it.

She pressed her lips on his mouth and kissed him passionately. "You won't spoil it this time," she said between kisses. "I'll never regret being with you. I love you."

"Are you completely sure?" he pressed her, craving for a positive answer.

"Yes. If you just allow me."

"I do," he sighed. "My lord, I do! I can't go on without you, darling. I love you, my sweet Margie. I love you!"

She closed her eyes and smiled secretively. He had finally admitted to it. It had been there all the time, but she had not been able to see it earlier.

Then came the moment she could think no more. His kisses became hotter and hotter and desire flamed into sweet surrender.

Twelve

During the following days, Marguerite found it more and more difficult to hide the happiness she was feeling. She had to act indifferently whenever Hilaire was present and only dared to dream about Anthony in the privacy of her rooms.

She was more than glad when a message from Cartouche spurred her into action. That way, she would have no more time to daydream.

"We know where Claude de Bassy drinks his beer," her friend wrote. "Shall we meet tomorrow evening? And no lady's attire for this adventure, please. Jeanot will bring you to the exact spot."

When darkness fell, she told her maid she wanted to retire to bed early because she felt a cold coming. As soon as the girl left her rooms, she changed her nightgown for a man's outfit which Jeanot had been able to find and smuggle into her wardrobe. Tight-fitting trousers, a white shirt, black jacket, knee-high soft leather boots, black velvet cape and a sword girdle.

She studied her image in the mirror and was satisfied with the result. Her figure was still slender enough to hide its femininity, and when she put on a wig and hat, she did resemble a young man.

She smiled, pushed the broad-rimmed hat somewhat better on her head and hurried down the backstairs to find Jeanot.

They left the house unseen and found their way through the dark streets of Paris. Somewhere in the neighborhood of Saint-Denis, Cartouche joined them.

"We'll go to Le Chat Gris," he announced. "It's a small tavern in de Rue Quincampoix. De Bassy spent a couple of hours in the taproom last night and the night before, so we hope to see him there tonight as well."

It did not take them long to reach the tavern. Jeanot entered first to make sure their man was present while she and Cartouche waited on the porch.

"We're lucky," Jeanot reported after a few seconds.

Marguerite immediately noticed de Bassy was drunk--and her hopes of finding out something diminished at once. Nevertheless, she walked over to his table. Cartouche remained near the door, keeping an eye on all that was happening around them.

Near the door leading to the cellar two tradesmen were seated, and another four craftsmen were throwing dice at a table near the fireplace. The corner in which Claude was seated was at the opposite side of the room, so there might be a chance their conversation would not be overheard.

"Some wine, mon ami?" she asked, while beckoning the landlord to give the man a refill and leave the jar on the table.

De Bassy raised his head with difficulty and fumbled with his goblet. With a hasty movement he put it to his lips and emptied it in one long draught. "Merci." He tried to make out who was buying him a drink, but did not recognize the disguised woman.

"More?" Marguerite asked. She did not wait for an answer but filled his goblet anew.

"What do you want of me?" It sounded resigned, as if it had happened to him before.

"I want to ask you some questions."

"Of course. Go ahead."

She pushed the jar of wine in his direction, more or less surprised that everything seemed to run so smoothly. "I would like to know more about Marguerite de Vallencieux," she started, talking slowly.

Claude giggled and spilled more than half of the wine. It dripped off his chin.

She could hardly keep herself from hitting him full in the face. Instead, her fingers ticked impatiently on the table. "Well? Do you know her?"

He read the determination in her looks and rubbed a dirty sleeve against his mouth in an attempt to control himself. "Little Margot, of Chateau Vallencieux?"

Angrily, she grabbed the jar and put it aside. "If you won't talk, you had the last of this wine," she threatened.

He shrugged and grinned like an idiot. "No need to get angry, man! Yes, I knew this Margot--I met her a long time ago. Never saw a girl who behaved so much like a boy. She came to Paris with me...rode better than most men."

"When exactly was that?" she urged him, becoming more and more intrigued.

He had to think over this question, making her even more nervous. "Oh, long time ago, when the old king was still reigning. She nearly begged me to take her along, yes sir! But I could understand her reasons to escape marriage--the guy was more than twice her age!"

"And then? What happened when the both of you arrived in Paris?"

Claude sighed. "I ran out of money. Tried to fix something for her...a rich guy, a count or so. But apparently she did not approve of it."

"What did she do then?"

"She ran away," he answered laconically. "Had to agree with her later on--that man was a true villain."

One and one make two. She assumed that the young Marguerite--she, in fact, before she lost her memory--had taken on Claude's name, perhaps pretending to be his wife or sister.

"Have you seen her since?" Her voice was terse and her nerves were on edge. So much depended on his answers. If only he could be sober--now there was no way of telling how much his answers were influenced by the wine.

He nodded vaguely. There was something in his attitude that told her he did not like this question. "Once," he murmured. In a sudden impulse, he leaned across the table and held his head close to hers.

His sour breath was revolting. She took out a handkerchief and held it before her nose.

""Poor lass," he whispered, full of regret. "I couldn't help her there. Armand shouldn't have…" Then his head sunk on his arms. He dozed off.

Marguerite tried to shake him, but he was too far gone into oblivion. She would not find out anything else this evening.

~ * ~

The following evening they paid a second visit to the tavern. With the passing of time, customers came and went, but Claude de Bassy never showed up. Finally, Marguerite signaled the landlord and asked him if he had seen him during the day.

"No sir, we haven't" the man answered. "He's probably sleeping it off-- he had more than enough yesterday. You weren't the only one to pay him a drink."

She quickly shot a glance at Cartouche and noticed the worried expression on his face. They were suspecting the same, it seemed.

"Was it after we left?" the gang leader inquired.

The landlord scratched his chin. "Wait a moment…yes, I think it was later that night. A stout man came in and asked for Claude. They sat talking and drinking for a while."

"I see. Do you know by chance where de Bassy is living?"

"He has a room somewhere in the neighborhood. I believe he once said it was only a couple of streets away. His landlady is a certain Madame Sauvignard, a widow."

They paid for their drinks and left the tavern in a hurry. They located Madame Sauvignard's house but only after a full hour had ticked by. At this late hour, all the doors and shutters were locked for the night and the street lay deserted. No wonder their loud knocking on Madame's door elicited some angry reactions. Marguerite, however, did not pay attention to them and kept on drumming the wood with her pistol. She stopped when she heard light movement inside.

Shortly afterwards a small window opened, and a terrified white face looked into hers. The widow tried to say something, but clearly fear left her mute.

"Let us in!" the young woman demanded, waving her pistol.

The door now opened and the widow waited on the threshold, wringing her hands in terror. "Please gentlemen, don't hurt me! I'm only a poor widow and I haven't got any money!"

"We don't intend to take your money," Marguerite replied. "We must speak to Claude. He has a room here, right?"

"I don't know where he is," the woman answered. She tried to slam the door shut, but Cartouche was faster. He put his foot between it and the wall and pushed it open once more. Jeanot leaped into the corridor and his mistress followed.

Expertly she pointed her gun at the woman. "I believe you are lying! If you don't tell the truth, you'll force me to use this, sweetheart."

Madame Sauvignard stared at the gun as if hypnotized. Her legs trembled so heavily they gave up their support. She sank to the ground in a formless bundle. "Have mercy, Monsieur! They threatened to kill me if I…"

Marguerite suddenly realized what she was doing and put away the pistol. She took the frightened woman by the shoulders and helped her to get to her feet. "Don't be afraid," she apologized. "We don't mean you harm. We don't mean Claude harm and we hope you can tell us what happened. Perhaps we can help him then."

The widow still trembled but appeared to have regained some calm. She decided to believe the young fellow. "Two men came searching for Monsieur this morning," she said. "I could see he did not like their presence, but he did leave in their company. Later on one of those men returned and made me promise not to tell anyone of their visit. It was a nasty man…called Gaillot, I think."

"Gaillard!" Jeanot corrected softly.

"Yes, that was his name. Gaillard."

Cartouche took Marguerite aside. "This doesn't look well, Marquise," he whispered into her ear. "They have probably killed him by now. They were afraid he'd tell you too much."

"You're right," she sighed. "We'd better leave. There is nothing more we can do here."

"And what will happen to me?" the widow piped up. She took the young man by the arm, and only at that moment she realized she spoke to a woman.

On hearing Gaillard's name mentioned, Marguerite had momentarily forgotten her earlier promise. Now she was reminded of her duty towards the innocent victim. "Go to the Hôtel d'Aubervilliers and ask for the housekeeper. She needs a kitchen maid and you'll be accepted immediately. You will be safe there," she promised.

"Thank you, Madame!" the widow whispered. "And God bless you."

Out on the street, Marguerite let go of her emotions. "Damn! What a stroke of bad luck. Claude hasn't told us everything, that's for sure. The only option left to us now is to talk to Armand. Claude mentioned him. I wonder what his role is in this drama."

"Hush!" Jeanot froze in his steps and signaled them to be silent. He appeared to be listening with full concentration.

"What's wrong?" she asked in a soft tone. The boy did not answer, and when she looked at Cartouche, she noticed the same awareness.

The gang leader took her by the arm and hurried her along through a tangle of streets and alleys. The boy kept up with them without effort. Finally, they arrived at L'Ange Noir where they would be safe among friends.

"I believe someone was behind us, trying to hear what we said," Jeanot explained once they were seated and enjoying a cup of warm wine.

His uncle nodded in agreement. "I think we are rid of them now. I wonder who'd dare to follow us."

"Do you think someone overheard our conversation?" she needed to know, realizing the consequences of this.

"Yes. If you have any plans to see your brother, Madame, you have no time to waste!"

In recent weeks she had won in determination, and thus it did not take her long to reach a decision. "Let's go to Newton's house," she said. "I need to talk this over with him."

She had not seen Anthony for some days and suddenly longed for his embrace--with the sure knowledge it would relieve her worries for the time being.

Her eyes betrayed the excitement she felt and Jeanot was quick to notice this. "You love him, Madame?" he asked.

Cartouche rose and went to speak to his lieutenant, apparently not very interested in matters of the heart.

"Yes," Marguerite admitted freely.

The boy nodded his approval and gave her a smile of understanding which showed his precocity. "He's of the right sort. This time you made the right decision, Marchioness!"

She laughed and pulled his ear. The little rascal!

~ * ~

The next morning, immediately after breakfast, she ordered her carriage to be readied and had Pauline, her new maid, pack some light luggage for her. Dressed in a comfortable gown and warm cape she descended the staircase to the hall where she happened to meet her husband.

"You're up early, *ma chère*," he remarked. "I'm just coming home."

"I have to go to Vallencieux," she explained briefly.

"Again? Didn't you once say that you did not look forward to your brother's company?"

"We have to settle some estate matters--my father gave me land there when I married Etienne, remember? It is possible I'll have to stay at Vallencieux for a couple of days."

"Do you as like, my dear. Give my regards to Armand and his bride, will you?"

Marguerite had received instructions. The coacher directed the carriage straight to the city's gates, where it was halted for inspection then continued on its way. If she was being followed, they would see this. But the possible spy needed to be very fast to notice that in the confusion of a traffic jam, the young woman slipped out of the carriage and mingled in with the crowd.

The coacher was one of Cartouche's men and Marguerite's place was taken by a young girl who vaguely resembled her. They would continue their trip for some hours until they were sure nobody was following then they could return to Paris.

Marguerite hurried through the streets, which she knew very well. Every now and then she threw a glance over her shoulder. She could not spot anyone suspicious. Perhaps they had succeeded in fooling Gaillard and his accomplices?

At last she reached Lord Newton's residence. Anthony was anxiously waiting for her. He took her into his arms and gave her a quick kiss. "Did anyone follow you?" he asked urgently.

"I believe not," she answered, feeling safe in his embrace.

"Hurry up and change, my sweet," he said.

She ran up the stairs to undress and get into her men's clothes. Then she hastened down again to the courtyard. Anthony was in the saddle, astride a strong stallion. Another equally fiery horse was being held for her. With the help of the groom she jumped on to it and spurred her mount forward. There was no time to waste!

~ * ~

The long ride was hard but uneventful. They needed all their energy to keep galloping. Newton had made sure fresh horses awaited at each baiting place--quite remarkable a fact, given the short time between the making of the plan and its execution. But everything went as planned. They reached Vallencieux when the next morning was about to break.

To their surprise most rooms of the chateau were brightly lit up and there were a lot of people about. Strangely enough, nobody seemed to take notice of their arrival. They led their exhausted mounts to the stables themselves and saw to it they were rubbed dry and fed. Only afterwards they entered the castle.

The hall lay deserted, but from one of the rooms came the desperate wailing of a woman.

"I'm afraid we have come too late," said Anthony. He took Marguerite firmly by the hand and pulled her along the corridors to the drawing room where the noise was louder.

What they witnessed made them sick. Denise knelt on the cold floor and cradled the body of her husband. Her white nightgown was red with his blood, which was pumping from a deep wound in his chest. In the background, the old housekeeper of the family was weeping too, her face hidden in her apron.

Marguerite swallowed a couple of times and finally managed to croak. "Marie?"

The old woman looked up, and hastened to wipe her eyes dry. "My sweet child, how pleased I am to see you here. You'll know what to do. Such a tragedy! Monsieur Armand dead and Madame Denise just sitting there."

Marguerite gently hugged her nurse. For a while the women were silent, unified in their grief. Then the youngest one asked: ""Can you tell me what happened, Marie?"

They both got a fright when it was Denise who answered. They had not noticed how she at last got up and kept staring at the stains on her gown.

"We were about to go to bed," she said in a monotonous voice, losing all sense of reality. "We heard a noise in the courtyard. A minute later the door to this room was kicked and three men burst in. They held guns at us. Armand threw himself before me. He wanted..." Her voice broke and tears streamed over her cheeks. She began to shake and turned white.

Anthony signaled Marguerite and together they escorted Armand's widow from the room. Marie followed them and offered to take Denise to bed.

"Have someone stay with her," Anthony ordered softly. He then entered the drawing room and looked for something to cover the corpse. A tablecloth will do, he thought. With respect he kneeled down and closed the eyelids of the deceased.

Afterwards he returned to the hall where Marguerite waited for him. He noticed at once how calm and determined she looked.

"I'll make them pay for this," she swore.

He went over to her and tenderly wrapped her up in his embrace. "Hush, my darling. Don't speak of this now. This is a time for grief."

Her mouth tightened. She clearly did not agree with him. "I can't grieve right now," she confessed. "You know I was not too fond of Armand. We had a lot of fights, and he kept things hidden from me. Perhaps I even had reasons to despise him…" She swallowed. "Nevertheless, he's my brother. His blood also runs through my veins."

"I understand," he said and pressed a comforting kiss on the warm flesh of her neck. "A foul murder asks for revenge."

"Justice!" she corrected. "And the truth."

He could only agree. "Do what you must, darling, but be careful. Don't allow this to rule your life. Don't do things you'll regret later on. It is a lesson I learned too late."

Thirteen

Marguerite and Anthony had no other choice. They had to spend the night at Vallencieux. A lot of things needed a firm hand, and it was better not to count on Denise. It was Anthony who saw to it that the body of Armand was brought into his bedroom where Marie and Marguerite washed the deceased and covered him properly.

Candles were lit around the bed. The old housekeeper volunteered to hold the nightly vigil. The three children Vallencieux were more precious to her than her own, and she felt it her duty to pray for Monsieur Armand. Father Ambroise, the *curé* of the small parish, would join her in these prayers.

Impressed by Newton's quiet authority and Marguerite's angry words, the servants set to work with vigor. Before that, they sought refuge in the kitchen; the women crying like frightened weasels and the men robbed of their bragging. Once Anthony convinced them of the necessity to leave the warm kitchen, they slowly returned to the drawing room where they cleaned the bloodstains off the floor. Here and there a muttered comment was heard, but nobody dared to leave until the work was finished.

When the last of the rumors died down, Marguerite sought her bed. She had asked one of the maids to prepare the rooms which once had been hers as a young girl, and it was there Anthony waited for her. He had looked after the fire, which now spread a cozy warmth, and had invitingly thrown open the covers of the bed. With a deep sigh, she undressed and allowed her tired limbs to sink down in the soft mattress. Anthony joined her and she crawled up close against him. He sensed her mood perfectly and made love to her in a passionate, almost violent way.

"It isn't wrong, is it?" she asked later, when all their energy was spent. "We are making love to each other while Armand's body is lying one floor beneath us."

He kissed her tenderly. "It isn't wrong, Margie," he ensured her. "Life and death form a unity which can't be separated. You needed this."

"Yes," she whispered, "I did. You give me strength, you know. When I'm in your arms, I have the feeling nothing can hurt me."

"You are strong enough, my love," he said with a faint smile. "You do rely on your strength, don't you realize? You are a woman of character, and I admire the way in which you deal with life, especially in poor circumstances."

"I wish I felt that confident," she sighed. "What bothers me is that now we'll never know what Armand's role was in the events before I suffered this loss of memory."

"Wouldn't there be a way to find out?"

"I honestly don't think so. Claude de Bassy is most likely murdered--and they got to Armand before we could ask any questions. I doubt even Cartouche will be able to match more missing pieces together. We've lost every clue."

"That's not right," he corrected. "I know one person who knows the truth."

She looked at him, puzzled. "Who would that be?"

He smiled again. "You, my dear. Your brain has gathered all this information. It is locked up in your memories."

"But I can't remember anything!"

"Just now. Who knows what will happen given time? "

She thought this over for a minute. "A doctor I once consulted said the same," she spoke at last. "He told me to wait patiently. One day I'd remember, he ensured me."

"And when you do, you'll be in even more danger," he realized, and his grip on her tightened. He was determined to do everything in his power to prevent her from being attacked.

"I do know that," she stated evenly, although she too had to fight the panic which threatened to overwhelm her. "I will be very careful, and I will ask Dominique for some of his men as protection. What else can I do?"

He bit his lips and was silent for a while. Then he hesitatingly asked: "Do you want us to be together forever?"--knowing he dreaded her answer.

She produced a sad smile. "That would be lovely," she answered, so very sorry because it would be impossible. "But I have a husband and marriage vows can't be broken. I'll have to remain Hilaire's wife until death releases us."

"It doesn't have to be so," he argued. "If you really love me, you wouldn't care about conventions and leave d'Aubervilliers. You'd follow me to England."

She pushed his hands away and turned her back on him. "I love you," she breathed into the cushions, "but never ask me that again. I am a Vallencieux and I could never bring shame upon our family's name. I know where my duties lie." She swallowed through her emotions and continued in a calmer way: "I would despise myself if I lived openly with you, Anthony."

Then something he said popped into her memory. Did he intend to leave France? Would he consider leaving her behind and rob her of the one good thing in her life?

She gave the cushion a vehement push out of frustration and came to sit upright, her knees pulled up to her breast. "Anthony, what did you say about England?" Her voice sounded hoarse and she almost stumbled over the words.

He looked her straight into the face. "I do have plans to travel to England soon," he declared. "My grandfather wrote to me some time ago. He's old and very lonely, Marguerite, and I'm his only grandson. He would like to see me."

"Then you'd better go as soon as possible," she reacted, deeply hurt. "I shan't beg you to stay here."

His arm slid around her waist and remained there, despite her resistance. "Margie, let's not fight," he begged. "I love you!"

"But you'll leave me soon."

"I won't go to England without you," he swore. "I could never leave you behind! Because my love for you is so strong I want to protect you as best as I can. Wouldn't it be great if I could persuade you to follow me across the Channel? You'd be safe in England."

"I won't run away."

Very gently he kissed her on the forehead, resigned and accepting her decision. "How I do know that, sweetheart. So I'll have to stay until all mysteries around you are solved then we'll see. Trust me, my love. Together we'll find a solution."

Their glances met and she read the sincerity in his eyes. She believed him.

"I could never hurt you," he stated.

She took his hand and put it to her bosom then pressed her warm mouth on his, full of demand and desire for him. This was her way of asking his forgiveness. She would no longer doubt his love for her.

Once more they became one.

Fourteen

Three days later, Armand was buried at the small cemetery of Vallencieux, next to the grave tombs of his father and mother. The parents of Denise came to Burgundy and proposed to their daughter to return with them to Compiegne.

Denise agreed. "After all," she confessed to her sister-in-law, "there is no urgent reason to stay. Armand hasn't fathered a child with me, which means the title and the estate will go to your brother René or otherwise to his heirs."

As a widow, Denise inherited a small amount of money and the use of the lodge on the border of the domain. Marguerite could well imagine how the young woman preferred the homeliness of her parents' house to this deserted lodge. The last person who inhabited it was an aunt of Marguerite's father, and since then the place had not been properly looked after for lack of money.

When they said farewell, Marguerite kissed Denise warmly. She did not think she would ever see her again.

Not much later, she and Anthony returned to Paris. Marie and a few trusted servants would remain on the estate. They would close up most of the rooms and await the arrival of the new master. Marguerite had sent him a letter, but had no idea how long it would take to arrive in Canada. Possibly months, even years?

~ * ~

"You have stayed away for a long time," Hilaire greeted her when she opened the door to the drawing room on her return. Apparently this was one of these days he decided to spend in his house. He was playing with an empty glass of wine.

"I didn't know what to think," he continued. "In my imagination, I saw you running off with a lover already."

Did that sound as a threat? She took off her hat and tidied her hair before a mirror. She felt Hilaire's glances pricking in her back, and it gave her an uneasy feeling. To give herself an air, she studied her reflection more attentively then managed to answer in a casual tone. "What if I had? Would you mind?"

He put down the glass and jumped to his feet. He walked up to her and placed his hands on her shoulders, in a possessive manner. "You're my wife, Marguerite. I wouldn't tolerate such an insult. It would be a blemish on the family name."

"I see. Doesn't the family honor suffer from your various escapades?" she shot back, ready to challenge him. The pressure on her shoulders increased and became somewhat painful. Yet she did not allow herself to show emotion.

"Whose fault is that? If I was welcome in your bed, I wouldn't have to look for comfort elsewhere."

She forced herself to remain calm. Starting an argument with Hilaire would not help her. "Armand died," she explained coolly, "which accounted for the reason I had to stay longer at Vallencieux than planned. I had to arrange a funeral." While speaking, she slowly rubbed the sores on her shoulder and knew that, by the next day, her skin would show ugly blue patches that would not go away immediately.

The marquis had the decency to look confused. "Forgive me, *ma chère*, I deserve your scorn. What can I say? I did not intend to hurt you."

"It is alright, Hilaire," she said, not wanting to offend him too openly.

"It is a great shock to hear your news," he continued. "Armand looked such a vital fellow."

She nodded.

"What did he die from? An accident?"

"Not an accident. Three bullets straight through the heart. Armand was murdered."

"What?"

"You heard me. Some men forced their way into the castle and attacked my brother and his wife."

"What about her? Was she also killed?"

"No, Armand protected her. But she's heart-broken, of course."

"I can imagine," Hilaire responded compassionately. "Poor Marguerite! It appears there is a curse on your family. First your life gets threatened, and now your brother is dead."

"Some curse!" she whispered, but he caught her words.

"Someone who bears a grudge against your family?" he suggested.

"No, I don't think that is the case," she shrugged. "Armand is--was--the only one who could explain certain facts of a ten year old mystery."

Her husband frowned, and suddenly she regretted the lack of confidence between them. "I'm sorry," she quickly said. "You have no idea of what I'm involved in. More importantly, I can't draw you along in it."

"Is it too late to share your trust, Marguerite?" he asked. It sounded casual but was a plea.

She shrugged again, totally helpless. He had nothing to do with it, but he did look honest in his concern.

"I don't want you to think you are on your own," he continued. "You can always count on me when you need support."

"I appreciate that, Hilaire," she answered, after carefully thinking over what she was about to say. "But it is indeed too late--for us."

He nodded his head in acknowledgement. He too was well enough aware of the fact they had grown apart. "I understand I have lost your affection, but have I also lost your friendship?" he inquired.

He seemed to mean it in earnest. After a short while she accepted his offer. "We can always give friendship a try," she said, with only the slightest of hesitation in her voice.

He kissed her hand and left the room.

~ * ~

Marguerite looked into the mirror and was well pleased with the creation the dressmaker had designed just for her. She intended to wear it at the costumed ball at Madame de Berry's residence, on occasion of carnival in the middle of February.

She was dressed in a translucent gown of fine gold lace, sewn with delicate rose petals, over a bodice and skirt of black satin. Her hair was coifed and adorned with real roses from the greenhouse. On top of her head, a golden veil was attached. It hid her face as efficiently as a mask.

Enthusiastic over her disguise and wanting to show off, she went looking for her husband. She found him in his study, deep in thought. One of the drawers of his desk stood open and on top of it rested an expensively inlaid box.

Hilaire only noticed her when she came quite close. "Marguerite, dear, you startled me!"

He tried to hide what he was looking at but was not quick enough.

She caught a glance of something shimmering, and would not be a real woman if she did not sense an instant curiosity. "What have you got there?" she asked. "It looks like diamonds."

Finally he turned around and faced her. He smiled, as her request pleased him. He picked up the box once more and held it in his outstretched hand. Then he teasingly opened it, and at last allowed her to admire the most perfect string of diamonds she had ever laid eyes on. Each stone was of equal size as the others, cut and polished to sheer perfection. The diamonds caught and reflected the light of the candles on the desk and seemed to burn into the velvet of the box. Her breath caught with a hiss.

"Words can't explain their beauty, can they?" Hilaire said it quietly as a mere statement. He took the necklace out of its container and asked her to turn around.

She could feel the warmth of his fingers on her neck and consequently the sudden weight of the necklace. She walked over to a window and stared at her image in the windowpanes. Her fingers touched the cold stones, which now appeared to shine even brighter because of the contact with her warm skin.

"Can I wear them?" she asked, very much impressed.

"Today and every time you choose to," he answered, his eyes shining with pride. "They fit you, Marguerite--but then this necklace was designed for the most beautiful of women."

She sought, and found, a small mirror and lifted the veil to get a better look at her present.

Hilaire contented himself by watching her excited moves. "Wear them with dignity, *ma chère*. They are the Medici Diamonds."

"What?"

She did remember the name, although not from where and when. At the same time, a shiver went over her spine and an inner feeling warned her of something evil. Automatically her hands went up to her neck and fumbled at the lock. It opened at last and with a sigh she put the necklace back in its casket.

"I don't think I'm going to wear them tonight," she said, all excitement gone from her voice.

Hilaire shook his head. "Don't tell me you believe all these crazy tales around the necklace, my dear! They were made up by people who envied us because they did not own the necklace themselves."

"I don't know of any stories," she confessed. "But nevertheless, I don't think it is right to show off such great wealth."

"It is told the necklace brings bad luck to the owner," he explained. "But in our case, it has brought fortune. The diamonds became ours when King

Henry the Fourth married off his young mistress to one of his barons, a fellow named d'Aubervilliers. When the girl gave birth to a fine son, the necklace was offered as a present and the boy became a marquis. Since then, our family has done extremely well."

"Until now." The words escaped her mouth. She could do nothing against it.

"Your problems have nothing to do with this necklace," Hilaire said. "Surely, you can't believe a thing of such beauty can have evil qualities? Just look at those diamonds: they reach sheer perfection."

Once more, he lifted the necklace out of its velvet cushion and let it slide through his fingers, caressing the separate stones.

She could not explain why, but this gave her an even worse feeling of fright. He seemed absorbed by the beauty of the diamonds, not his usual self.

"Did I tell you about my father?" he asked her, the diamonds dripping through his fingers. "He was a big admirer of the arts, and the necklace fascinated him. He spent a great deal of his life and his fortune in research of its origins. Apparently, the necklace was originally designed for Eléonore d'Aquitaine, the mother of Richard the Lionheart. The ruler of Antioch, Raymond de Toulouse, gave them to her when she went crusading with her first husband, King Louis of France. Raymond and Eléonore were lovers, of course. Rumor has it each diamond stands for one perfect night of love. Later on, Eléonore sold the necklace to pay for Richard's ransom. It is still not clear how the diamonds found their way to Italy, but they ended up in the treasury of the Medici family."

"Didn't some of those Medici's die under mysterious circumstances?" Marguerite asked.

"Those were violent times, my dear. Anyway, they came to France with Catherine de Medici and she gave them as present to her daughter, Marguerite de Valois, when she married."

"And that marriage was followed by Saint Bartholomew's night."

"Which would have happened, even if she had not worn the necklace-- what are you trying to prove, Marguerite? I thought you admired the jewels."

She had to admit he was right, but still the nagging feeling of unease stayed with her. She could not explain it, but she felt it had something to do with the necklace. "It is exquisite," she said. "Still, I'd rather not wear it."

He gave her a sharp look. "You disappoint me, Marguerite. I had expected you to be proud to be permitted to wear the family jewels!"

"But I *am* honored, Hilaire," she stressed softy.

"It is your right as marquise d'Aubervilliers. Please wear them tonight-- my mother and grandmother have worn them before you. Imagine how jealous the other ladies at the court will be!"

"The court doesn't interest me," she declined. "I have told you this before. Shining there is not my purpose in life."

His lips curled into a smile. However, his eyes told another tale. "Do I have to beg you, my dear?"

An unmistakable threat was put into the smooth plea, and she realized she could get into serious problems. Because she wanted to avoid trouble with Hilaire at any cost, she sighed deeply and finally agreed to wear the necklace.

He fastened it around her neck a second time and deliberately caressed the soft skin beneath his fingers.

He did not succeed in thrilling her. She stepped aside and made it obvious she wanted to leave the study. "I need to finish my toilet. Please excuse me, or else we won't be able to leave for the ball on time."

He held her back. "Let me admire you, my sweet Marguerite. How beautiful you look! And how different you are…"

These last words warned her to tread extremely careful. She knew he referred to someone in particular, a person who might also be of interest to her.

"Different from whom?" she popped the question, as she knew he expected this.

He laughed. It did not sound very pleasant. "Perhaps not that different! You're just as curious as the others to find out secrets."

"Do you mind telling me?" she dared to remark, wanting to find out if she was right in her suspicions.

"Of course not," he said with a smile. "I referred to a former mistress of mine."

"The girl you mentioned before--this Bassy woman?"

He shrugged. "She was not important, just a simple whore. No, the one I talk about was a lady of fine birth and married of course. She was very beautiful, alas also enormously vain and stupid. Imagine, she announced to her friends she was going to divorce her husband. Oh yes, she wanted to advance in life, become a marchioness!"

So she had been wrong, after all. Who could be that other woman? Would she also be part of the mystery, or did this only concern Hilaire's past?

Her husband went on. "I was very much infatuated with her at first and wanted to please her. So I once showed her the Medici diamonds and even allowed her to wear them on occasion. What a fool I was! The lady thought she could use them to get what she wanted. She threatened to lock the necklace in a secret place if I did not consent to marry her."

"I don't suppose you'd give in to blackmail," she stated with certainty.

"Never!"

"What happened then?" she had to prompt him.

Hilaire gave her another smile while reaching to open the door for her. "Nothing special," he said lightly while he showed her out. "The lady died. She was found murdered a couple of days later. She had a very jealous husband."

She could not help it. Another shiver went over her spine and brought back all the terror.

Fifteen

A Pierrot took hold of Marguerite's hand and dragged her away from the old nobleman whose company she had to endure throughout a wild round dance.

She gladly accepted this new dancing partner. She followed his light-footed movements and laughed heartily at his witty remarks. He was a very good dancer, and she felt like an elf in his arms. The rhythm of the music bemused her and for a while she forgot what worried her.

Suddenly she stiffened in her movements. There, that creature dressed in a black domino! He stared right into her face. The lips, not covered by the mask he wore, formed one tight line and she could read naked hatred in his eyes.

Her heart began to beat faster. Some primitive instinct told her this man was her enemy and his only desire was her total destruction. She trusted this instinct as she knew it had protected her before.

It was not the first time that evening she caught sight of the man in domino. Over and over he had popped up at unexpected places while she circulated in the different rooms of the palace of Madame de Berry. At first she had not paid a lot of attention to it, thinking he was an acquaintance or a possible admirer, but later she had looked at him with suspicion. He appeared to follow her wherever she went, waiting for his chance.

She loosened Pierrot's hand.

"Madame, don't leave," the man said, clearly disappointed. "Let's have one more dance, yes?"

She did not listen to his protests. Her gaze shot through the room and surveyed the people in it. Where was Hilaire? They had gone their own way once they had greeted their hostess, and right now she could not spot his pirate costume among the crowd of celebrators.

Driven by instinct, she wove her way towards the exit, every now and then casting a furtive glance over her shoulder.

The domino went in the same direction and mocked her useless attempts to free herself from his presence.

She moved faster. In her hurry she almost collided with someone and nearly lost her balance. She would have fallen were it not for two strong arms that immediately got hold of her slender frame. She looked into the broad smile of a caliph.

"*Chère dame*, may I have this dance?"

She could not refuse, for despite his disguise, she recognized His Highness the Regent without any problem.

The domino posted himself against one of the walls and smiled sarcastically. When the dancing couple passed close by, he made an eloquent gesture along his throat.

Marguerite's fear grew. What could she do? Was there any chance of escape? The prince whirled her round and round. Now they went into the direction of a passage to another room. The idea suddenly popped up. This was her chance.

"Your Highness, I'm ever so sorry," she said quickly, while she gave the astonished ruler a deliberate push. It made him stagger backwards.

She neglected the raised eyebrows of the bystanders and began to run towards the other room--her rose-strewn skirts lifted with one hand and showing a good part of silken leg to the men

At last, the hall!

Before the startled servants could react, she opened the heavy front door and flung herself out into the street. There she was surrounded by a suffocating silence. She shivered in the cold night air, for in her distress she had forgotten to put on a cloak. She tore off her veil and wrapped it over her bare shoulders. Then she hurried down the street, taking cover from houses that lined it.

~ * ~

She did not get far. Only seconds later she heard footsteps behind her, closing the distance. At that moment she realized she had willingly stepped into a trap. She should have stayed in the palace. The man in the domino had acted with only one purpose in mind: to drive her away from the safety of the ballrooms, out into the night where his accomplices were waiting for her. This time there would be no escape.

She wanted to cry out her anguish, but no sound came over her bitten lips. She ceased to think as a reasonable being. She felt like a hunted animal who could feel the hot breath of the hounds on its neck.

Tears dripped out of her eyes and wetted her cheeks. She did not notice them. She ran blindly, trying to keep ahead of her pursuers. She did not see anything and heard nothing. Her foot hooked behind some left-behind trash and she fell to the ground. No time to feel sorry for herself. She paid no attention to the bruises she had caught nor to the blood that stained her dress.

A new surge of energy brought her to her feet again and she continued.

The sounds now became more audible. Not only running feet, but those of swords and knives being pulled and held ready.

She ran as fast as she could. In the end though her breath came with more and more difficulty, and her legs were about to refuse further service. She stumbled a second time, managed to crawl into an upright position once more and still succeeded in putting one foot before the other.

Someone nearly caught up with her; she could feel his breath. Then a hand landed heavily on her shoulder. It brought her to a standstill--and finally she gave way to a scream. It echoed loudly in the night.

Immediately another hand closed over her mouth and suffocated the noise. She was not granted the mercy of unconsciousness--on the contrary. Her senses seemed to register everything more sharply. The man leaned over her. Now he would cut her throat. She struggled with the last of her resources.

"Margie, for heaven's sake!"

The words were whispered, but she recognized Anthony's voice. The relief was so sudden she felt more distressed. She burst out into weeping, her body began to tremble violently. Her lover's arms cuddled her.

"I thought it was…it was…" she hiccupped. "Oh, Anthony!"

"You're scared to death," he said. "I saw how you left the palace in panic and instantly realized the danger of your action. I followed you, thank God. Now try and be courageous for a few minutes longer, my love, and I'll get you away from here."

She trusted him and wiped the tears from her eyes. At the moment when she lifted her head to whisper her thanks, she caught the reflection of a knife's blade.

"Anthony, behind you!"

Newton turned just in time to escape the thrust of the knife. His hand closed around the scoundrel's wrist and exercised so much pressure the weapon slipped out of the paralyzed fingers. One well-placed blow of the fist brought the hireling to his knees.

Then two more men popped up from the darkness. They were armed with cudgels and attacked the lord from two sides. Anthony jumped out of harm's way and hastened to draw his sword.

Marguerite's gaze shot from one person to another. It looked as if Newton had a clear advantage over his two opponents. One of them already showed a deep wound to the arm and the other sighed and puffed under the forceful wheeling of the sword.

A premonition made her look over her shoulder to check if the first man was still unconscious. What she witnessed made her blood freeze. The man was reaching for his knife. His intention was obvious.

115

She opened her mouth, but only a hoarse whisper left her dry lips. The only thing she could do was launch herself forward with no consideration to her own safety. She fell against the villain, clung to him and bore him down to the ground.

Her long skirts covered him and did not make it easy for him to move. He had a tough job keeping away from her sharp nails. They tore painful scratches over his face. Then he managed to free one hand. With it, he hit her hard in the face and made use of the short moment of pain to swing a leg over her wriggling body. He pinned her down with his greater bodyweight and grinned. Slowly and totally enjoying it, he laid his hands around her neck.

When it grew dark before her eyes, Marguerite's hands fell to the ground. The cobbles felt very cold and something cut in her groping fingers. It took her numbed brain some time to register the meaning of this: her fingers were not touching the cold stone, but the metal of a knife. She had the knife! While her assaulter was pressing away the vital air from her lungs, she concentrated to perform the one task that could save her. She pressed her fingers around the knife and managed at last to lift it up.

When the man felt her movement, it was too late. The blade came down between two ribs and lanced into his heart--killing him instantly.

In the meantime, Anthony had dealt with the other villains. Now he kicked away the body that covered Marguerite and knelt down beside her. He did not hide his fear. He had watched her attack the man and had cursed himself for not being able to come to her rescue sooner. He took her shaking body into his arms and pressed his face against her shoulder. "Don't ever attempt to do that again, Margie," he said between his teeth. "Never, you hear!"

Then he kissed her and held her close. She lay quietly in his embrace and answered the kisses with only half the ardor she normally showed. He soon became aware of that so he stopped kissing her.

"Be brave for a little while longer, sweetheart. Don't let this distress you."

She stared at him with eyes wide open, still shaken with horror. "But I feel terrible, Anthony! I did not mean to kill that man--only I had to, otherwise he would have hurt you. Isn't it dreadful? This is the second time I have killed someone."

He did not shrink away from her. His face only expressed sympathy and acceptance. It gave her courage once more, a reason to go on.

"You did what was right and saved my life," he acknowledged. "It is over now. Come, let me escort you home."

"Do you think it is safe," she asked, still feeling uncertain. "Won't there be others, waiting for us in the dark?"

Why was she so sure the events of this night had not come to an end yet? She knew she had to face what was coming, but she grew very tired of it. The constant fright diminished her willpower and she realized she could not go on forever. Could she give up the fight?

There, in the deserted street strewn with corpses, she was willing to grant Anthony what he wished most.

"Take me to your house," she said with sudden determination. "I want to be with you, forever. This town makes me sick! I'll accompany you to England, even tomorrow if it has to be."

He could not understand what made her say this. It hurt him physically to see her in such a state of bewilderment. It looked like all the spirit had been taken from her. "Do you realize what you say?" he asked urgently.

She tried to smile, but the smile turned into a grimace. "I know perfectly well what I'm doing," she said. "I have made up my mind. I can't--won't--stay in France, where my life is threatened every day. This tension becomes too hard to bear. Honor and family lose their meaning here. You are the man I love, and I want to be with you." Then, uttering her secret fear aloud, she blurted out: "I couldn't stand losing you! When I saw that man reaching for his knife, I nearly died."

He pressed his mouth against hers. This time, both shared the passion.

"I'd lie if I said your decision doesn't please me," he confessed some time later. "But have you really thought it through, darling? Will you never regret it?"

The smile she gave him told him everything. "Never," she swore solemnly.

"I love you, " he whispered after another intimate moment. "From now on you can leave everything to me. Come, let's go home."

~ * ~

They walked down the street until they found an empty cab. Anthony ordered the coacher to take them to the Hôtel d'Aubervilliers, despite Marguerite's protests.

"You'll be quite safe in your house," he explained to her. "Go straight to your room and call your maid and Jeanot. Have them pack all the things you need. You wouldn't leave the country without any luggage, would you?"

Hesitatingly, she shook her head. Why did he need to tease her at such moments? And what did she care? She had no business in that house anymore--in fact, had she ever?

On their arrival at the residence, Anthony waved aside the lackeys and overtook the task of accompanying Marguerite inside. The maid Pauline was waiting for her mistress. She had tended to the fire and the room was invitingly warm.

"Madame, what has happened!" she cried out, when she noticed the state of dishevelment in which her mistress showed up. Both her mistress and the stranger accompanying her were covered in blood and mud and their clothes were torn. Who was that man?

"Something to drink and quick!""

Pauline did not react immediately.

"Hurry up, girl. Don't you see your mistress is in dire need of a warm drink?" It was said with authority, and finally the maid responded to it. She hurried to a side table where wine and glasses stood ready.

Marguerite accepted the glass of wine with gratitude. She gulped it down and at last some warmth filled her body. "That's better," she sighed. "I could do with a bath as well. Will you prepare one for me, Pauline?"

"Immediately, Madame."

Not long afterwards the perfumed water filled the tub, and she helped her mistress to undress, every now and then casting a look over her shoulder to the strange man. Her mistress did not seem to mind his presence.

"Pauline, I want you to prepare for a journey," Marguerite ordered her maid, as she sunk down in the warm water. "You know what to pack. Enough gowns for the day, some warm capes, a couple of evening gowns."

"Yes, Madame," the maid said and left the couple alone.

"I won't insult your husband by using his bedroom," Anthony joked. "Although I need a bath myself. I'll return home and have it there. Besides, I have to make preparations for our journey to Calais--I do suppose you'll want to set off as soon as possible?"

"The sooner the better," she replied.

"Shall we say then that I'll be back for you in three or four hours' time? Can you be ready by then?"

"Of course. I don't want to take that much. If Pauline wants, she can come along. I needn't ask Jeanot; I know what his answer will be."

"You're quite fond of that boy, aren't you?" he said affectionately. "He's a clever lad. I'll love having him in my service."

She leaned her head against the rim of the tub, and realized she was still wearing the Medici necklace. The villain's attempt to strangle her had pressed the diamonds deep into her flesh and left blue marks which showed clearly against the whiteness of her skin. Without looking at it, she threw the necklace aside. "This is certainly one of the things I won't take along," she remarked. "Hilaire can keep his precious necklace! Those Medici diamonds do bring bad luck!"

She was stunned by Anthony's reaction. During the evening, her veil had hidden the necklace, and during the fight he had been too busy with other things. Now his eyes clung to the magnificent string of diamonds--and he froze.

He had seen this necklace before. Missing pieces of the puzzle fell into place.

"What's that weird look?" Marguerite asked. "Haven't you heard of the Medici diamonds? They are quite infamous."

"I have," he said shortly. "Did you say it belongs to your husband?"

"It is part of his heritage," she explained. "He presented the necklace to me earlier this evening--oh my god, it seems ages ago! I'll gladly leave those diamonds here where they belong. They have a deadly reputation."

She expected he would contradict her, as Hilaire had done. To her astonishment, he completely agreed with her.

"I know of their reputation, and what's more, I believe in it," he said roughly. "Get rid of those diamonds, darling. Later on I'll buy all the jewels you need."

"The only thing I need is your love," she answered. "Go now. I'll be ready by the time you come back."

~ * ~

The house was quiet; all the sounds had died down. The servants had gone to bed with the exception of Jeanot who was sitting half asleep next to Marguerite's trunks. His mistress, wrapped in a fur-trimmed cloak, suppressed a shiver and kept staring at the big grandfather clock that slowly and teasingly ticked away the seconds. *Hurry up*, she prayed wordlessly, *oh please, hurry up!* Despite the familiar surroundings and Anthony's promises, the feeling of coming disaster still had not left her.

At last there was the sound of wheels rattling over the boulders and a carriage coming to a standstill before the house. She ran towards the massive front door and had it open before Anthony could knock. Just like her he was dressed for the journey.

"At last, there you are!"

"Are you still afraid?" he informed.

"Yes," she admitted. "I'll only feel better once we have left this house and this town."

"We leave as soon as my coacher can load your luggage."

He signaled his man who began to carry away the various trunks, helped in this task by Jeanot. Together they fastened the luggage on the roof of the carriage.

Marguerite watched their movements with anxiety. She held her breath when another carriage rolled through the street and got hold of Anthony's arm when it halted before their door. The sound of approaching footsteps echoed loudly through the stillness. Then the door was thrown open.

She had a premonition it would be Hilaire. And indeed, it was he who entered the mansion, followed by a groom. Her fingers, cold as ice, pressed into Newton's flesh--a thing she was not aware of. Still as a statue she awaited the final blow of misfortune.

Hilaire took his time. He tidied the lace on his cuffs and put aside his hat. At last he turned his gaze towards the couple who were waiting near the staircase.

"Madame d'Aubervilliers, Lord Newton."

His greeting was polite but cold. The fear Marguerite experienced now turned almost physical. It felt like a thousand needles were being stuck into her flesh. She could not move, even if she wanted to.

The only one who appeared to keep his composure was Anthony. "A good evening to you, marquis."

"I see you are going on a journey, *mon vieux*," the marquis answered. "I pray, don't let my presence bother you. Go ahead and kiss my wife farewell."

Bit by bit, Marguerite took in the implication in these words. Hilaire offered to review her decision--as always he acted as the perfect gentleman. Then her eyes met his, and with a shock she realized it was only a pose. His glance revealed his true nature: cruel and unmerciful.

The indignation she sensed as a result of this gave her new energy, and she looked up, in a very proud way. "I am leaving with Lord Newton," she said clearly.

"So I've heard," Hilaire responded. "My valet came looking for me at the Hotel du Berry and told me an incredible story--or so I thought. He said my wife was packing her belongings and planned on leaving me, like a thief in the night. Of course, *chérie*, I told him he was wrong! Madame d'Aubervilliers would never do such a thing, I said."

Even when his tone remained cordial, the words held a threat. Anthony put his hand over Marguerite's cold fingers and pressed them comfortingly. His touch drove the chill away.

"I'm afraid I must disappoint you, Hilaire, but I am really leaving you. My mind is quite made up," she told him plainly.

He smiled in a cruel way. "So is mine, my dear. I am prepared to forget what I just witnessed, but I'll never tolerate you running away and bringing shame upon our name. I am your husband and I do have rights. Have you forgotten that?"

While he spoke, he approached her and took her brutally by the arm. He clearly intended to drag her away from Newton.

"Leave me be, Hilaire!" she protested.

At that moment Anthony decided it was time to intervene. "One moment, d'Aubervilliers! There's something you should know." His hand locked around Hilaire's pulse and forced him to let go of his wife.

The marquis did not appreciate this action. "Don't mix yourself in our affairs, Newton," he warned his rival. "You too are familiar with the law. Marguerite is my wife and consequently she has to obey me in every way."

Anthony smiled, which confused Marguerite even more and succeeded in unnerving the marquis. A dangerous light danced in his eyes. "The law grants a husband every power, indeed. You are quite right in this, *mon cher marquis*. However, we have a problem here." He waited an instant, and the tension grew. Then he added explosively, "The lady is not your wife."

Two pair of eyes were pointed at him, full of wonder and disbelief.

"Your claims can't hold any truth," the marquis stated furiously.

Newton now gave way to a loud roar of laughter. "You don't have to take my word for granted," he said after a while. "But, it is so that I happen to know Marguerite married for the first time in Saint-Denis, when she was a young and inexperienced girl. The man she married then is still alive, which condemns her later marriages as bigamy."

"No!" Hilaire repeated.

"It is the truth. And what is more--I can prove it."

He searched his pockets and dug up an old document, very much wrinkled by age and use. He unfolded it with respect and held it to the marquis, so he could view it. "As you can testify it is a legal document. It says here that Marguerite de Vallencieux and Anthony St. Lawrence, your servant, were wedded in the presence of witnesses on the second of April, in the year of our lord 1711. No law can prevent me from taking Lady Newton with me to England!"

Hilaire studied the document for one brief moment. Then he clenched it to a ball with his fist and threw it to the ground with a disdainful gesture. "I should believe you?" he sneered. "Everyone in Paris knows your reputation, Newton. I don't put my trust in people who were condemned of murder. Without any doubt you have ways to produce fake documents."

None of the men paid attention to Marguerite. She let go a soft cry and hastened to pick up the creased document. Her fingers trembled while she slowly ironed out the wrinkles. She, the wife of Anthony… She stared so long at the words the letters began to dance before her eyes. Tears dripped down on them.

She did not understand anything anymore. Anthony would be her husband? According to the document it was the truth and had been for ten long years. Why had he never mentioned anything about this? Why had he led her to believe she was lawfully married to Hilaire? Why, oh God, why? The questions whirled around in her brain and distracted her from what was happening further down the hall.

The sound of steel meeting steel brought her back to reality. She looked up with a start. Anthony and Hilaire had drawn their swords and were settling their argument in the eldest fashion.

"Stop that! For heaven's sake!"

Neither of the men listened to her tormented cry. The two adversaries opposed each other in deadly earnest and intended to use their weapons to kill.

Marguerite's eyes shot from one to the other and her lips uttered a silent prayer. The marquis had the reputation of being one of the best swordsmen in the country--he used to brag about if often enough. And Anthony? As far as she could judge, he was not the weaker of the two. But he had been in a fight earlier and had put a lot of energy in it. Most likely he would tire sooner.

She became paler and paler and sought support with the boy Jeanot, who had come to her side as soon as the fight started.

The clatter of steel continued. The two men moved through the entrance hall and soon they neared the front door. As this was still opened wide, the fight eventually moved to the street.

Marguerite closed her eyes, caught in the grip of terror. Suddenly images flashed, becoming sharper and clearer with the second--and she was part of them.

Two shady figures at first. Then she recognized Anthony and Armand. They were fighting, and she was watching the duel, with the same anxiety she felt now. She stood huddled in a dark corridor, somewhere in a narrow house. An older women, which she made out to be the housekeeper of Lord Newton, had an arm around her shoulders.

The vision carried her away to another point in time. It hurt, but she had to know what was kept buried for years.

She did not realize she sank to her knees and all the blood left her face. Jeanot watched her with worried eyes. He tried to help his mistress, but she did not hear him.

So the doctor was right after all, Marguerite thought. *My memory is coming back. It took this moment, where I find myself in an identical situation--worried sick the man I love would come to harm.*

1710
One

"Race you to the castle?"

Marguerite did not wait for an answer. She pressed her heels into the flanks of her horse and spurred it forward. A thundering noise behind her meant her brother took up the challenge.

She laughed with glee and wiped away the strands of hair that blew into her face. Then she leaned deeper over the neck of the animal. Their speed increased.

"I'm going to beat you this time, sister!" she heard René yell.

In a flash the two youngsters raced through the offshoot of the forest. Marguerite looked over her shoulder and noticed her younger sibling was right behind her. He gave her a cheerful grin.

Neck to neck they dashed through the village of Vallencieux, scarcely avoiding the free roaming chickens and some playing children. Then they continued their way uphill to the medieval castle which dominated the landscape.

Just before the malfunctioning drawbridge, the girl pulled in the reins and brought her prancing horse to a standstill. She won by a hair's breath.

"You are just a bit too fast for me," René panted. "The way you ride a horse makes me forget you're only a girl."

"Thank you for the compliment, dear brother."

They exchanged a look of understanding then smiled openly. Marguerite did not resemble a lady in any way. Her figure was very much boyish and most of the time she dressed with nonchalance. When she put her legs in pants and long boots then hiding her long black hair under a broad-rimmed hat, she could easily pass for a young man.

Marguerite hated the long skirts she was supposed to wear. She also managed to forget the rules of behavior the good nuns of Dijon had tried to impose on her and frequently searched the wardrobe of her older brother for some of his clothes.

Of course her father and Armand often rebuked her for this. But the youngest one, René, just thought it practical she should wear trousers when they went horseback riding. She appreciated this attitude, and it was natural she felt more affection for him than for Armand, who was twenty-two years of age and was their father's heir. She and René did everything together and indulged in the wildest adventures.

Marguerite was seventeen years old, turning eighteen in November of this year. She had spent three long years at a *pensionat* in Dijon--a boarding school run by nuns which came highly recommended by her aunt de Salanges. Her father had listened to the advice of his sister-in-law and had sent his only daughter to the nuns, in the vague hope she could learn some respectable manners.

Luckily for Marguerite, those long years had come to an end. She felt relieved to know that after this summer, she need not return to the school where she had the feeling of being locked in a prison.

"I hope Marie has our supper ready," she said. Marie was the woman who had nursed the three children de Vallencieux and who now stayed on as cook. "I must confess I'm starved!"

"So am I," acknowledged René.

They led their horses over the bridge and rode under the massive gate tower which gave entrance to the ancestral home.

The foundations of Chateau Vallencieux were laid in the Middle Ages, and some of the sturdy walls and towers still bore proof of this. The living quarters were renovated in the early sixteenth century when their family was rich and powerful. Now the roof leaked when the rain came down and some of the walls had gaping holes in them. The once so proud building stood in deplorable state. The present count simply had no money for even the most urgent repairs.

The cause of this misery was the children's grandfather, the tenth count. He was a player in heart and bones and gambled away the entire fortune at the card tables of Paris. His son Jaques did what he could. He married Elisabeth Anne de Salanges, an heiress. He was able to pay back most of his father's playing debts with the dowry she brought along, but this left him nearly a beggar. Right now, the estate produced just enough to beat the everyday costs of living and to settle the annual taxes.

"I think we have visitors," René said when observing the unusual bustle at the courtyard. The young kitchen maid ran to and fro, obeying Marie's orders, and Martine, the stable lad, showed a rare industriousness in fetching loads of hay for the stables.

"Yes, you must be right," Marguerite agreed.

Their assumptions were confirmed when they noticed the strange horses in the two first boxes. Indeed, visitors had arrived--a very rare occasion. As soon as they had seen to their own animals, they hurried into the house.

In the hall, they ran into Armand, who was obviously waiting for them. Tall and blond--the only of Anne's children who had inherited her looks--he stood there and blocked the way to the stairs. A disdainful look was plastered over his face.

"If I hadn't thought so," he greeted them coldly. "Been riding, dear sister? And you had nothing against it, did you René?"

The smiles died away. Armand's cool attitude always had the effect of a splash with chilled water.

"We have guests," he continued. "Go immediately to your rooms and tidy up! We'll sit down to dinner in less than an hour and father expects impeccable behavior. And Marguerite, he also requests that you wear your best dress. Rosette will help you."

~ * ~

While the maid Rosette was trying to fashion a modern hairstyle--she had the intention of leaving this godforsaken chateau and become the chamber maid of a rich and powerful lady in Paris--Marguerite watched her reflection in the mirror with a critical look. *No, I'll never be a beauty. My skin is too much colored by the sun, my face lacks significance and my hands are not soft enough. Even my eyes don't draw attention, despite their rare emerald color.*

"If Mademoiselle will stand up?"

Rosette held up the silk gown and threw it skillfully over Marguerite's head and shoulders. She pulled on the strings of the bodice until the waist was narrow enough then closed up the dress. "*Et voilà*, Mademoiselle is ready!"

Marguerite took a deep breath and began to pace through the room. The many skirts bothered her and made her feel uncomfortable. "How I hate being a girl," she sighed and pulled a sour face.

The maid giggled. "Mademoiselle will think otherwise soon enough. It won't take long before a handsome man will court you and then...oh la la!"

"Nonsense! Who'll look at me?" she said. She put a hand against her bodice to indicate how flat it was. "Here should be something, am I not right?"

"Mademoiselle!" Rosette responded indignantly. "Don't ever say such a thing in public. You'll change in due time--some girls just take longer than others. And while we are waiting for this to happen, we can correct your figure with the help of a fichu." Her quick fingers tucked the linen in its place. "There, you see? You look very pretty, Mademoiselle. Very pretty indeed. And now, remember to take smaller steps, that is much more elegant."

When the maid left her, Marguerite did not immediately go down to the dining room. She lingered deliberately. Her father's urgent request cast a shadow over the pleasure she had over the unexpected arrivals.

It was the first time ever he cared for the clothes she wore. When they went to church and she donned her black dress with the white lace collar, he did not seem to take notice. So why was it imperative now she wear the new pink dress he had given her when she came home from the convent and which was meant to wear at the ball they always had after the harvest was brought in?

When she finally arrived downstairs, the men were waiting for her. Jaques de Vallencieux, despite his fifty years was still a handsome man. He came forward and elegantly offered her his arm. With a proud air he walked her over to the two strangers and thereby showing a fatherly affection Marguerite had not witnessed before.

"*Ma petite*, may I present to you Monsieur Laneuil, a lawyer from Dijon, and his cousin, Monsieur de Bassy. Gentlemen, my daughter Marguerite."

One after the other the men bowed over her hand and kissed it. Etienne Laneuil was a stout man, well into his forties. He had a reddish complexion, kind brown eyes and thinning hair. Claude de Bassy, on the other hand, was young and dashing and dressed as a beau. Both held on to her hand a bit longer than required.

"It's a pleasure getting to know you, Mademoiselle," Launeuil said pleasantly.

"A real privilege," de Bassy added, while his eyes studied her freely.

His licentious glances gave her an uneasy feeling. "Thank you," she said softly.

"*Messieurs*, dinner is served," the count announced, now that the introductions were completed.

Jean-Michel, the count's personal attendant, opened the doors to the dining room. There a richly decorated table invited the guests to sit down.

With a courteous gesture, Armand pulled away his sister's chair which elicited another moment of confusion on her part. Etienne Laneuil found a seat next to her and de Bassy on the opposite side of the table.

The dinner was excellent. Marie had surpassed herself in the preparation of the various dishes. Carp in rich dill sauce followed stuffed pigeon; veal cutlets with fresh vegetables and cheese ended the meal. Later on Jean-Michel served sweetmeats and fruit. The wine that accompanied every dish belonged to the special reserve of the count. As a result of all this eating and drinking, the atmosphere around the table soon became less formal.

129

"Monsieur Laneuil is an old and trusted friend of mine," the count announced, toasting to it. "Moreover, we are distant relatives."

"Oh, really?" Armand responded.

"My beloved wife--God have her soul--was linked to the de Salanges," Laneuil explained. "I consider it an honor to be reckoned among the friends of *Monsieur le comte*."

"You live in Dijon, Monsieur?" Marguerite inquired politely, nudged by her father to say something.

"Indeed, Mademoiselle. A beautiful town to my taste; I enjoy residing there."

"Dijon is not half as magnificent and exciting as Paris," de Bassy remarked.

"Ah, Paris!" Jaques sighed. "You are quite right, de Bassy. No town on earth can equal Paris and is there a court that compares to Versailles?" One more sigh. "How I remember the days I spent there... As captain of the guard I came into contact with all the people in high places. King Louis the fourteenth in all his glory, Madame de Montespan, the prince of Condé... Now it's Armand's ambition to once occupy the same position."

"It won't take long anymore," stressed Armand.

René and Marguerite exchanged a quick glance. Had they missed out on something? Up to now Armand's plans had never been discussed, and although they both realized their brother was pretty ambitious, this announcement came as a surprise.

Where are we to get the money? Marguerite wondered shortly. But the conversation continued, and she had to pay attention. Her father's slight push against her leg made that obvious.

"Well, everyone of us has wishes for the future," Laneuil smiled. "Personally, I hope for a promotion in my professional career. I'd like to become attorney-general of this region."

Claude leaned over the table; "Dear cousin, why not admit you really want a title?" he said teasingly then he explained to the others: "Etienne thinks he's not dignified enough to enter society."

While the older man looked rather embarrassed, the young man now directed his attention to Marguerite and asked her boldly: "And you, Mademoiselle? What are your ambitions?"

She could not prevent that a slight blush colored her cheeks. This young fellow was so different from her brothers, much more world-wise.

"I only wish life doesn't have too many surprises for me," she answered at last. "I am quite satisfied with my present situation."

"Satisfied?" de Bassy responded indignantly. "Mademoiselle! Life at the countryside is utterly boring. It appears to me. Nothing ever happens."

René watched the flirtation. Now he considered it his duty to intervene. "Monsieur, you are quite wrong," he put in. "Why should our life be boring? We don't give boredom a chance. I can assure you country-life has many interesting aspects."

"My brother and sister still tend to consider life as one big adventure, my dear chap," Armand said in a condescending manner. "Of course, they are still very young."

"I'd give a lot to be young once more," Laneuil sighed. "*La jeunesse!* The most beautiful time in one's life."

"Come on, dear friend, you are a man in the prime of his life," Jaques grinned. "I dare say you are a desirable party as far as the ladies are concerned."

"It surprises me, cousin, that you have never married again," Claude mentioned, on purpose.

"I mourned my late wife for a long time," Laneuil acknowledged. "Only recently the thought of remarrying has begun to interest me."

"May I inquire if you have plans in that direction, Monsieur?" René wanted to know, sensing something was going on behind their backs.

"I have set my hopes on a certain party, young master," Etienne answered. Over Marguerite's head, his glance met that of the count, who nodded shortly.

When everybody was totally satisfied and all the dishes were cleared away to make room for the men's port, Marguerite asked to be excused. She returned to her room, feeling drowsy. She did not call for Rosette but managed to loosen up the bodice of the gown so she could step out of it. Then she quickly sponged her skin and donned a nightgown.

Although she was tired, sleep did not arrive too readily that night. Because she did not know any better, she put the blame on the presumptuous meal and the rivers of wine.

Two

"Mademoiselle, your father wants to speak with you," Rosette announced on entering Marguerite's room. It was two days after the dinner party and the guests had left the castle for Dijon the day before. "He is waiting for you in his study."

At that moment, no feelings of ill-boding warned her. She obeyed the request and ran down the stairs where her father had his office. The count sat behind his desk, studying some papers. He looked up when she entered and asked her to take a seat.

"I have good news for you, daughter," Jaques said, looking pleased with himself.

"Yes, father?"

"Monsieur Laneuil has offered for your hand in marriage." It was said with a smug smile, which clearly showed his pleasure about it.

Marguerite's eyebrows went up in surprise. "Surely, that's a joke? That man is much too old for me, isn't he, father?"

She could not believe what she heard then.

The count shook his head and gave her a stern look. "Of course he's not too old to become your husband, daughter. He has a fortune to spend on you and your needs."

When she noticed he meant what he said, she became furious. "I refuse to accept that offer!" she announced. "I won't marry that man."

133

"You will do as I say," her father ordered, slightly irritated because his daughter could never act as any normal girl.

"No!" She stamped her foot out of frustration and her green eyes filled with anger. She held up her head in a proud fashion and did not want to admit to herself that her father was deaf to her pleas. She soon found out why he was so determined.

"I have given my word, so no more protest!" he said sternly. "You will marry Monsieur Laneuil, like it or not. He was very modest about his wealth when he came to visit, but I have since learned he is part owner of a business which imports silk from the Middle East. His mother, a de Bassy, left him these shares."

"What do I care about money!" Marguerite sneered. "I don't want that man. He's old and besides, he's a commoner. I thought you wanted me to marry a man with a title."

"That's true," Jaques admitted. "But I have changed my mind. I have no doubt Etienne will succeed in getting that position of attorney-general. In time he could even become attorney-general of Paris! Then the Regent won't deny him a title."

"Of course. I've heard money means everything to His Highness."

"So be it. That is none of your concern. What matters is that Etienne will be able to provide you with everything you need. Clothes, jewelry--all the things I can't afford to give you. To show his good intentions your fiancé already agreed to finance Armand's army training. Your brother will soon be leaving us. When he completes his studies, he'll hopefully enter my old regiment and occupy a position at the Court," he explained.

Now she understood what it was all about--and she had to admit her defeat. Armand had always taken the first place in their father's affections. She was only a pawn in his great plan to launch Armand's entrance in society. He did not care for her feelings. He would gladly sacrifice her so his eldest son could obtain a glorified post at Versailles, and thus restore the family's fame and fortune.

Jaques shook his head, pretending to pity her--but she knew it was only make-believe. "I swear it was not my intention to make use of you in this way," he said with false concern. "But alas! We all have to strive for the well-being of Vallencieux. Once you are married, Etienne will not deny his father-in-law a loan. With those funds we'll be able to do the necessary reparations to the roof."

"Of course," she answered flatly.

"You're still very young to marry, I know… On the other hand, eventually you would have married anyway and become a wife and mother. Laneuil's proposal came somewhat unexpectedly, but I never dreamed I'd succeed in finding you such a fortuned party. Imagine, he doesn't care that you only bring a small dowry."

"Oh, I easily see how fortunate *he* is, but what about me? I'll have to endure the embraces of an old man."

"Old?" her father protested. "Laneuil is eight years younger than I am. He's a man in his prime, who knows how to look after the needs of a young woman. You may count yourself extremely lucky in getting him."

Marguerite considered this conversation closed and rose to her feet. Without asking her father's permission, she went to the door. Before she pulled it shut behind her, she glanced over her shoulder and remarked wryly, "You know what bothers me most, father? That you didn't even care to ask how I felt about this. You may marry me off to Monsieur Laneuil, but it certainly will happen without *my* consent."

"To your room, young lady!" Jaques shouted, finally losing his temper. "You will obey me in every way. You shall become Launeil's wife if I have to drag you to the altar myself. And to prevent you from any mischief, you will remain in your room until you become more reasonable."

~ * ~

Marguerite felt as if she could walk up the walls out of sheer boredom. She was not allowed to leave her room and her food was brought upstairs. The only person she saw was Rosette. Unfortunately, this one seemed afraid to answer any of her questions.

"I can't bear this any longer," she decided at last, after having thought out a strategy. She rang the bell.

Rosette did not take long to appear. "Yes, Mademoiselle?"

"Please go and tell my father I will no longer refuse to marry Monsieur Laneuil," she told her.

"Yes, Mademoiselle."

Half an hour later, the door opened again and her father entered the room. "The maid tells me you seem reasonable at last," he greeted her.

She cast down her eyes and pretended to be meek. "Yes father. I have thought about it, and now I think you are right," she said in a small voice. She hoped she did not overdo these false sentiments.

"I'm pleased," the count answered. "I am going to see our solicitor and have a contract drawn up. And of course, I'll warn Etienne."

He did not take long to get familiar with this commoner, Marguerite thought. But on the outside, she nodded her approval.

"And you are allowed to come down again," Jaques added. "But don't play me for a fool. You will be watched all the time."

As if I did not know that myself! Anyway, it's better than being stuck in this room. I'm bound to find a way out of this mess.

"Yes, father," she said aloud. "I do understand that. I can assure you my behavior will be impeccable."

"I do hope so," the count sighed, not really trusting her on her word.

The following days, Rosette constantly accompanied her mistress. Also Armand sought her company more than once. At night, her room was still locked.

Then Etienne Laneuil arrived back at the castle where he was cordially received by the count and his eldest son. Marguerite pretended to be glad to see him. Again, they sat down to a sumptuous dinner which was followed by a walk in the garden to settle the stomach.

Monsieur Laneuil offered his fiancée his arm and led her outside. Her father and brothers followed them outside but had the decency to keep a little distance between them and the couple. After a while, they withdrew inside and allowed them some privacy.

Laneuil guided her to a very pretty part of the garden. There he spread his cloak over the grass. "Pray take a seat, my dear."

Quietly, she did as he requested. He sat down beside her. She noticed his face was covered in perspiration and was unable to tell if this came from the lingering heat of the day past or because he felt nervous.

After a short while, he took her hand into his. He looked very pleased with himself now, and she had to restrain the urge to slap him in the face for it.

"How do you feel about our engagement, Mademoiselle Marguerite?" he asked.

"Do you really expect an answer?" she said, raising her eyebrows.

He seemed surprised at her attitude. "Why yes, of course," he hastened to assure her. "I understand it all has been somewhat of a surprise to you. I did ask your father to wait until next year, but he thought it would be stupid. I take it you don't have any objections?"

"No," she answered, keeping her voice even.

"*Voyez!* You will soon get used to your new situation," he responded. "I am your humble servant, Marguerite. My only desire is to make you happy."

"My wish is to be happy, too," she sighed. Fortunately he could not read the thoughts behind her serene brow.

"We have to set a date for the wedding," he continued. "What do you think of August the fifteenth, Assumption Day? If the wedding takes place then, I still have plenty of time to make some necessary arrangements, like drawing up a nice marriage settlement for you."

"Spare me the details, please," she interrupted sharply, feeling more and more the urge to run away and make a fool of herself.

Her response shook his self-confidence, but then he began to laugh. "How right you are, *ma chère.* I shouldn't trouble you with business matters.

They are not of your concern. Probably you will be more interested in redecorating your new home?"

"I am sure I can rely on your good taste in that matter.'

"Why yes, if you insist. Rest assured and know I will spare no money in the decoration of your rooms. Everything will be brand new."

~ * ~

It flattered him more than he could express to see how his youthful bride relied on his judgment. *This marriage promised to become the best deal he ever made*, he reflected. *Not only would he experience a positive change in his personal life, but marrying the daughter of a count did have other advantages. It would give him more respect and the support of mighty people in Paris, like the girl's uncle. The money that Jaques de Vallencieux wanted in return was, compared to all these benefits, a small sacrifice.*

He searched the contents of his coat's pocket for the surprise he had prepared for her. "I have something for you, dearest."

He opened his hand, revealing a small box. She accepted it and pried it open. In it she found a beautiful ring, set with brilliants and a single emerald. Involuntarily, she released a sigh of surprise.

He smiled tenderly and took the ring out of its box. Then he carefully slid it over her ring finger and allowed her to admire it. Making use of her confusion, he quickly put his arm around her waist and pressed a light kiss on her cheek.

She was only too pleased when he left it at that, and instead suggested they return and join the others.

~ * ~

Three days later, the village of Vallencieux celebrated the betrothal of their count's only daughter. Neighbors and friends of the family arrived at the castle to take part in the big garden party the count offered to the neighborhood.

One of the new arrivals was Claude, Etienne's cousin. Armand was certainly glad to see him. The two young men had become quite friendly on the previous occasion and again spent most of the time in each other's company.

With all the hustle, those who had to watch Marguerite became a bit careless--and the young woman gladly took advantage. She had waited a long time for this opportunity, but finally she managed to exchange some quick words with her youngest brother.

"You are the only one who can come to my rescue," she told him.

"How then?" René asked, not sure if he could be of help. Speaking up for her meant he had to defy his father's will, and he was not sure he would dare to do that. He felt a lot of pity for his sister, surely, but would it not be better if she accepted her fate? Nothing could be done against it, anyway.

"I have a plan," she announced. "I am sure it can work out, with your help. The only thing you have to do is find a long rope and smuggle it into my room. I'll use it to climb out of the window."

Réné shook his head. "Marguerite! Do you really think you can do that? And how am I supposed to bring that rope into your room?"

"I'll leave my riding gloves in the stable," she said, having thought about it for hours. "Then you can come up and bring them to me. Wind the rope around your waist and wear a coat that is somewhat bigger. Nobody will notice anything."

"Fine," he grumbled. "But where in heaven's name will you go? You don't have anyone out there who can help you."

Now she smiled. "Didn't you hear Claude mentioning at lunch he's leaving for Paris tomorrow? I'm sure he won't mind taking me along. And once in Paris I can ask our uncle to help me. You know he's quite fond of me. He won't throw me out."

René thought for a moment. "I'm not sure about this, but I'll help you, sister," he finally said.

She pinched his cheek. "Thank you, brother. I knew I could count on you."

~ * ~

When all the sounds in the castle died down, Marguerite exchanged her nightgown for a pair of trousers and a shirt then took the bundle of rope out of the closet where she had hidden it behind her clothes. Within a couple of minutes she managed to secure it firmly around one of the legs of the bed. Then she opened the window with care. She let the rope down with as little noise as possible.

When she felt sure everything was ready, she climbed onto the windowsill and threw her legs over it. Her feet easily found support against the worn-out and crusted walls and soon she reached the deserted courtyard. From there, she made her way to the kitchen entrance. The door there, she knew from experience, would not be closed. She was right. She hurried through the kitchen then up the stairs, not needing light.

~ * ~

Claude de Bassy woke up, startled. His room was dark and nothing moved, but he was certain there *was* something. Trying not make any sound, he pushed himself to an upright position and tried to remember where he had laid down his sword. Before his fingers could touch it, however, a dark figure popped up beside the bed and a small hand closed over his mouth.

"I beg of you, not a sound, Monsieur! It is I, Marguerite de Vallencieux."

At once he felt wide awake. "Mademoiselle," he said, "what are you doing here, in the middle of night?"

"Hush, please. I had to speak to you, and there is no other possibility," she said.

He shrugged, taken aback by her boldness. "*Eh bien*, speak up then."

"You are leaving for Paris tomorrow, aren't you? I want to accompany you, for I certainly have no intention of becoming your cousin's bride."

He could not withhold a faint smile. The arrogance of the brat. He had noticed it before in all of the family. Poor but proud, thinking everyone would bow to their wishes. "But this is utter foolishness, my dear girl," he then said. "I have no wish to be hunted down by your dear brother Armand for kidnapping you. Besides, you would be in my way."

"Oh, you!"

Her small hand, now turned into a fist, gave him a nasty punch. She had so much hoped he would be willing to take her along. She bit her lip and swallowed through the tears of frustration. She did not want to make a fool of herself when he could witness it.

Claude watched her with growing interest. It suddenly occurred to him she had beautiful eyes, especially when they were wet with tears. And she had guts. He could not deny that. "What do you intend to do, once you reach Paris?" he wanted to know, despite his better judgment.

She looked up, hope springing in her face. "My uncle lives in the neighborhood of Saint-Cloud," she answered. "I don't think he will refuse to take me in. He's quite fond of me, as my mother was his favorite sister."

"I see."

"Are you going to take me along, then?" she asked again, a smile suddenly back on her lips. "I promise you I won't be a burden to you. I can stand being in the saddle for an entire day and I don't often complain. Please, will you take me along?"

Later on, Marguerite would learn that her unsuspecting, slow smile created a magical attraction to men. Claude was unable to resist it. "All right then," he agreed.

"Oh thank you, thank you!" she whispered gratefully, ready to embrace him.

"Calm down a bit, dear," he hurried to restrain her. "We have to make some practical arrangements. We can't just ride off."

"Of course not. Listen, I'd thought we could do it like this…"

Her head came closer to his, and in a low voice she began to share her plans with him.

Three

"*Messieurs, Mademoiselle*, I bid you farewell for the time being," Claude said when taking leave of the Vallencieux's. In the courtyard, he jumped into the saddle a stable lad held ready for him.

"A safe journey, and don't forget you are invited to the wedding," the count said.

"After the wedding, I am coming to Paris as well," Armand added.

"Well, I'll be looking forward to receiving you there," Claude replied. He saluted them then spurred on his mount. He trotted over the drawing bridge and soon disappeared out of sight.

"A well-mannered fellow," Jaques commented. "I do like his company."

"His mother taught him well," Etienne said. He too would be leaving later that day, as it was not fitting to stay in the bride's house before the wedding.

The party entered the castle again then sat down to breakfast. To Marguerite, the seconds seemed to tick away too slowly. She did not know how she would suffer passing away the time.

For that reason, she showed some signs of enthusiasm when her fiancé invited her for a ride. At least that would carry her through the morning, she thought.

They rode through the lush green countryside for an hour or so then Etienne invited his bride to step down from the horse and join him in a stroll along the river.

"I wanted another opportunity to be alone with you, my dear," he told her while he offered her his arm. "I thought you wouldn't mind, as it seems your father and brother are quite possessive and won't let you out of their sight."

She had to admit he could be a sharp observer at times. Probably that was the reason why he made his career as a prosecutor. He was also kind. If he were not so old, she would at least have thought over his proposal.

"I was rather wild when I was younger," she answered. "That is why Papa is worried I won't behave properly."

Etienne laughed. "Well, I wouldn't mind some recklessness, from time to time. Rest assured, my dear, once we are married I shall not be a harsh husband."

She thanked him for that. In fairness, his character seemed fine enough. What bothered her most was that her father had not left her a choice of her own. She should have been able to meet different men, make their acquaintance then form an opinion. She did not want an old man for husband, but this feeling was not pointed solely at Etienne. As a person, he was better to deal with than her family.

"I'm sure you are very kind," she remarked.

"Why thank you, my dear," he replied, flattered she told him so. His hopes grew that this marriage could turn into something he had not really expected. Would it not be lovely to win the love and respect of this young woman?

"I do have another present for you," he said, to change the subject. He handed her a purse in quality leather. "You don't have to open it straight away, but I thought you could use money of your own, seeing how your father deals with you."

"You shouldn't do this," she said, surprised at the weight of the purse.

He smiled. "I just like to pleasure you, sweet Marguerite. Go and buy something nice for yourself, yes?"

"Of course, I'll do that," she said.

The sun went up higher in the sky and it was time to return to the castle for luncheon.

~ * ~

In the afternoon, Etienne in turn took his leave from the family. When she kissed him goodbye, Marguerite felt a pang of remorse. The poor fellow did not know what was going to happen, and for a short moment, she felt bad about it. *He'll get over it,* she tried to reassure herself. *Once his disappointment ebbs away, he'll look for another bride. There are plenty of young women around.* She gave him one more sweet smile then turned away to enter the castle.

Finally, evening came. Dinner was the ordinary quick affair now that the guests had left, and she could excuse herself soon enough to go to her room. She allowed Rosette to help her wash and get into her nightgown, crept into bed and waited for the now familiar locking of her door.

Only after she heard the click she sprang into action. She donned her riding outfit--the one she 'borrowed' from Armand--and pressed her legs into the boots. Then she put up her hair with the help of some sturdy pins. Over it, she pressed a three-cornered hat. Her vanity mirror now showed a slender young man who laughed with perfect white teeth.

She folded clean underwear, some shirts and one of her gowns into a bag, hiding the purse with the money and her engagement ring between the clothes. She left the room the same way as before. As silently as possible, she made her way to the stables and went to her favorite mare, Marquisette. To prevent the animal from whinnying, she quickly put a hand over its nostrils and hushed it into silence. She saddled the mare then wound some straps of cloth round the hoofs.

The big stable door creaked when she pushed it open. A dog began to bark, and she froze. But nothing happened, and the castle remained quiet. At last she mounted and guided the mare in the direction of the village. Only there she dared to remove the windings from the hoofs. Mounted again, she set her heels into the animal's flanks and at a steady pace, they continued to the next village where Claude had agreed to wait for her.

"You made it," he greeted her once she arrived at the inn where he had taken a room. He was ready for the journey, his horse held at the reins. "We best get as far as possible."

They rode for the greatest part of the night. As the new day dawned, Marguerite felt sure there was a safe distance between them and possible pursuers--should her father decide to try and bring her back. Better still, with a bit of luck her disappearance would not have been spotted yet. Who in the castle would even think Claude was taking her to Paris? She had too often displayed her dislike of him.

A gnawing in their stomachs warned them they had not eaten since the previous evening. Claude exchanged a look of understanding with Marguerite then pulled his horse to standstill.

"Let's have breakfast!"

He found a suitable spot under a big tree, tethered the horses nearby and spread his cape over the grass. From one of his saddlebags he produced a loaf of bread and a hunk of cheese. Then he sat down and invited Marguerite to do the same.

The breakfast tasted good. Once their hunger was satisfied and washed down with several gulps of fresh water, they both stretched out and closed their eyes. Not long afterwards, they were sound asleep. Only when the sun was high in the sky, did they wake up.

They used the nearby brook to wash their faces and hands and gulped down more water. Then they unfastened the horses and continued their journey. By dusk, they reached the town of Auxerre. Claude knew his way around the town and guided them straight to a tavern.

"One moment, I'll check if they have a room for us," he said to Marguerite.

While he disappeared inside, she took the opportunity to look around a bit. A stagecoach was about to leave and this created quite a fuss. She admired the skill of the driver who had to maneuver through the narrow streets.

"You can dismount, Marguerite," Claude called out in a cheerful manner.

With easiness, she jumped to the ground, happy to stretch her legs after the long ride. She handed the reins of her mare to a young lad who promised to take good care of the horse.

The tavern was quiet now the stagecoach had left. It was still too early for the country folk to come in for a drink after work. So they had the choice of where to sit down and picked a table near a window.

A waitress approached them. "You two gentlemen must be hungry," she said with a smile, directed at Marguerite. "We have a fine stew of mutton tonight."

"Two big portions of that, my dear," Claude winked, "and a jug of wine." He pinched the soft flesh of her buttocks.

The girl, who was used to this sort of treatment, just shrugged and threw another look at the man's companion.

As soon as she moved away, Claude began to laugh. "You've made a conquest there, Marguerite. But well, you do resemble a cute lad!"

Embarrassed and to hide the red on her cheeks, she lowered her head. She wished he would not act this way.

The food was surprisingly delicious, although the wine was of a lesser quality. They did not linger at the table for too long. The efforts of the last day made themselves felt, and Marguerite knew it was high time she rolled into bed.

Claude seemed to notice it too. "Into bed with you, lad!"

He signaled the innkeeper who brought her to a small but tidy room. The bed had a soft mattress, and with a deep sigh, she let down her weight on it. She slept before her head hit the pillows.

The creaking sound of an opening door woke her up. She raised her head from the pillow and stared at Claude, who entered the room. He removed his coat and flung it over the back of a chair. "What the hell...?" she stammered, but shut up in confusion as the young man continued to undress.

She closed her eyes in embarrassment once more and thus only felt how he climbed into the bed with her. Instinctively, she moved to the far edge of the mattress.

"What are you doing?" she cried out. "Get out of this bed!"

"Don't make a fuss, my dear," he said softly. His brown eyes studied her carefully. "I am not going to spend my good money on two rooms each time we stop for the night," he explained. "I'm not going to rape you, if that's what you're afraid of," he added with a minor sense of compassion. "You wanted me to take you along, so you have to compromise."

She did not answer. She had to think. With him so close, it was not at all easy to do. She knew she could chase him out of this bed and remain on her own for the rest of the night. But what would happen afterwards? Would she come down the next morning to learn he had left? How would she continue her journey in that case? She did not know the way to Paris and a lone traveler would make an easy prey to every villain along the road. Somewhere Claude was right. She would not make it on her own. If this was the price to pay for it, *eh bien*, so be it.

When she did not give away any form of protest, he turned his back to her and soon was asleep.

Marguerite did not manage to sleep a wink. Claude's snoring and his close proximity kept her awake until the day broke. She realized she had made a big mistake in choosing Claude as her companion.

Perhaps I could better have stayed in Vallencieux and marry Etienne after all, she mused. *I'm sure he'd be much kinder to me than this lout. He treated me as a lady, which is as it should be.*

Four

"Please, not the horses!" Marguerite cried out, literally begging. But this time Claude could not be persuaded by her pleas.

In fact, he threw her a disdainful look. "Stop nagging, Marguerite. That crook of a tailor wants an advance in cash--the impertinence of these people! I favor him with my *clientèle* and even recommend him to my friends. Just because I'm a bit slow in paying his last bill, he has the nerve to ask me for an advance before he starts on my new coat."

"It was several bills," she whispered vehemently.

He did not listen to her. "I need this coat for the *comtesse's* ball next week, so I really see no other solution but selling the horses."

"No! Why don't we go to Saint-Cloud once more?"

"I can't wait until that uncle of yours finally decides to return to Paris," the young man sneered.

"The concierge said it was only a matter of days."

"Leave it, Marguerite. I have made up my mind."

He girded on his sword, put on his hat and left the room without one look behind.

Marguerite's slipper, aimed at him in anger, only missed him by a hair's breadth. She did not care to pick it up but flung herself on the squeaking bed and wept tears of pure frustration. *The bastard!* How well he knew that her only joy lay in the rare trip she made on the back of Marquisette. Those rides reminded her of home.

Being in Paris was not quite the adventure she had imagined it to be. How could she know she would miss having her father and brothers around, even when they were not so close? She even missed Etienne.

Right now, she knew with certainty that having married him would have been far better than her life here. The man she had run off with proved to be an egotist and totally untrustworthy.

She recalled what had happened since her flight from Vallencieux.

~ * ~

After Auxerre, they had spent two more days traveling and reached Paris in the course of the third day. The new environment made Marguerite forget the sleepless nights she had to spend with Claude--which did nothing for her temper. Every day she felt more irritated and hardly could smile anymore.

As soon as they were settled into their lodgings--a second-rate boarding house close to the town center--she saddled Marquisette and rode to Saint-Cloud where the Count de Salanges owned a magnificent mansion. There she met with the first disappointment.

After ringing the doorbell several times, the concierge came to answer it. "*Monsieur le comte* is not present," he said, in a not too friendly tone.

"Where has he gone?"

The man looked her over for a while and at last deemed her worthy of an answer. "He's left to attend his niece's wedding in Burgundy," he said.

"And will he be away for long?"

"Of course, I don't expect him back before two weeks have passed."

"I am a relative of the count," she told the man. "I need somewhere to stay. Could you not allow me into the house?"

The concierge shook his head. "The master gave explicit orders to close up the house until he returns," he said. "And excuse me for not knowing who you are, girl. As far as I'm concerned, you belong to a gang of crooks and you plan on robbing this place."

149

She turned and ran off. She would not dare to return until her uncle had returned from Burgundy.

The following moment was not pleasant either. She had to tell Claude her uncle was out of town and beg him if she could stay under his wing for a while longer.

He shrugged his shoulder. "I don't mind, dear girl, but you must understand I can't afford to pay for everything myself. I expect you to pay your part in the costs for lodging and food."

"Of course," she promised, eager to please him. His protection was better than nothing, after all.

The following days were tedious. Most of the time, Claude went to pursue his own business after breakfast and left her on her own. Because she did not know the town, she was afraid to venture out too far and felt thoroughly bored after a couple of days. When she finally worked up the courage to ask him where he spent his time, he answered he 'was earning their living'.

Of course, when at the end of the week the landlord came asking for his money, he was nowhere to be seen and she had to pay the full amount out of Etienne's purse.

She intended to ask him for his contribution as soon as she saw him, but did not get the opportunity. He surprised her at breakfast--a meal he mostly skipped because he stayed in bed until noon--and grinned at her cheerfully. "Come on, Marguerite," he told her. "We are spending this morning in town. Wait and see how wonderful you're going to find it!"

He dragged her along to their rooms and made her dress up in the one present he had ever bought her, a simple muslin gown. He had gotten tired of seeing her in men's clothes or the simple black dress she brought along.

During their walk he told her about the night he had spent out. "I attended a game of cards at a friend's house and sitting next to me was the *Comtesse* d'Arcourt. She's a widow and loaded. With a bit of persuasion I can convince her to spend some of that money on us."

"I'm not interested," she replied.

"Oh, but you should," he retorted. "I told her I have a sister, and she had no objections to the fact that you accompany me to the ball she's having next week."

"Your sister?" she arched her eyebrows. "Do you think she'll believe that? Why can't you introduce me under my own name?"

Claude sighed. "You don't want your father to find out where you're hiding, do you?" he asked, and now his concern seemed genuine. "No, no, from now on you are Mademoiselle de Bassy, my sister. You'll get a chance to meet interesting people at this and other balls. Make sure you don't make a mistake. You can't afford a slip of the tongue!"

She did not get the opportunity to ask other questions. He dragged her along to a seamstress and ordered three different evening gowns. Despite herself, she felt thrilled. She had not often been presented with new clothes. The only thing that bothered her a bit was that the dresses should have a low neckline.

When the seamstress had taken down her measurements and had promised the gowns should be ready within a few days, they went to a tailor's workshop where Claude ordered a new coat for himself.

During that first ball at the countess's mansion, Marguerite felt ill at ease. First of all her new frock was much too flamboyant with its heavy coral-red shades and a *décolleté* that was so deep she almost did not dare to breathe. It made her look like a child in her mother's dress, and when she noticed the disapproving looks--or those of hidden pleasure--from the other women, she felt even more miserable.

And what about the people who attended this ball? They all made a rather awkward impression on her. Their artificial conversations and false courtesies were quite new to her and she soon had a distaste for such affairs.

Moreover, she could not find any liking for the *comtesse*. She did try her best to be polite, for Claude's sake, but she could not help thinking the woman was *ordinaire*.

From the bits of conversation she picked up during the time she had to spend at the balls, she learned that Madame d'Arcourt was a former *courtisane* who had besotted an old count and got him to marry her. The count had not lived long after the marriage--coincidence?--and the widow was left with his fortune, which she now spent on luxuries and expensive parties.

The first invitation was followed by a second and a third. It happened that Claude stayed at the Hôtel d'Arcourt for a couple of nights, and although Marguerite counted her blessings on such occasions, she also considered it as some sort of treason towards her. Her dislike of the countess grew by the day.

The seamstress and the tailor presented their bills. She had already emptied Etienne's purse by paying the landlord and was forced to bring her engagement ring to the pawnbroker's. The amount of money she received for it was just enough to settle the bills and pay for one week's rent to go. The innkeeper had already mentioned something about having to ask for his money each week. She believed him when he threatened to throw them out if they did not pay promptly.

With each day that came and went, she became more and more ashamed of her appearance and her way of living.

~ * ~

Three days after he sold the horses, Claude walked into their room and announced they were going to another party at the house of the Comtesse. She pulled a sour face.

"Try to smile, Marguerite," Claude said. "You're going to a party, not to your funeral!"

Her eyes shot fire. ""I don't give a damn about your parties," she shouted at Claude. "Nor about your precious *comtesse*! You're a bastard and I will never forgive you for selling my horse."

He took her brutally by the arm and squeezed if painfully. She had to bite her lips not to scream out in pain.

"You will promise to behave, and do as I say, won't you?" he threatened her softly.

"Only because you are stronger than I," she answered. "And now, release me. I won't run away."

She allowed him to accompany her to a rented coach and in silence they drove to the residence of the Comtesse.

With a recently acquired nonchalance, she greeted Madame d'Arcourt. "*Bon soir, Madame.* So nice to be here again."

On this occasion, the former courtesan wore a stately gown in poison-green, lined with cherry-red lace. In her hair, which could be best described as having the color of a carrot, she wore three feathers in the same red coloring. The result of it all was revolting, to say the least, but the woman seemed quite happy with her appearance.

"My dear friends, welcome," she smiled when she saw Claude and his sister.

She held up her hand to Claude, so he could kiss it, and blew a kiss beside Marguerite's cheek. "How sweet you look, my dear child," she said with a false smile. "Quite a nice dress you wear."

I'm not an infant, Marguerite thought angrily. She was wise enough, though, not to show her true feelings. In a voice just as sweet she said, "Why, thank you Madame. You are stunning, as always. You must certainly give me the name of your seamstress."

For a change, she did not feel unhappy about the dress she was wearing. By now, she was used to wearing long skirts, and when a new gown was ordered, she had for once been able to persuade Claude to let her have her way in choosing a design. Tonight she wore an evening dress in soft pink satin, with only a modest neckline and few decorations. It made her look extremely young and pure in this place of utter decadence.

With a possessive air, Madame d'Arcourt took hold of Claude's arm. "*Mon cher*, I insist you help me with the reception of our guests," she cooed. "I don't doubt we can put the protection of your little sister in the capable hands or Marquis d'Aubervilliers."

On hearing his name mentioned, a tall man joined their party. Marguerite had seen him in the countess's house before. If she was right, he too was one of the *amants* of the lady. He was certainly handsome and good-looking, and had perfect manners compared to many other guests. He never said an unpleasant word to her yet she could not prevent a shiver every time they met. Instinctively, she recognized his true nature: he was a wolf in sheepskin.

"If you permit me, Mademoiselle."

He bowed to her and apparently docile she allowed him to escort her to the dance floor. It was still warm for September, and the temperature in the rooms was suffocating. She opened her fan and waved some coolness into her face. "*Mon dieu*, I won't survive this night!" she exclaimed.

The marquis immediately summoned one of the lackeys to bring her a glass of cooled wine. She thanked him for this attention and drank gratefully, although she realized that with such temperatures, she should not drink too much.

"Mademoiselle de Bassy, I admire your good taste," d'Aubervilliers said. "You look so...refreshing and charming. A rose among the daffodils."

"You are flattering me, Monsieur," she replied. "I'm just a country girl, for once wearing a gown I like." She wished he would not make further compliments, as she was at a loss of what to say.

"It suits you nicely. That delicate pink against your dark hair almost makes you a beauty."

"Please, Monsieur, you embarrass me. I am certainly not a beauty!" she tried to persuade him from saying anything else.

"Perhaps not in the literal sense," he said, clearly not wanting to recognize her signals. "You are different." Then he smiled. "But now, no more talking. Let's dance."

They took part in a couple of dances. The ballroom was crowded, for this was an informal occasion. The countess frequently opened her doors to everyone who wanted to come, and by doing this, the place had established the reputation of being a *rendez-vous* house. Gentlemen of noble birth could openly bring their mistresses while masked ladies of the court came looking for a gallant adventure. Everything was possible and everything was permitted.

The heat and the smoke, produced by hundreds of candles, made Marguerite feel unpleasant. She felt relieved when the marquis proposed to take a stroll in the garden and eagerly agreed--the heat being responsible for her lack of alertness.

"I have a light headache," she told him in truth. "I'm sure fresh air will do me good."

When they left the crowded rooms behind them, it felt like a cool shower. Dusk was falling and a fresh breeze rustled the leaves of the trees. Here and there a lantern spread some diffuse light over the path the marquis took, and she could spot various other couple walling around. "Ah, this is wonderful," she sighed. She welcomed the coolness on her cheeks, and already the pressure in her head began to diminish.

The marquis guided her along a lighted path to a small pavilion at the far end of the garden. It was encircled by low bushes and looked truly peaceful. She was so involved with breathing in the air she did not notice there were no other wanderers in this part of the garden.

"I do have a key to this place," she heard the marquis say. "Do you wish to go inside and rest a while? We can open the windows to let the air in."

He pressed her fingers lightly, revealing his true intentions. Cold anger quickly took possession of her. "I am not tired, Monsieur," she said, careful not to show her rage. "I prefer to walk a bit longer."

The marquis stopped abruptly. He gave her a look of disbelief. "My dear Mademoiselle, you seem to be afraid of me! I mean no harm to you; you must believe me. Has your brother not entrusted me with your safety?"

She could only decline. "Why should I be afraid of you?" she remarked lightly. "You are always the perfect cavalier."

"So why don't you follow my suggestion? It will be much quieter here than in the big house."

He released her arm and took a gilded key out of his pocket. The lock opened instantly--apparently oiled by frequent use. "So convenient," he mentioned. "I often come here to escape the crowds. The *comtesse* knows I don't enjoy them, so she has given me this key."

She allowed him to escort her inside. The small room was surprisingly decorated in a nice fashion, even when a large bed dominated the space.

The marquis closed the door behind them then began to open up the windows, as he had promised.

There were no chairs to sit down on, so Marguerite remained standing. Her mind was busy with finding a way out of this situation.

One more window then d'Aubervilliers turned to her again. "Why don't we sit down? We can use the bed as a sofa."

He approached her, and she had to restrain herself from drawing back. Now he was quite near to her; their bodies were almost touching. His face came so close she could feel his breath. Yet she was not thinking about his nearness. It was his eyes that caught her attention--they held a secretive look which made her afraid.

"Do you find me repulsive, Mademoiselle?" she heard him ask, as if he was aware of her feelings. She refused to look away.

"You know pretty well you are a handsome man," she said, trying to sound as if she knew her way around.

He laughed then wrapped his arms around her waist.

She allowed him to do just this and also did not protest when he pressed his lips onto her mouth for a searing kiss. She responded to it, because she had figured out how to escape his unwanted attentions. She shut her mind off and allowed him more freedom; until he was convinced she would allow him to bed her.

At that exact moment, she threw up her knee and kicked him in the groin with full force. She noted with satisfaction what such a simple trick could do to a grown man. The marquis's face turned white as a sheet and he rolled over the floor, tortured with pain. Making good use of it, she quickly grabbed hold of a statue, which stood in a niche, and broke it to pieces over his head. The force of the blow rendered him unconscious.

With a sigh of relief, she wiped the loose strands of hair out of her face then checked if her dress was wrinkled. She waited some time longer to allow her breathing to calm and finally made her way back to the house. She did not meet anyone in the garden for which she felt thankful.

When she went inside the mansion, the heat almost knocked her off her feet. Nevertheless, she crossed the various rooms in the hope of finding out where Claude was. When she could not immediately find him, she found the major-domo, whom she suspected of sharing the secrets of the house.

"Gerard, have you seen my brother?" she asked him.

"Last time I saw him he was in the library," the man answered.

She headed for the library, which acted as gambling room tonight. If possible, the heat was even more intense here. The room was crowded with people. Dozens of feverish eyes concentrated on the cards that brought fortune or ruin.

Her tour around the room brought no result either. When asked, some of the men who frequently visited Madame d'Arcourt's *soirées* told her that her brother and the countess had played some games of faro, but had left the library about half an hour ago.

She was glad to leave the greenhouse's humid atmosphere, but at the same time, she felt ill at ease because she desperately wanted to talk to Claude. She had to persuade him to take her home!

When she crossed the hall, she noticed how a young couple crept up the stairs to the higher floor where the bedrooms were situated. On a hunch, she decided to follow them. The couple reached the first floor and disappeared into one of the rooms. Now she was alone on the sparsely lit landing.

She looked around. Almost all of the doors were closed and behind them she could distinguish muffled voices and sighs of delight. She put her ear against each door; trying to identify the voices of the people she was looking for.

Then she advanced to the last door in the corridor. Coming closer, she saw a small ray of light beneath the partially shut door. The voices sounded louder as well. She could clearly understand what was said inside. A man--whose voice she recognized as Claude's without any doubt--was laughing at some joke. "Yes, *ma chère,* I agree that it is settled nicely!"

A woman--the *comtesse*--said complacently: "Haven't I told you to count on Antoinette? You finally get rid of that silly girl and d'Aubervilliers pays you a handsome sum for her on top of it."

"I take it he won't harm her in any way?"

Did that sound as a change of heart? If so, it came rather late, Marguerite thought.

"Of course not," Madame d'Arcourt answered. "He promised me he will set her up with a house and some capital, once he tires of her. By the way, is she really your sister?"

Marguerite's fingers pressed into the skirts of her gown so harshly her nails went straight through the fabric. *The bastards! Those damned bastards....*

She turned abruptly and ran down the stairs. Tears dripped down onto her cheeks and made wet stains on her dress.

In a flash she stood outside--she did not remember how it happened. All at once, she found herself in an empty street, where only darkness reigned. She kept running.

A coacher yelled something at her, but she did not catch his words. Only when she became aware of the gnawing pain in her side, did she slow down. To her surprise, she had reached the neighborhood where their lodgings were.

She managed to enter the establishment without the landlord noticing and hurried to the room she shared with Claude. She realized she had to leave. If Claude returned to find her, he would turn her over to the marquis. How deep he had sunk. She was only merchandise to him; something he could trade in to pay for his luxuries.

She opened up the buttons of her dress and quickly stepped out of it. Skirts would only hold her up. The old riding outfit still felt trusted and comfortable. She knew her pursuers would be looking for a girl, not for a boy.

Money! She needed money if she was to survive life in this town. She went through their belongings and came up with a couple of *sous*, barely enough coins to pay for food once or twice. *Merde*, she thought, *if only I still had Marquisette!*

The sound of an arriving carriage startled her. She propped the money into her pocket and searched for an another way out. She opened the window that looked out on the back alley behind the inn and threw her legs over the sill. One quick glance convinced her the alley was deserted. Like a cat, she landed well on her feet, pressed the hat lower to hide her face and began to walk off in a lazy stroll.

Five

The Pont Neuf, as usual, was crowded with people and animals. Merchants loudly praised their wares, gipsy's and artists performed tricks, quacks tried to cheat foolish believers out of their money. Well-to-do citizens and beggars alike moved in all directions.

The slender young man who lingered near one of the stalls did not attract special attention. Agreed, his face looked not too clean and his clothes looked as if they had been slept in. But there were many poor students like him.

Marguerite--the student--directed her looks from one stall to another. She had to be careful not to alarm the vendors. The smell of bread, still warm, tortured her nostrils, but the baker's boy looked too alert and hard-handed.

Disappointed, she walked on. Since she'd run away from the inn, she had not had a lot to eat. The few pennies she stole could buy her some bread and cheese, but these were long gone. The nights, which she spent under one of the bridges, were easier to bear because the temperatures were still reasonably warm for the time of year.

By now, she had figured out the best way to get food would be to steal some--and for that purpose she came to the bridge. Here were so many people no one would notice her--or so she thought.

She still had not decided what to do after she had eaten. What choices did she have? Either she had to face her uncle, who she now believed would bring her back to her family--where her father and Armand would make her pay for her reckless deed of running away. Or she could return to the inn and risk her luck with Claude. Would she be able to persuade him not to sell her to the marquis?

Her nostrils picked up the scent of fruit. A woman sold apples and pears and oranges from Spain. She lingered somewhat and calculated her chances, the water almost coming to her mouth when she stared at those delicious apples. The merchant was helping a customer and did not look her way. One apple disappeared into her pocket. She reached out for a second time and got hold of a pear.

Then a heavy hand landed on her shoulder. She dropped the pear and looked into the face of a sturdy woman.

"Caught in the act, you thieving scoundrel!" she cried out, drawing everyone's attention.

Marguerite panicked. In her mind she already saw herself arrested and carried off to prison by the guard--she, a Vallencieux! The fright gave her unusual force and she managed to wriggle out of the woman's hold. She pushed her away and started to run to the other end of the bridge.

"Hold the thief!" she heard behind her. The woman and the vendor began the chase. Their loud cries alarmed the guards who were posted along the bridge. One of them tried to bar her way. She dove under his arm and ran even harder.

"Pst, this way!"

A man grabbed her sleeve and she was quickly pulled into a narrow alley. She hardly realized what happened. Her persecutors ran past.

Her savior now let go of her arm and showed her an encouraging smile. "Still an amateur, *non*?"

She looked up and slowly returned his roguish smile. She studied the face of the stranger who had kept her from being arrested. He was a young man, only partly outgrown his boyhood. Most likely he was not much older than she. He was half a head taller though and had an athletic body with firm shoulders and strong legs. His irregular features--the nose was too big and the lips too sensual--were framed with shoulder-long curly brown hair. All in all, his looks gave her a good feeling--they reminded her of her brother René.

"I suppose I should thank you," she said, "although I don't know you."

He raised his eyebrows, which gave his face a comical look. "Hello there, what a posh language! Where do you belong, mate? Are you a member of the brotherhood?"

He crossed his index and middle fingers--surely a sign she ought to know--and held his hand up, so she could see it clearly.

"Brotherhood?" she repeated. She was completely at a loss and shook her head. This slight movement made her hat, which already stood unsteady on her head, tumble to the ground.

"Good heavens, you're a girl!" The young man produced a whistle full of surprise and his grin became even wider. Then he made a dashing bow, which could only be bettered by a courtier.

"Your servant, Mademoiselle! Allow me to introduce myself. I am Louis Dominique Bourgignon. Pickpocket by profession, and member of the renowned Parisian *confrérie* of thieves and beggars."

She returned a *révérence*, involuntary amused by his speech. "How do you do, Monsieur? My name is Marguerite."

Simultaneously they both burst out into laughter. Afterwards, he fished a still warm loaf of bread out of his sack, broke it, and offered her a part. She set her teeth into it, showing how hungry she was. Then she remembered her manners and offered him the apple. "We can share it," she said.

"You're quite something," Dominique told her. "Won't you tell me where you come from?"

"Burgundy," she replied, her mouth full of apple.

"I see. Got attracted by the fame of Paris?"

"Sort of." Even though she felt at ease with this young man, she still was not prepared to give away her identity or mention any of the events which had brought her to the capital.

He did not seem overly interested anyway. "Do you have a place to sleep?"

She shook her head.

"I may have something for you," he then said. "At least, if you are not afraid to trust me."

The past couple of weeks had been a harsh learning school for Marguerite. By now, she recognized the look of sincerity in a man's face. She decided she could trust this young fellow, in spite of his 'profession'. He inspired much more confidence than Claude or the marquis. "I do," she answered.

"It's a place where you will be completely safe," he announced. "I live there too."

"Gladly."

Without hesitation, she accepted his hand and felt how his fingers pressed hers comfortingly.

"Friends?" he asked.

"Friends," she acknowledged.

A friendship that would last for years was born.

~ * ~

Through a tangle of small streets and alleys, Dominique brought her to L'Ange Noir. It was a dark and dubious tavern in the immediate neighborhood of the old Tour de Nesle, in the heart of Saint-Denis. Outside the entrance hung a signboard with a fading angel painted on it. It was covered with layers of dust and barely attracted attention.

"We like to keep it this way," the young man explained to his newfound friend. "We are not too keen on strangers visiting here."

He pushed the front door open. This entrance, in all its shabbiness, did not indicate that behind this poor front an enormous building lay concealed, taking in all the nearby premises and outfitted with secret getaways to the river Seine.

"Young Cartouche, who have you brought with you?" someone asked. Marguerite looked surprised when she heard her companion named otherwise.

"That's my nickname here," he quickly mentioned. Then he addressed the man who had spoken. "Ronchard, I've found this young lady on the streets and she needs shelter."

The innkeeper, who was tall and skinny, studied her for a while then nodded his approval.

"Fine by me," he said. "But remember you need to present her to Meurice."

"I'll do that as soon as she's settled in," Dominique promised.

"Right, then I'll show you where the young lady can sleep."

He brought them to a small but tidy room, which had a good bed and even a cupboard to place some clothes in it.

"Who's Meurice?" Marguerite wanted to know as soon as Ronchard left them alone. "And what do I have to pay for this room?"

Dominique smiled. "Curious, eh? You'll have to restrain from asking too many questions from now on. But for once I'll make an exception, your being new to this. Meurice is our leader. He's the strongest and most cunning of us all, and so we obey his orders. I already told you we're a brotherhood. We all contribute to our cost of living. What we find on the streets, we bring home with us then Meurice decides what to do with it. So no, you don't have to pay anything for your bed and board, but later on you'll be asked to make a contribution of your own, you understand?"

She nodded, although she was not completely sure of what was being expected of her. For the moment, she had everything she needed; warm food, a place to rest.

The next day, her new friend showed her around. He introduced her to some of his friends, also thieves and beggars, and told her about their habits. He also began to teach her how to pick someone's pocket. Because she had a good mind and made good use of her eyes, it did not take her long to pick up how he did it, and after a while, she was willing to try it for herself.

It's just a game; she tried to quench the pangs of conscience. She knew what she did was wrong. *But what am I to do? At least here I don't have to be afraid of being discovered.*

163

Two nights later, Cartouche--even Marguerite now called him so--introduced his new friend to the *confrérie*.

The nightly meeting of all its members took place after dusk. The previous night, she had witnessed with wonder how, one by one, every member came in, was provided with a drink by Ronchard, and then presented the 'harvest' of the day to the leader. This one calculated their share and handed it over to them.

"Do they never fight?" she asked Cartouche.

"No," he answered, "that's how things are done here. Meurice is the boss."

"And what happens when someone questions his authority?" she went on, trying to get a better idea of how things were in her new world.

"They fight," Cartouche smiled. Then he continued: "Shall I share a secret with you? One day, I'm going to be the boss here. Then the orders shall be given by me."

She looked up at him. "Do you mean that?"

"You can bet on it. The whole of Paris shall know the name of Cartouche."

"And the entire police force will hunt you down," she could not stop from saying. She was fond of the young man and when she considered his future, a feeling of sadness took possession of her. She could already picture him dangling from the gallows.

Dominique himself did not seem to be bothered by this idea. "We all arrive at the Place de Grève--sooner or later," he said.

That specific night, the brothers entered the inn as usual. Marguerite could already distinguish the different types of criminal--although they did not consider themselves to be so. The ones with stern faces and repulsive manners were the cut-throats, she knew, who could be hired to perform any crime. The ones with dishevelled clothes and apparently missing limbs, were the beggars, who could mostly be found near the churches. The robbers and pickpockets, like Dominique, looked quite innocent, because they needed to be able to mix with the crowds and not draw attention to themselves.

When all the loot was split up and everyone was enjoying his drink, the young man took Marguerite's hand and led her to the high table where Meurice and his lieutenants sat.

"This young lady wants to become a member of our brotherhood," he said. "And I can vouch for her."

"Very well," Meurice answered. His clever eyes took in the girl, who looked ever so innocent. Then a slow smile appeared on his face. "I think she'll fit in rather nice. She will go by the name Duchesse."

And so it was done. When Meurice spoke, everyone accepted his decision. From that day onwards, Marguerite became Duchesse, the girl who could talk like she belonged to the nobility and who could fool people just because of it.

When she brought in a well-filled purse of gold and placed it on Meurice's table, some days later, she felt proud of herself. The five coins in gold, which she received as her share, were the first money she ever earned by herself. *With a bit of luck,* she mused, *I'll be able to save enough to buy a horse then I can return to Burgundy.* She was wiling to face her father, whom she trusted would, by now, be willing to forgive her for her thoughtless deeds. Of course she kept these plans to herself. She did not even talk of them to Cartouche.

The weeks went by, and Marguerite felt as if she had been living in Paris for ages. She knew the town well enough by now and also its many secrets. Her new friend was her guide and her teacher. Nothing special ever happened, until that one night.

~ * ~

One by one, her new friends entered the inn and they cheerfully greeted Marguerite. First came in Louison and Jaquot, two highly skilled thieves. Then Michot-Wooden-Leg, a man who had the use of both his legs, but who pretended to miss one to raise pity. Pierre the pimp with his troop of hookers followed. Mira the Egyptian, a gipsy with a sharp tongue and a virtuosity in robbing a man from his money; was already a bit late. Finally arrived big Romain, the quack who sold all kinds of worthless potions and salves at the Pont Neuf.

Then, all of a sudden, another man entered. He appeared to be six foot tall and was completely dressed in black. With a haughty air he strolled through the tavern and beckoned Ronchard to bring him some wine.

Marguerite's attention was raised because he seemed so completely different from the others. She had not seen him enter L'Ange Noir before. He seemed to be lost in thought and had no eye for his surroundings. She looked at him once more.

As if he sensed someone was studying him, he suddenly raised his head and directed a wondering glance at Marguerite.

Smoke-gray eyes pierced inquiringly into hers, and she felt a physical shock. A fireball shot through her body and confused her. Embarrassed by these strange sensations and because she was being caught at prying, she turned her head and moved to another part of the room. God, who was this man?

Meurice announced the division of the goods was going to begin. In due course, the stranger stepped forward and handed over a heavy purse with a royal gesture. The leader of the gang smiled his approval and winked at the stranger. "Looks like the profits were good this month."

"Of course," the man answered. "The ladies and gentlemen of the gentry are returning to town." He spoke with a hoarse voice, which had a strange attraction.

Despite herself and her intention of spending no more thoughts on the stranger, Marguerite pushed her elbow into Dominique's side, thus diverting his attention from the reddish-blond damsel who had just joined Pierre's harem of girls and who was making tempting moves towards him. "Who's that man?" she whispered. She desperately wanted to know, and he was the only one who could provide her with an answer.

Dominique did not reply straight away.

166

~ * ~

"Well?" she insisted, pushing somewhat harder.

"That guy? That is Le Chevalier, my dear." Cartouche finally banned the maid out of his thoughts and paid attention to what Marguerite was saying. When he saw where she was pointing, he felt some unease. Hell! Was she interested in him? He did not like that look of expectation on her face. He wanted to remain the one she looked up to.

"The Chevalier," she repeated slowly. "Yes, that's a fitting name. Is he a real nobleman?"

"Who knows, maybe. You know full well we don't ask too many questions. Whatever people may have been or done is of no significance here."

Marguerite threw another long glance at the man. "I think he's a nobleman," she finally said. "He behaves so…refined."

Takes one to know one, Cartouche thought. He began to feel more and more uneasy. His new companion seemed quite interested. He so much hoped to win her affection, even her love… Damn! His self-confidence underwent a crisis when he considered how he would be able to obtain that goal.

"It's not important whether or not the Chevalier is a nobleman," he stated at last.

However, Marguerite's curiosity was not satisfied. "How come I only see him tonight? Where has he been all this time?"

He sighed deeply. He knew she would not give up until he answered. "Because he only comes to our gatherings once a month. He runs a gambling house in the Rue Quincampoix, and Meurice shares a percentage in the profits."

"Why?"

Now she was really going too far! He began to lose his temper. "Don't ask so many questions, Duchesse!" he reproached her, not too kindly.

"But I'd like to know more," she held on. "Please, Dominique!"

She looked up at him with begging eyes--and all of a sudden, his anger melted away, like butter in the sun. He too was not immune to the intensity of her green eyes. "Alright then," he shrugged at last. "Years ago, the Chevalier arrived in Paris, totally ruined. To make it worse there was a prize on his head. He needed and found a place to hide in our midst, and bit by bit he was able to improve his situation. He is very clever at cards and a while ago, he decided to take over a gambling house. He has become very rich now, you know, and it would not be difficult for him to buy back his way in society and act as a seigneur. Yet he remains a member of our *confrèrie*. That is our rule: whatever you do or wherever you go, you pay tributary to the leader of the gang. Don't ever try to release these ties, or else…"

"I understand," she answered softly. His words brought her into a reflective mood. When, some time later, the young man asked her to dance, she denied decisively and left on her own for a stiff walk through the deserted streets. She did not realize she was trying to escape the memory of predominant gray eyes.

Six

Shortly after Marguerite's eighteenth birthday, which fell on November 15th, Cartouche announced a party was about to be held in L'Ange Noir, something big and festive.

"I'm so honored," Marguerite called out, to tease him. "I did not expect my birthday was so important to everyone."

His eyes turned big. "You had your birthday? My goodness, I owe you a present then!"

Willingly, she allowed him to take her into his arms and she received a couple of warm kisses on her cheeks. The only thing that bothered her a bit was that he held her unusually long close to his body and that she could feel the tenseness of his muscles. His fingers touched the soft skin of her neck and hesitatingly stroked the lines of cheek and jaw. Although the sensation was not at all unpleasant, she felt embarrassed over this display of friendship. She had never experienced the like of it at home. Even René did not demonstrate his brotherly love this openly. And now she wished Dominique would release her. Being a virgin, she did not understand the underlying sexual desires her companion was undergoing at the moment.

Dominique had to struggle not to press her even closer, had to keep his hands from wandering and taking possession of her budding breasts. He longed to kiss her with fierceness and make her want him as badly as he needed her. Luckily, his good sense got the better of him and at last he dropped his hands and stepped back. He knew too well he would frighten her off if he kept doing this.

Unconsciously, Marguerite's hand went up to her cheek. She was thinking of her previous birthday at the convent. Not much later she had come home to spend Christmas there, and there were presents from her father, from René, from Marie, even from Armand. Every now and then the longing for home overtook her. What would René be doing at this moment? Was he galloping across the fields with Armand, or locked up in that stuffy classroom with Père Duthot?

"Do you think you like me, Duchesse?"

Cartouche's voice broke off her contemplations. "What? Oh--of course," she answered automatically. "You are my friend, aren't you? I almost love you as a brother--in fact, you often remind me of my brother René."

Her honest words diminished his hopes for the time being. She was not ready yet. Still, he refused to be pessimistic and felt confident enough about his own capacities. He would not give up easily. There had to be a way to make her realize he was the right man for her. He was able to smile pleasantly. "That's worth a lot to me, Duchesse. Look, I want to show you something."

He took her hand and brought her to his room in the attic. From the small window, one was able to look out over the entire *quartier*, which made it an ideal lookout post.

The young man invited her to sit on the bed and began to fumble at his belt. Out came a small package.

"I always keep valuable things here," he explained to Marguerite. "Meurice doesn't know I have this. Look, here's a present for your birthday!"

He handed the package over to her. It was surprisingly heavy for being so small. She began to unwrap it. When its contents were bared, a sigh of disbelief escaped her lips. Even in this gray attic room, the diamonds seemed to live a life of their own. They sparkled and blinded the eyes with their splendor.

Marguerite carefully lifted the necklace up. "Oh, these are beautiful!" she cried out. "They must be worth a fortune!"

Her green eyes reflected the flickering a thousand times and appeared to transform themselves into emeralds. This was the best reward Cartouche could think of. "Diamonds for a duchess," he whispered, just as much spellbound.

"And you really want me to have them?" she needed to make sure. "Don't you want to save them for your sweetheart?"

"I'm too young to get involved," he stated, not wanting to reveal his true intentions. "They are for you, Duchesse, only for you."

"Then I must thank you properly," she said, as she neared him. Her fingertips touched his skin, light as a butterfly, and her lips left a tender, furtive kiss on his lips. With a newly acquired female intuition--was it the influence of the diamonds?--she suddenly realized this young man had more than brotherly feelings for her. She felt she had to do something to prevent him from getting hurt.

"Don't fall in love with me, Dominique," she said quietly. "It wouldn't work out. I can't love a man just now."

He bit his lip, taken by her sudden insight. He also understood she wanted some reassurance from him. "Treated roughly, right?" he told her knowingly. "Not all men are such bastards, Marguerite, remember that. I will remain your friend, and nothing more, if that is what you want. But you can't keep me from dreaming."

"Oh, dreams!" she exclaimed, suddenly impatient. She did not value dreams any longer. Dreams were shattered in this harsh world. Better hold on to reality.

With an inviting gesture, she turned her back to Dominique and held up the necklace. "Will you fasten it for me?"

He did as she asked. She turned again, now to look into the small mirror he used to shave. She admired the necklace for a while.

"I shall wear it at the party," she then decided. "I've never had anything as beautiful as this. Thank you a lot, my friend."

"You'll be the queen of the ball," he knew. "Especially when you wear a silk or satin gown. Shall I ask Louison to have a look in the atelier of Madame Berthe?"

"Oh fine," she grinned. "Better still, I'll accompany him. Dresses need to be fitted!"

~ * ~

The night of the party arrived.

Light as a feather, Marguerite swirled from one pair of arms to another. The cream-colored satin of her dress suited her to perfection, making the blackness of her hair stand out even more. Her eyes shone with a brilliance that swept up images of the deep ocean, and the blushes on her cheeks had the healthy shade of sun-ripe apricots.

For the first time in her young life, the promise of beauty manifested itself in its full glory. The graceful movements of her fragile body, with the long limbs and the first showing of budding breasts, combined with the still innocent look on her face, placed her far above every other woman in L'Ange Noir.

A number of men became aware of their feelings of desire. Meurice followed her movements with a greedy eye and licked his lips. He wondered if he would take this piece of candy for himself or share it with the others. Pierre donned a wide grin and calculated her worth in hard coins. He would soon talk to her, he said to himself, and convince her of the benefits working for him could bring. Romain ran to and fro with drinks and sweetmeats, which he shyly offered to her--quite unusual for a man who always had a comment.

Cartouche leaned against a doorpost in a reflective mood. Duchesse was definitely changing into a woman. Soon the ugly duckling would turn into a magnificent swan, and once she became aware of her power over men, she would solely turn to him in distress. There certainly would be others. He was not blind! Would it be worth fighting for her favors and put their friendship at risk, or would it pay to stand in the background and await the right moment?

There was another point to consider. Becoming more confident, Marguerite would learn to face the frights that had chased her away from her trusted surroundings. As well as she fitted in, she really did not belong in this place of crime and she should not remain here forever. She belonged in some castle or manor, encircled by her family and their trusted servants. Who could her father be, a duke? Despite himself, he smiled at this thought.

~ * ~

Two members of the gang left the party unusually early. When the rest of the *confrèrie* was more sober, they would have noticed the faces of Jaquot and Louison were very pale. They hurried to the room they shared. Jaquot put down two beakers and filled them with brandy. Louison emptied his in one gulp.

Jaquot patted him on the shoulder. "I know, *mon ami*. Those wretched diamonds seem to lead a life of their own!"

"For heaven's sake, how did they come into the possession of sweet little Duchesse? You can bet on it, there will be trouble," Louison said. He poured himself another drink.

Unexpectedly, he found himself back in the dark bedroom, staring at the dead woman on the carpet. The diamonds laying there.

"Scarron died because of them," Jaquot recalled. "Remember that gipsy girl he was involved with in those days? I'm sure she was the one who cut his throat. The next day both she and the diamond necklace had disappeared."

"You're probably right. But there is something else. Did you know the old Jew, Rosenthal, came to see Scarron the day after we handed him the necklace? Later, I had to call on him for advice in another matter, and he mentioned something about the necklace. Mind, he did not dare to call it by its real name, but he said there was no other string of diamonds of exactly the same size, and its history was written in blood."

"Bloody hell!"

They had another drink and remained silent for a while. Then Louison raised the important question: "Shall we warn Marguerite? Should we tell her that already two people died because of this necklace?"

Jaquot sighed. "Now you tell me something. Do we have the right? We don't know how she came by it."

~ * ~

Unknown by the two thieves, Marguerite's fate was already decided.

One of the revelers, who arrived somewhat late at the party, caught a glimpse of the sparkling necklace around the young woman's neck--and stopped moving.

A bitter taste came into the Chevalier's mouth and time stood still. He found himself in the past, back to that fateful night when Isabelle had deigned to turn up for dinner. Caught back in that moment when he swore he would kill her for being unfaithful to him. Back to that specific night, which had been the first in a disastrous course of events. The body at the foot of the stairs, the trial, the years of banishment...

With some difficulty, he shrugged off those gloomy thoughts and decided on his course of action. He paced in Marguerite's direction. "I will have this dance."

Her joy came to an abrupt end. She looked up into his smoke-gray eyes and shivered. Yet she did not dare refuse him. His voice had such an air of command she allowed him to take her to the dance-floor without any form of protest.

He put his arm around her middle and swirled her round on the tunes of a farandole. He did not utter another word and did not release her when the farandole ended. He just pulled her closer against his tight body.

She was not sure what his intentions were. Did he want to kiss her, or what? And why did he study her so intensely?

The Chevalier stared into her eyes and in his mind their emerald color changed into deep-blue. The dark hair turned into gold-blond, the shy smile into a defiant grin. Oh, Isabelle! How he had loved her, and how she had betrayed that love. She mocked him for his true love and was overcome by greed to have the Medici diamonds, sacrificing everything to obtain them. Unconsciously, his fingers pressed deeply into the soft flesh of Marguerite's shoulders hurting her.

"Take your hands off me," he suddenly heard an angry voice. With a shock, he came to his senses. Isabelle was dead. The girl they called Duchesse who seemed furious now was wearing the missing piece of evidence, the diamond necklace. He had lost control over himself, he cursed. This should not happen again! If he was to succeed in his plan, he should keep his wits together and not allow subversive feelings to play their tricky part.

Impatiently, Marguerite pulled herself loose from his grip. She raised her hand to slap him in the face, but before she could succeed in it, her wrist was caught in an iron grip.

"You behave like a wildcat, *petite*," the man mentioned lazily. "You don't give me the chance of telling you I'm sorry for having hurt you. Do you always react so violently?"

She frowned. "I'm puzzled, Monsieur. One moment you look as if you want to kill me, and the other you are trying to put the blame on me."

"You don't understand," he said--then he left her alone on the dance-floor. Feeling abused, although she could not fully explain why, she too turned around and intended to fetch a glass of wine to help her through the strange emotions. She was met halfway by Cartouche.

"What did that guy want of you?"" he asked. He sounded not too pleased. "Did you come to any harm?"

She almost laughed at his violent reaction. Then she shrugged. "Well, he did nothing I can't deal with. You don't need to worry over me."

"Don't talk rubbish, Duchesse. Your shoulder obviously bears his mark! He *has* hurt you!"

She saw he was working up a rage. His fists were clenched and his mouth became a tight line. She knew he wanted to get his revenge, and she realized as well she had to do something to prevent this.

"Don't seek a fight with him," she told her friend in a firm tone. "I don't want it!"

It was the truth. Somehow she understood she was getting involved in a dark conflict seeming to focus on the person of the Chevalier--and in which Cartouche had no participation at all.

~ * ~

The evening held other surprises. Not very long after the incident on the dance-floor, Meurice beckoned Marguerite to his table.

"We should talk about an important matter, my dear," he told her. "Take a seat. This concerns your future here."

She did not immediately feel the danger. She was curious to learn what the leader of the gang had to say to her, so she obeyed his request and sat down.

"Look, Duchesse," Meurice began, "you've lived here long enough by now to understand we live by strict rules."

She nodded.

"It's a necessity," he went on. "And it's needless to say the presence of a young and beautiful lass like you can lead to problems of various kinds. Our men are no saints. Some of them will want to possess that girl, and as long as she doesn't choose her protector, the rivalry may cause fights and uneasiness. Do you get this?"

Now she was vaguely getting worried. "I think so."

"Therefore I have decided," said Meurice. "The moment has come for you to announce to us which of our men you'll take to be your companion. The others will respect your decision, so you are free to choose whomever you desire."

Two dark red blushes appeared on her cheeks and betrayed the sudden nervousness she felt.

Meurice chose to neglect this. ""Four of our brothers already came forward to announce their intentions. It is up to you now--either you pick one of them, or else there will be a fight. The winner will then have earned his rights to you."

A silence fell in the room. Everyone present appeared to be listening to what Meurice was saying. The musicians put down their instruments and waited. Slowly, a circle was formed around Meurice and Marguerite.

Fully aware of the tension he created and secretly enjoying it, Meurice beckoned some men forward. One by one, they stepped into the open space created for them.

First came the Chevalier, whose decision had only been made a couple of minutes ago. He looked arrogant and fearsome.

Next was Romain, behaving in a shy manner and feeling somewhat embarrassed because now his intentions were revealed to all of the others.

Pierre stepped into the circle. He felt sure of his charms and his easy ways with women.

And lastly, young Cartouche took up his place. He could not hide his anger but nevertheless raised his head proudly.

Marguerite closed her eyes. *This cannot be true*, she prayed. *It's only a bad dream. When I open my eyes, I'll be awake and then…*

Her daydreaming came to an abrupt end when Meurice laid a hand on her shoulder. "Come on, Duchesse. Who is it going to be? If you are unable to choose, we'll certainly have a good competition. Who will be the strongest, you think?"

She pushed away his hand and finally opened her eyes. She focused her attention on each of the four men and she knew her destiny when she met the commanding stare from the smoke-gray eyes. This man, she felt, would do everything it took to possess her. Romain and Pierre were certainly no match for him. Cartouche would put up a good fight, but he had barely outgrown his boyhood and although he was fierce and angry, he would be no equal to the other man.

No, she knew what answer she should give. His eyes worked like magnets. She could not fight this strange attraction.

She took a couple of steps forward, in his direction. Cartouche watched her with amazement and pain.

"I choose him," she said softly, but the silence had become so complete that everyone heard her words.

Seven

The rest of the evening seemed unreal. On hearing her answer, the Chevalier smiled in a confident manner then he joined her, placing a possessive arm around her middle. He held on to her while he accepted the congratulations of Meurice and the others. Then he announced, "We must go now."

Marguerite wanted to scream. She had not expected this. Where was that man taking her? She struggled a bit, but one look at Meurice told her to keep quiet once more. She allowed the Chevalier to take her outside into the street where his horse stood tethered. He jumped into the saddle then reached down to allow her to mount as well. She felt how he wrapped his warm cloak around her to protect her from the November cold. He nudged the horse into a trot and they were on their way.

She noticed how they headed towards the Rue Quincampoix--then she remembered how Cartouche had mentioned the Chevalier had his gambling house there.

The house was rather big, to her surprise. It had a courtyard, which was concealed from the street by a high wall and a dark gate. Her new companion steered the horse towards the gate and let his fist come down on the wood. The gate opened instantly and a silent servant lifted her off the horse and took the reins as soon as the Chevalier dismounted as well.

She did not have time to look around. The man took her arm and pulled her along. They crossed several corridors and a dark hall, after which they mounted a narrow flight of stairs. Finally they entered a cozy room with rather nice furniture and a welcoming fire smoldering in the hearth.

When she put out her hands to the warmth of the fire, she fully realized the impact of her decision. She had completely surrendered herself to the mercy of a man who was a stranger to her. What would happen now? She knew she would have to tread carefully.

The sound of ringing glasses made her turn around. The Chevalier was busy pouring wine. "It is cold outside," he remarked. "This will warm your blood."

She accepted a glass and brought it to her lips. The wine was of superior quality.

He emptied his glass in one gulp, poured himself another one, and let himself down in one of the easy chairs that were placed before the hearth. When he noticed she did not join him, he beckoned towards the chair next to his. "Don't remain standing there, girl. Sit down and drink your wine."

She did as he requested. Because she was nervous, she too drank thirstily from her glass. As soon as she had emptied it, he took it out of her hand to fill it anew. When he reached to do this for a second time, she protested. "I've had enough, thank you."

His eyes immediately showed his dismay. "Do I hear well? Do you refuse to drink to our--how shall we say--agreement?" he asked in a pleasant tone, although there was an underlying sharpness to it.

She rose from the chair. Suddenly, she felt tired and not able to face the rest of the evening. "Of course not, Monsieur," she answered. "I am just not used to drinking. Too much wine makes me drowsy." His glance became softer again.

Now he smiled. "So, no more wine for you then. I don't want you to fall asleep. The night is still young."

She sat down again, deciding it was wiser to indulge his moods. The minutes ticked away. He sat in his chair, sipping more wine, and appeared to be lost in thought. He turned the stem of the glass round and round in his hand, and the constant movement made her more aware of her fatigue. At long last she thought she could not possibly offend him by telling him she wanted to go to bed. "It's getting late, Monsieur," she whispered. "It is long past my usual bedtime."

Although she spoke softly, her voice startled him. He jumped up and stared at the clock on the mantelpiece, which showed almost two o'clock. "Yes, it's late," he agreed. "Let's have one last glass to toast our agreement."

She nodded. "I'll have one more then I'll go to sleep."

This time he did not bring the full glass to her. She had to cross the room to where he was standing and take it out of his hands.

"To us," he toasted.

These two small words had such a definite undertone, sounded so meaningful, so threatening. She knew she had walked into a trap and it could get difficult to free herself from it. Once again, she would have to adjust to a new way of living, to learning new rules. Duchesse was getting further and further away from the aristocratic girl she had once been in Burgundy.

"White suits you nicely," his voice interrupted her train of thought. "You almost look beautiful in this dress."

"Cartouche chose it for me," she said defiantly, stung by his condescending tone.

"Has he? I'm surprised he shows such good taste," the Chevalier commented. "You rather like that fellow, don't you?"

"He's my best friend," she answered. It was the plain truth.

He laughed. "It was clever of you not to take him. Know why? He adores you too much. He would always want to please you."

"And is that so wrong?" she dared to remark, forgetting her earlier intentions.

"For you it would be. You need a stronger rein, that of an experienced rider."

That stung. "I'm not a horse, so please don't compare me to one," she said in a sharper tone.

He shrugged at her critique. "As you like, *ma chère*. Come, let me show you to your room."

He took quick steps and she almost had to run to keep up with him. He guided her through a corridor and opened the door to a small but cozy room in which a huge four-poster bed took in most of the available space. It was decorated with pink satin drapes and had the same hued coverlet on the bed.

He gave her barely a second to look around. Then he took her by the wrist again and pulled her out of the room, which he then locked. "Tonight, of course," he said, "you will sleep in my room."

She opened her mouth for a cry but he quickly smothered it by closing his hand over her lips. Willingly or not, she had to follow him to another room on the other side of the corridor--a very sober place with a definite male atmosphere. He pushed her backwards towards the edge of the mattress and made her fall upon it.

He laughed loudly when she immediately jumped to her feet and confronted him with an air of abuse. "Is my bed not acceptable to you?" he asked mockingly. "Do you prefer to make love in clouds of pink?"

"I prefer my own bed, "she sneered. "And I don't intend sharing it with you!"

"Alas," he replied. "That's not done. Are you forgetting we both belong to the brotherhood? The rules imposed by Meurice count as the law here. When you chose me, it meant that from now on we are husband and wife, or something very close to it. You owe me obedience."

That was the moment when she lost all caution. She stomped her foot in anger. "I refuse to obey the rules of a highwayman!" she called out, completely the aristocratic damsel. "I refuse to be treated like an object by you or any other man!"

She attempted to rush past him to the open door. Of course she was no match for him. He easily grabbed her by the middle and again pressed her close to his body. With one strong arm he held her fixed, while he used the other to tilt up her chin to kiss her.

Her eyes shot fire and she wriggled furiously in his grip--although she knew it would be in vain. She was his captive and she could not prevent his mouth coming down on hers. No more time to tell him she was an innocent.

He kissed her slowly and deliberately, paying no attention to her resistance. His tongue did not assault her lips. No, he was experienced enough to realize he had to be careful, so his tongue gently teased her. His ways were so refined that after a while he sensed she was giving up her wriggling and relaxed in his arms. Then he slowly maneuvered her in the direction of the bed, pace by pace, until at last they sank into the soft mattress.

Marguerite could do nothing to prevent it. Her mind told her she should push him away, but her body told another story. This was pleasant, oh so pleasant. It so felt right--how could that be? Why had nobody ever told her lovemaking could be so wonderful?

The weight of his body covering hers, made her come back to reality. No, not that! She panicked and discovered her will to resist was not completely broken yet. With sheer force, she managed to tear one of her hands loose then let her small fist come down on his back. She tried to kick him everywhere she could.

"My, my, what a wildcat!" he laughed and easily caught her hand and kept it--for security reasons--pinned above her head. She turned her face into the pillow when his mouth neared hers once more. "Please, you must know…"

He only heard some mumbled words and laughed even harder. She was putting up a good show of innocence.

Seconds later, she sensed stroking warmth on her neck. His warm mouth found a path from the hollow there to the gap between her breasts. It confused her to the extreme. She halfheartedly wanted to fight him, but on the other hand something inside forbade it. Looking back, she could not remember when exactly her feelings of disgust and resistance made way to acceptance. Bit by bit she became aware of a sensation of heat, a heat that spread through her limbs and melted down her last attempts at defiance. She did not realize he released her hands, so he could use his own to caress her further. With an unconscious gesture, she put her arms around his neck and pulled him closer to her, to feel every inch of him

He did not try to hurry her--or himself. Slowly he broke past her resistance and kept his own desire in check. Only when he felt she began to cooperate, he peeled away clothes. With an easiness that betrayed his skill, he untied the strings which fastened her bodice and held up her skirts. Layer by layer of cloth he pulled over her head, until she only wore a thin chemise. When he removed this at last, he made it feel like one long caress enticing her senses.

Marguerite sighed, a deep sigh of contentment. She was completely happy now and wanted this perfect feeling of sensation to continue.

The Chevalier looked down on the exposed body with its perfect coloring. In a wink, he disposed of his own clothing. Then he joined her in the bed. Her arms welcomed him.

She again panicked when she felt something hard nudge against her most private parts. She opened her mouth to speak, but he pressed his lips on hers while driving his cock into her dampness.

Both their eyes opened wide. She felt a sweet pain, and he realized she was a virgin.

With ultimate softness he continued to caress her until she forgot the pain and felt a whole range of new sensations. After a while, she became a willing participant in this new game.

~ * ~

It was late at night when she fell asleep, completely spent. The Chevalier smiled when he noticed how she curled up against his body. So this was a real wedding night after all. Who could have thought the girl had never been touched before? But then he shook his head, blaming himself for these feelings of desire. They would not serve well if he wanted to continue with his plan. But by God, he wanted the girl!

Her sleep was so deep she did not sense when he finally got out of bed, lifted her gently in his arms and carried her to her own room.

When he pulled back the pink coverlet, he remained standing next to the bed for a short time. He looked down on the sleeping girl, and suddenly felt unsure about himself and the task he had set out to perform.

Eight

Marguerite opened her eyes. Still a bit sleepy, she became aware of a pink glow around her. She registered this then yawned and stretched in the bed. Only when she was fully awake did she find she was lying in her own bed and the Chevalier was not sleeping at her side anymore.

She worked herself to an upright position and swung her legs over the edge of the mattress. Her feet touched down on a thick carpet and the room did not feel chilly. When she looked around, she saw a cozy fire burning in the hearth. On the big clothing chest positioned at the end of the bed, a dressing gown lay ready for her.

She wrapped herself in it and walked to the window where she opened the heavy curtains. The cold light of a winter sun fell into the room and illuminated it, showing more of the luxuries inside.

She pressed her nose against the window and looked down on the street below. Judging by the activity there, and by the grumbling in her stomach, she guessed it must be near noon. Oddly enough, she did not hear a single sound coming from the house. When she opened the door to the corridor, she still could not distinguish any sound. Was she alone in this house?

She decided she best leave the room and start looking for somebody to bring her breakfast. She crossed the corridor to the room where she had spent the night but found it closed to her touch. Most of the other doors were closed as well, apart from one that immediately opened. The room she entered was the drawing room where they had drunk their wine the previous night. The curtains were open, and she noticed a table was set near the enclave of the windows.

She suddenly became aware of soft footsteps nearing the room. A woman entered. She was dressed in a severe black gown with a white apron and bonnet to cover her hair. Her face showed no emotion and the mouth was tight. She appeared to be somewhere in her forties.

"I see that Mademoiselle has woken up," she said as she approached the middle of the room.

Marguerite supposed she would be the housekeeper. "You made me startle," she told her. "I assumed I was completely alone here."

The woman pressed her lips even tighter. "The master has requested you should be permitted to sleep as long as you wished. I shall bring you breakfast right away, and when you desire it, I can also provide you with warm water for a bath. There are clean clothes in the wardrobe. Just have a look at them, there should be something in it that has your size."

"My own dress will do," Marguerite said.

"I'm afraid that won't be possible. I noticed there were some stains of wine on it, so I ordered a maid to wash it."

She turned her back to the young woman and clearly wanted to walk away.

Marguerite's voice held her. "One moment! I don't even know who you are."

Their eyes met. The older woman was the first to give in as she recognized the authority of the younger one. "*Eh bien.* I am Marthe Dumoulin and I am the housekeeper and cook of Monsieur le Chevalier."

Marguerite nodded her head in acknowledgement. "I'm called Duchesse," she mentioned, "although my real name is Marguerite. I come from Burgundy. Are there any servants beside you, Madame Dumoulin?"

"Yes. Upstairs there is Claudine, a foolish girl who cleans the rooms, not too bright but willing. And we also have Robert, a pensioned soldier who looks after the fires in the hearth and fetches water or does chores which require some male strength. Of course there are other people for the downstairs rooms where our master has his gambling salons. Luckily, I don't have to bother with them. They are the sole responsibility of Monsieur."

Madame Dumoulin shrugged her shoulders to express how she thought about gambling. This movement reminded Marguerite of the unyielding manners of Père Duthot's housekeeper, for whom she had feared as a child. Involuntarily, she began to wonder what a god-fearing woman such as Marthe was doing in these less than righteous surroundings. She obviously did not belong here. Alas, she did not seem very talkative. These questions would have to wait until later. There were more urgent matters to discuss.

"Has the Chevalier gone out?" she asked.

"The master has left town," the housekeeper answered. Her voice seemed to gain in warmth when she referred to the man. "He'll probably be away for a couple of days. You are free to move about as you like, but he requests--for the sake of safety--you do not enter the gambling rooms without his permission. If there is anything you require, let me know." She did not mention how the master had trusted her with his problems and how he felt it better to stay away from the girl for a while.

She left Marguerite to her own reflections.

Not much later Claudine entered the room with a tray of freshly baked bread and croissants, accompanied by a pot of deliciously smelling cacao.

Marguerite sent the girl away before she started to eat. To her surprise, she was famished. Before she knew it, she put the last crumbs into her mouth. While finishing a second cup of cacao, she returned to her bedroom and opened the wardrobe to have a look at its contents. Like Madame Dumoulin had said, it contained gowns and dresses in various colors and different fabrics. *Did these clothes belong to former mistresses of the Chevalier*, she mused. She took out some of those that appeared to be more or less her size and held them before her body.

Finally, she decided on a light woolen dress in an olive-green shade that colored nicely against her skin, she noticed, when she crossed the room to the big standing mirror. She tossed the gown on the bed, as it would probably need some stitching to fit, and thought she could have a bath while she waited.

She had not had the luxury of a warm bath since leaving Vallencieux, and she longed to wash away the smell of shaving-water that still clung to her skin. With every move she became aware of *him*.

She looked around for the bell-rope and found it hidden behind the drapes of the bed. She pulled it. Claudine entered. "What does Mademoiselle wish for?"

"Tell your man to bring me some hot water."

Seconds later, the door opened and a sturdy, gray-haired man entered with two buckets of steaming water. He put them down and produced a bathtub out of a cupboard. He poured the water into it. "Here you are, Miss. I was told you'd need a nice hot bath. Will you be wanting more water?"

He gave her a cheerful grin, did not wait for an answer and left to fetch two more buckets. When he emptied those, she thanked him cordially. His was the first friendly face she had come across in this house. "You're Robert, are you not?" she asked.

"*Aye, Miss.* Robert McFarlane, that's me name."

"McFarlane? It sounds Scottish."

This is indeed a strange household, she thought. *A housekeeper that could better work for a priest and a Scottish hireling?*

"*Aye Miss,*" Robert answered. "I'm from Inverness in the Highlands."

Apparently, old McFarlane did not mind a chat. "It's a long way from Scotland to France, Robert," she dared to remark, wanting to find out more about the people who lived in this house.

"A long way indeed. It carried me from the Highlands to England--I was in the army, with the grenadiers--until our good king Jamie was driven out of the country and sought refuge here in your country. My commander followed the king in banishment, and I remained his servant to the day of his death."

"And now you've come here."

Her tone invited him to share more confidentialities, but suddenly he became aware of her motives and straightened himself. The friendly smile was wiped away. "*Aye Miss.* Now I'm here."

~ * ~

Although Marguerite desperately wanted to return to L'Ange Noir, she decided against it. Cartouche was certain to take her under a crossfire of questions, and it would hurt her pride far too deeply having to admit the man she had chosen in his place had left her already!

She had trouble in admitting to herself the Chevalier's behavior did not suit her at all. *Why did he have to go away?* It took some time to understand this was an irrational question. She should feel relieved he had gone; glad she could return to her normal routine. To no avail, She still felt abused and hurt.

She shortened the time on hand by checking out each room on this floor of the house. Beside the two bedrooms and the drawing room, she found an intimate dining room and even a library. When obviously the servants were only there to serve her and not to keep an eye on her, she felt confident enough to take a close look at the exquisite walnut *sécretaire*. She lifted up papers and opened every drawer in the hope of finding a key to the Chevalier's true identity.

At first she only found accounts and notes concerning the activities in the gambling rooms downstairs. They were all interesting in a way, but not what she was after. She sighed then began to look in less obvious spaces. She pullrf out the drawers and put her arm inside to feel for secret compartments, as she suspected this desk had to hide a secret.

More than an hour passed before one of her fingers touched a spring hidden at the back, and a narrow flat drawer shot forward. It contained a box that was wrapped in a faded piece of velvet.

She carefully took out the tips of the cloth and lifted the lid of the box. Her eyes lit up when she disclosed its contents. A set of dueling pistols--laden with a bullet each. And with them, the miniature of a beautiful woman, the name 'Isabelle' engraved in its frame. *Who was this woman? What role had she played in the Chevalier's life? Whey did he hide her image from curious glances?*

She took her time in studying the painted face of this woman and imagined how she would look in reality. With a feeling of envy, she had to admit such a beauty came close to perfection. The stranger's face was heart-shaped and had a delicate bone structure. The hair resembled spun gold. The lips were full and sensual and the eyes of the deepest blue.

Yet, on a closer look, she somehow sensed there was no real warmth in the gaze, only calculated shrewdness and cold-heartedness. *Will we ever meet*, she asked herself. *In that case, I don't think we can become friends.*

She put the portrait back in the drawer but kept the pistols. They were precious pieces of craftsmanship and she knew how to use them. When she was younger, René had once brought two such pistols to the garden, and they had used old marks on the trees for targets. Soon it became obvious she was a better shot than her brother. She took the pistols to her room and hid them under the mattress of her bed.

After dinner, which was served in the dining room and where she had eaten in silence, she began to feel bored. The servants had retired to their rooms after asking her if she needed anything. She felt more and more frustrated for having nothing to do and slowly something urged her to defy the Chevalier's wishes and take a look downstairs.

Carefully, she opened the door and when she did not spot or hear anything, she sneaked down the stairs. She arrived in a dark hall, which she remembered to have crossed the other day. She remained standing in its shadows for a while, not knowing what to do next when she heard a noise. She pressed her back tighter to the wall and waited.

One of the doors to this hall opened, and out rushed a footman in black and yellow livery. He hurried to the big entrance door and threw it open, to allow a company of players to come in. He showed them into the other room and for a short while Marguerite got an impression of the rich red and golden interior.

Two men and a woman, only their backs visible, threw off their cloaks and shared jokes. *Those voices!* Her heart stopped beating for a second. *How can this be? I don't know the other fellow, but what are Claude and Madame d'Arcourt doing here?*

For a second, bile rose into her throat. Then the panic ebbed away. *Don't be a ninny,* she said to herself. *This is a gambling house, right? Don't you remember how those two loved to play the dice?*

On the other side, she now understood she had better not come here again. Not because the Chevalier had forbidden it, but because she could not run the risk of being spotted by anyone she knew from her previous life.

Not minding the noise she made, she hurried up the stairs and got into bed.

~ * ~

As one long day after another passed, Marguerite's humor grew worse. The heavy rains and the cold of these late November days did not invite her to leave the house, and her restless nature could find no distraction in trying on the many dresses in the wardrobe or reading the books from the shelves in the library.

Bit by bit the conviction grew stronger she had committed a terrible mistake in choosing the Chevalier. She should have shown more character, she now thought, and should have defied him by naming Cartouche as her protector. He too wanted to have her, but she would have felt much safer in his company. Indeed, she could wind him around her little finger--and was that not better than having to endure the whims of a man she could not control at all?

As time advanced, she began to long for his return. She felt they had to settle this impossible situation.

One evening, when she had already retired to bed, she heard unusual noises in the corridor. There was a running to and fro and a banging of doors. It did not take her long to wrap her naked body into a dressing gown then run to the door.

At last, he was home! Then she remembered what she had decided on the previous night, and first went to her room to fetch the set of dueling pistols. She tucked one safely away in a pocket of her gown.

She found the Chevalier in the dining room, still wearing his dirty traveling clothes. He hungrily consumed a cold platter of chicken and beef. To her surprise--she was on bare feet--he raised his head and gave her a slow smile.

"Ah, there is my little Duchesse," he said in a friendly way. "Why don't you sit down, sweetheart? Do you also want something to eat?"

Marguerite was in no mood for friendliness, nor did she want to play games. "I have already eaten, thank you," she answered in a cool voice.

He grinned, not allowing himself to be bothered by her obvious bad temper. "Some wine, then?" He rose to his feet, remembering the lessons in polite conduct from an almost forgotten childhood, and pulled back a seat for her.

Marguerite accepted it because it would be rude to refuse. She allowed him to pour her a glass of burgundy, after which he returned to his meal. "I believe we have matters of importance to discuss, Monsieur," she said at last.

His only visible reaction was a narrowing of the eyes. The rest of his face did not betray emotion. "Matters of importance?" he repeated. "Alright, but it'll have to wait until I am finished with my meal. It surely cannot be *that* important."

Teasingly he picked up a chicken bone and drank his wine, daring Marguerite to lose her composure. He was well succeeding in it, as she became more nervous by the second. At long last he put down his glass and leaned back in his chair. "Go ahead, *ma chère*. What do you desire of me? New clothes, perhaps?"

This last casual remark was the trigger to a violent outburst. Marguerite's eyes shot fire and automatically her hand went into the pocket of her gown and produced the pistol. Her reaction was so swift it surprised the Chevalier. She jumped up and pointed the weapon at his heart. "Make no mistake, Monsieur," she warned him in a hoarse voice, "I know how to handle a gun."

"I don't doubt it, " he answered dryly. "You certainly have many talents. Can I get up? I rather feel at a disadvantage sitting behind this table."

She eyed him cautiously while he slowly stood and moved backwards. "You're far enough," she warned him. "Now Monsieur, let's talk. I demand from you some explanations."

"Of course. Anything you say." It occurred to him there and then the girl was far more intelligent and dangerous than he had expected her to be. Before that, she had looked so innocent and naïve, so easy to handle, a willing prey to carry out the plan he had in mind.

Something in him urged him to be gentle with her. He realized he needed her if his plans should have any success. So he calculated his chances and took advantage of a short instance of distraction on her part.

He moved so fast she did not see his foot coming and not much later the gun lay on the floor, kicked out of her hand. Before Marguerite could pick it up again, he was next to her and caught her wrists in an iron grip.

"Now we can talk," he hissed. "What am I to explain, my dear Duchesse?"

She bit her lip. If she had dared, she would have spit her scorn and anger into his face, but she instinctively knew the dangers such an action would evoke. Yet she did not think of surrendering herself to his mercy. "For instance why I'm here," she said instead, looking straight into his face.

"Oh, that's easy," he joked. "You're here because you're a pretty lass and I desired you."

"You want me to believe *that*?" she taunted. "First you practically raped me then you left me for days on my own. Is that a sign of desire?"

The grip on her wrists became firmer and began to pain her.

"Aw, you're hurting me!" she screamed, forgetting her composure.

Abruptly he loosened his hold and pushed her away, which made her fall into a chair. Yet her spirit was not broken. "I refuse to believe you only want my body," she told him. "You have brought me here for another purpose."

Her gaze challenged him to hit her, while she rubbed the painful spots on her arms. Two strong minds crossed swords and it was he who had to give in at the end. "You are right," he finally conceded. "I need you for the execution of a certain scheme I've made up. I am not going to explain my reasons or intentions, but I can tell you this, if you voluntarily agree to cooperate, you will be richly rewarded and will be free to go as you please. What do you think of my proposal?"

She had to think it over for a moment. She did not very much like what she was hearing, but she had to admit it intrigued her. Besides, did she really have a choice? "I'll cooperate," she decided.

He nodded. "That is settled then."

She pushed her chair away and pulled her dressing gown tighter around her body. In the heat of the previous moments it had loosened and was now showing generous portions of naked flesh.

"I'm tired. I think I'll return to bed now," she said.

He rose up and made it to the exit before she could lay a hand on the doorknob. He leaned into the doorway and blocked the passage with his body. "One moment, my dear," he whispered. His right arm slid around her waist and held her tight. His left hand moved between the velvet of the dressing gown and the silk of her skin and captured the roundness of a breast.

Before she could protest, his mouth closed down on hers. His kiss was as demanding as his attitude, and soon desire overtook both of them. This was the only thing she could not fight, did not want to fight.

Between kisses and caresses, he softly spoke into her ear. "You were wrong in one way, *chérie*. Somehow I *do* appreciate that delicious body of yours."

She had no answer for it. She knew he was attracted to her--and she to him.

Nine

"Isabelle!"

His voice called out and woke Marguerite with a start. Not knowing what was happening she opened her eyes and looked around. Then she remembered she was lying in the bed of the Chevalier. As a matter of fact, he had her in a firm grip and his face looked distorted. His fingers dug into her shoulders as he attempted to shake her.

"Isabelle, Isabelle, wake up!"

At last she realized he was having a nightmare. She bit her lip and was not sure of what to do. She simply had no experience with such things.

While she was still contemplating her next action, he suddenly pressed his head against her stomach and began to cry violently. His upper body shook and hot tears wetted her skin.

A wave of deep sympathy and pity overwhelmed her. Suddenly she saw the man who always bullied and challenged her in an entirely new light. While witnessing his vulnerability and total weakness, she instinctively knew what to do. She began to stroke his dark-brown curls in a tender fashion and whispered soothing words into his ear, like a mother would comfort her child. "Hush now darling, everything is fine," she breathed. "You are having a bad dream. Don't be afraid, I'm here."

Whether or not he heard her, he did calm down and soon afterwards his quiet breathing proved he had found peace in his sleep again. Carefully, as not to disturb him, she wriggled her body from under his weight and sought a more comfortable position. She felt how his arm went around her middle and she heard a faint sigh of contentment. Her eyes were wide open though, and she knew she would not be able to fall asleep again.

The fire in the hearth died down. It would probably be hours before Robert would come with new blocks to feed it.

Although she was awake, she had no wish whatsoever to leave this warm bed. She quite liked the way he held her tight to his body. It gave her a feeling of belonging--although she would be a fool ever to admit the fact.

~ * ~

Time went by. The New Year 1711 announced itself with heavy showers of snow, followed by a long spell of extremely cold temperatures. Lots of people complained about it, but not Marguerite. She spent the greatest part of the day indoors kept busy by the hard training schedule the Chevalier had entered her into.

When he woke up in the morning--after that night in which he had the nightmare--he did not remember anything of it.

"Good morning, my sweet," he greeted her. "Get your lazy butt out of bed! We'll have to start work today."

"Did you sleep well?" she asked, to make sure he did not remember.

"Of course," she answered. "Why do you ask?"

She laughed. "I just try to be polite."

"You'll need that," he told her. "Come, let's have breakfast and afterwards I am going to present you to the people who work downstairs."

"I thought I was forbidden to come there," she could not resist to remark.

"I don't like the idea of it very much," he admitted, "but it can't be changed. You are expected to work there in the near future, after you master certain skills."

Her eyebrows went up. "I hope you don't expect me to play the whore," she said.

He looked surprised, as he did not expect her to have such thoughts. "No, of course not," he hastened to assure her. "You will act as the hostess of the Domino club--which is how we name the salons downstairs."

"Ah, yes, that's better." *The foolish man doesn't know I'm pulling his leg*, she thought, still feeling good after a night of revelations.

"You will welcome the guests as they arrive and see to their needs," he went on. "You will also have to know something about cards and the different games played."

"I'm sure I can master that."

He did not seem to hear her. "More importantly," he went on, "you need more education. You definitely have an accent. You need to be able to talk like a lady of the court, and you should be able to play music and dance, and talk about literature."

So now her days were filled with daily lessons. In the mornings, the Chevalier invited her into his library, where he taught her how to play at cards. He also initiated her in some of his tricks. One of them consisted of keeping the tips of your fingers as sensitive as possible, to make them able to 'feel' what card was in your hands. Once she mastered this, he showed her other tricks. Bit by bit she became better and after a while she was almost as accomplished a player as he was.

Three times a week, a certain Madame Lebrun came to the house at the Rue Quincampoix. This impoverished lady had spent most of her youth and middle age in various classrooms, trying to bring young children some education. Alas, their parents had shown their gratitude by throwing her out once she became unable to handle them properly. Madame was ever so grateful to the Chevalier for the generous amount of money he paid her to teach his young fiancé.

Marguerite grew quite fond of her teacher. She enjoyed the afternoons she spent with Madame Lebrun and did not mind she showed her how regional her speech was. *What would Papa think of that*, she often asked herself. *He always thought the nuns in Dijon had such a great reputation. And my cousins talk the same way-- would they know it's not the proper way to speak?*

Madam Lebrun, on the other hand, soon discovered her pupil was not as illiterate as her employer seemed to think. But by then she began to love the girl and would not think of telling this to him. After all, their lessons bore fruit. The young woman behaved impeccably and nobody would be able to tell she came from Burgundy anymore.

The other two afternoons were spent with Signore Coretti, an Italian teacher of music and dance. Those lessons were not so successful. Although Marguerite loved to dance and had a good voice, she had no liking for a musical instrument. At home, no one had paid any attention to culture, and the spinet in the drawing room was never used. Signore Coretti tried and tried, but she always played out of tune. At long last, the Chevalier mercifully decreed she should no longer attempt to play an instrument but keep to singing instead.

The evenings she had to herself. After dinner the Chevalier disappeared to the rooms downstairs, where she was not to go yet. At first she felt relieved to be left on her own and relax a bit, but after some time this situation began to nerve her. She hated to be alone--she had given up trying to induce Madame Moulin into a non-committing conversation--and after some days she started to listen for the sound of his nearing footsteps. Once she heard him mount the stairs, she waited tentatively and prayed he would come to her bedroom and spend the rest of the night with her. His caresses and lovemaking thrilled her far more than she was ready to confess, and she thoroughly enjoyed their shared moments. She could not understand why he remained so distant during the daytime; at night his desire for her was evident and fierce. One thing she had learned however, the Chevalier did not like questions.

She seldom saw her former friends from L'Ange Noir. When she occasionally walked over the Pont Neuf, the presence of Robert McFarlane kept her from running off. She still could not tell whether he was there to protect or guard her, but it did spoil the pleasure she would have in revisiting her old environs.

~ * ~

To her astonishment, the Chevalier begged her to accompany him when he had to deliver his monthly contribution to Meurice. She was thrilled to attend the meeting, but once they entered the tavern, she realized the gathering had not the same character as before.

Although everyone greeted her cordially, she soon got the impression she did no longer belong there and automatically she began to act more distant. In a way she could understand now the nature of the Chevalier's attitude when he mingled among the members of the *confrèrie*.

Of course she could not avoid meeting up with Cartouche, whom she had not seen since the evening of the ball. She could tell from the look on his face he was angry with her.

"So, Marguerite," he greeted her in a grim way, "what an honor to be granted your presence!"

"Hello, Cartouche," she answered, with an obvious lack of enthusiasm.

"Is this how you greet an old friend?" he asked, very much abused in his manly pride and wanting to hurt her for it.

"Damn it, what can I say when you treat me so unkind?" she gave back, losing her temper.

"You could at least tell me how you're doing," he called out, impatient as well. "We don't see you anymore."

"I'm fine," she said, finding her composure. "The Chevalier is teaching me how to cheat at cards and how to behave as a lady. I find his company inspiring," she could not withhold herself from adding, as she wanted to get back at Cartouche.

"You start to sound like him already! I must say you two form a fine pair."

Her gaze shot fire. "Whatever you say."

She turned her back to him and walked away. She would not go as far as apologizing.

Luckily for her, Cartouche felt some remorse over his harsh words and came looking for her. He waited until the Chevalier went to speak with Meurice then put his arm around her shoulder. "I'm sorry, Duchesse," he whispered softly.

When she looked up at him, he gave her a roguish smile. "I know I have behaved badly," he admitted. "I should not solely put the blame on you."

"I accept your apologies, "she told him, realizing she did not want to lose this old friends over a silly quarrel. His friendship was too valuable to her.

"I still find it hard to accept you have chosen the Chevalier as your protector," he said in an honest voice. "I guess I'm jealous."

"Don't say that," she was quick to return. "You know, Dominique, it's not easy to live with the man. I know now that it was mistake to pick him. Just like everything else I did wrong in my life. I seem to heap up one stupidity after the other," she complained.

Her face betrayed some of the pain she felt and appealed to his friendship. He immediately responded. "Don't be so negative," he tried to cheer her up. "Why don't you run away from him? I'll help you to find a hiding place."

"I can't do that," she denied his offer. "I have given my word."

"Men should stick to their word--but women?"

"A word given by a Vallencieux is holy," she blurted out then she realized what she said and put a hand to her mouth.

He grinned at her shocked expression and squeezed her arm. "But I've known for a long time, sweetheart. Be assured your secret is in good hands. I won't tell anyone, I swear. We too have a code of honor."

"No questions, right?" she smiled. "I must thank you for not spreading this around. And you must promise me to remain my friend, will you?"

"You can count on that," he agreed. "I'll always be there, somewhere at the distance, to keep an eye on you. And you, Marguerite, have to promise me not to let that fellow bully you, do you hear?"

"I'm constantly trying to avoid that," she smiled, gaining back her good mood. She gave him a furtive kiss on the cheek and finally returned to the Chevalier's side.

~ * ~

The Chevalier moved restlessly, in that stage between sleep and consciousness. He yawned widely.

Marguerite, who sat watching him, had to smile. She was already washed and clothed, had enjoyed her breakfast and was now waiting for him to wake up as well. "No lessons this morning," she said in a contented way when he finally seemed awake. "It's almost noon."

He rubbed his eyes, but when he registered what she said, he immediately became alert. He pushed himself into an upward position. "Why haven't you woken me?" he demanded.

She shrugged, which unnerved him. "Oh well, you were sleeping at last. After that awful nightmare, I thought you could use a bit of extra rest."

His entire body tightened when she spoke. She noticed it but did not pay a lot of attention to the fact.

"A nightmare?" he repeated. "Did I wake you up, then?"

"You almost killed me," she smiled, although she was exaggerating. He seemed in a panic when he woke her, and at a given moment his hand had touched her throat. She had been able to remove it before any harm was done.

She crept up close to him and slid her arms around his neck. With her head resting on his shoulder, she began to caress the firm muscles of his arms and played with the hair on his breast. Her nipples became hard and prickled his skin in a sensual manner.

With a supple movement he turned his body, pulled her closer and lazily began to nibble at her lips.

She encouraged him in every way. While his mouth continued its exploration and the blood in her veins flowed faster, her feeling of being in control grew stronger and stronger. At last she found the courage to ask the question which had kept her curiosity for so long a time. He would not refuse her now, she contemplated, she had him entirely in her power. "Who's Isabelle, darling?" she whispered.

The last syllable still hung into the air when his hands flew around her neck and started to press.

Totally surprised by his sudden attack, she was unable to do anything but stare into his gray eyes, in which she could read the desire to kill and destroy. So this was her end, she thought vaguely, still not resisting.

The room began to disappear under a veil of fog, and only his eyes seemed to light up before her. Her arms fell back as she drifted away in oblivion.

~ * ~

The Chevalier suddenly returned to reality. To his horror, he realized the woman he was strangling was not Isabelle but Duchesse. What was he doing, in heaven's name? Disgusted at his own behavior, he removed his hands and kept them hidden at his back.

She did not move for some time. Seconds went by. At last she started to breathe once more, although with some difficulty. One of her hands went to her throat to rub the painful spot.

After yet another eternity she managed a sitting position, looking dizzy and weak.

Her vision still was not very clear. She tried to support herself against one of the bedposts and hoped the shaky feeling in her legs would go away.

"Let this be a lesson to you," he grumbled.

Although she was terribly shaken and had come close to death, she showed the true fighting spirit of the Vallencieux family. "Why don't you answer my question?" she brought forth, in a hoarse voice. "Otherwise you could just as well have finished me off."

He came a few steps closer, in a threatening manner. "Don't tempt me, Duchesse. You have a slender neck."

"You won't kill me," she said. No, you won't do it. You've told me yourself you need me."

Involuntarily, he had to admire her daring. She did not cast down her eyes and challenged him. Although it was not easy, he too had to admit she was right in one way. Damned woman! His anger suddenly rose up again. "Isabelle was a whore, my dear," he hissed. "A whore and a bitch--just the same as you are, for that matter. Shall we continue what you started before you asked that silly question?"

She shook her head, sensing he meant her no good. "I'd rather prefer to leave," she said in an attempt at lightness.

He did not respond but grabbed her and threw her on the bed. He was over her before she could put up a defense and pinned her down with his weight. He was fully aroused and he had to find satisfaction. His knee spread her legs.

Then he saw the look of contempt in her eyes--and another instinct told him to stop. She was no whore and he knew it well enough. At once he felt a deep shame. What would his mother have said if she saw him like this? He jumped from the bed and raced from the room.

~ * ~

Marguerite began to cry. This had gone so wrong. She felt sorry for herself, but also for him. *Why can't he see I'm not Isabelle, she thought between her sobbing. I don't wish to hurt him and I'm certainly not a whore. I care for those I love.*

Ten

From then on, Marguerite and the Chevalier slept apart. The intimacy--how sparse it might have been-- had been growing in the nights they spent together. Now that intimacy disappeared they hid their feelings behind a polite façade and tried to avoid the other as best as possible.

On a dull morning in February, the Chevalier ordered the young woman to his library.

"How is your progress with Madame Lebrun? Have you learned how to behave in a civilized way?"

"When a lady can become a whore without any problems, then a whore can just as easily turn into a lady," she replied. Her only weapon against his physical dominance was her sharp tongue. She had quickly learned to apply it whenever the need.

He appeared to have no defense against her scorn. "Soon you will have to take on the task for which I need you," he said, not reacting to her words.

"I'll be ready."

"Do you suppose you'll be up to it?" he asked.

She gave way to a disdainful laugh. "Don't you remember I'm a country girl, Monsieur? Herding swine is one of our daily activities." She intended to further hurt him with her statement, but to her astonishment he smiled.

"The gentlemen will be enraptured by you, *chérie*. Most of our customers are bored to death and welcome everything that doesn't fit into the ordinary pattern. Maybe you will start a new vogue in some circles."

"I have no ambition in that direction," she snapped.

"Fine with me," he agreed laconically. "Fetch your coat darling, because we are going out. I can't tolerate that my hostess runs around in borrowed clothes."

A rented carriage brought them to a narrow street near the Tuileries. The houses there had three or more floors and seemed to lean over, which made the street darker than normal for the time of day.

When Marguerite got out of the coach, a nasty smell hit her nostrils. The steps leading to the *souterain* of nr. twenty-eight were slippery because of the steady rainfall of the last days. For a second she did not pay attention to where she put her feet and slipped. She felt how the Chevalier steadied her. His tight grip sent an electrical shock through her body. Rather taken by it, she shook herself loose again. "Thank you," she murmured.

"At your service," he gave back, just as polite.

He was still standing next to her when he knocked at the door of the dressmaker's. A servant allowed them to enter the basement apartment, which was transformed into a workshop. A fellow who looked like a gnome sat on one of the tables, legs crossed, and sewed on a piece of clothing.

At the sound of their entering, he directed his scrutinizing glance at them. When he recognized the Chevalier, the inquisitive look gave way to a broad smile. "Monsieur, you are welcome," he greeted.

"Meet Patou, a wizard with the needle," the Chevalier introduced him to Marguerite.

"Is *he* going to make my clothes?"

Patou slid from the table and made an elegant bow before the young woman. "I'm a master dressmaker, mademoiselle. Do you doubt my proficiency?" His voice was unexpectedly melodious and civilized. "If so, I can assure you making dresses is my *métier*. Once my customers were ladies of the highest rank and position. My creations were renowned and desired, even in the rest of Europe. Years ago I dressed Madame de Montespan and the Duchess of Portsmouth. Alas, fame is so furtive. Other generations showed other tastes and I finally landed in this awful place."

"The lady needs a variety of evening gowns," the Chevalier interrupted. He knew Patou's tendency to talk about his past glory and did not particularly crave to hear it once more.

The dressmaker knew when to keep silent. "*Parfaitement*, Monsieur. Perhaps Mademoiselle can undo her cloak?"

Marguerite did as was requested of her and laid the cloak over a chair.

"And now turn around, but slowly," Patou asked her. He watched the young woman as she slowly swirled then nodded. "Perfect! You do have a fine figure, mademoiselle--just like I always imagined Diana, the goddess of the hunt."

"My bosom is too flat," Marguerite could not withhold herself from saying. She still considered herself an ugly duckling.

"Have you ever seen a Diana with a heavy bosom?" her companion intervened now. "Patou is right, my dear."

"No heavy skirts and deep necklines for the mademoiselle," the dressmaker spoke. "She should wear tightly closed gowns in a manly fashion, and the colors she needs are light pastels, to accentuate her youth."

But here the Chevalier did not agree. "No, Patou. Full colors. Don't forget she has to act as the hostess of my club. She shouldn't look too innocent."

Patou sighed and Marguerite pulled a face behind his back. Then the dressmaker pushed open a small door to a closet, in which an abundance of textiles were stowed away. He invited the young woman to come in and have a look.

Carefully she fingered dozens of rolls of ultra thin silk. One in particular caught her attention. It had garlands of pink roses on a cream-colored fond. It was so delicate it was almost transparent. *This would look well on me*, she knew. *I've never seen anything as beautiful as this.*

While she was dreaming away, the Chevalier spoke. He looked at velvets, satins and heavy silk in golden, deep purple and wine hues.

When they were done, Patou took notes and at last noted Marguerite's measurements.

~ * ~

Three days later, a messenger boy delivered the first of the finished gowns. When Marguerite opened the packages, she could only bear witness to the fact the dressmaker had a superb way with the needle. The gowns fitted perfectly and showed off her slender figure splendidly.

This first delivery consisted of three packages. The first two contained evening gowns in burgundy red and golden and white--beautiful enough, but they made her look older than she was. However, the last package held a surprise. When she undid the wrapping, she found a dress in the flowered silk she had so much admired.

She immediately tried it on then went to gaze at her reflection in the standing mirror. Was it really she whose image appeared in the glass? Because she saw an elegant woman, wearing a magnificent dress. The tight lines and the abundance of Valenciennes lace around her sleeves and neckline accentuated the slenderness of her figure. The skirt swayed gently around her hips. The blackness of her hair contrasted superbly against the color of the dress, and the blushes on her cheeks matched the shade of the silken roses.

Delightedly she turned a few pirouettes and watched in the mirror how her dress swirled around her. This, she decided, would become her favorite one.

So he did notice, she mused, *even when I thought he was only looking at those other rolls. Somewhere he must have a kind heart. He doesn't always show it, but I'm certain it's there. I also know he doesn't trust women. That is why he behaved so strangely the other night. Should I tell him I'm willing to forgive him?*

So, on an impulse, she picked up her skirts and hurried down the stairs to the gambling rooms where she would find the Chevalier. She neglected the astonished stares of the servants she passed and only had eyes for him.

"How can I thank you, Monsieur?" she said in a voice that sounded warm and promising. "This gown is delightful!"

He looked up from his business. Her changed attitude was new to him, and he was not sure as how to respond. He had never learned to read a woman's thoughts. Therefore he restrained himself to a cool smile. "I'm glad my little surprise seems to bring you so much joy," he said.

"I didn't realize you knew how much I admired that silk," she added, coming closer and speaking less formally.

He shrugged. "There is nothing wrong with my eyesight, Duchesse," he remarked. "I suppose you understand you can only wear this dress upstairs?"

He readily expected his last words would make her angry again, but to his surprise she nodded.

"Of course I realize what you mean," Marguerite said. She could understand him well enough. "In these surroundings you have to make a show of yourself... inwardly and outwardly. Here you have to appear strong and flawless. Nevertheless I am very grateful for your gesture. It shows you are a kind man, *au fond*."

She let this piece of sharp and sudden insight go accompanied by a light kiss on his lips.

Before he could say anything--and no, it would not be something unfriendly--she had left the room again. With a rather brusque movement, he turned around and began to scowl at one of the lackeys.

Later that night, after Marguerite had retired to bed, the door softly opened and the Chevalier entered after a slight hesitation.

She watched him from the bed, secretly happy to have won him over, but outwardly not wanting to show it. So she pulled up the blankets and covered her body. "Have you taken the wrong door?" she asked, not able to resist this bit of teasing. She was glad enough he'd returned to her bed, but he should not know it right away.

He shook his head and even felt less sure of himself. Finally, he leaned against one of the bed's posters and studied her. More and more he grew ill at ease.

"What are you doing here?" she insisted. "If you don't say anything, you can leave."

"Back to your old self, Duchesse? This afternoon you left another impression."

An older and more experience woman would understand how deceptive his acted nonchalance was. She would know how hard it was for him to forget his suspicions and come to her freely. She would welcome the opportunity of giving their awkward relationship another chance--and she would open her arms and accept him.

But Marguerite was still very young and distrustful of the male race. And most of all, she was proud. So she felt attacked and responded to it. "Did I give you the impression you would be welcome in my bed?" she said. "It only shows how badly you understand women."

He still did not say anything, only looked somewhat shocked--or did she imagine that? "Anyway," she went on, "it was only politeness that compelled me to thank you for your gift. Yes, perhaps I acted on impulse. But this should not lead you to believe I closed my eyes on your disgusting way of behaving."

He could only stare at her. Her imitation of *grande dame* was reaching perfection.

His fists began to itch and he had to fight the urge of giving her a good shaking. What did she find wrong in his behavior?

"It is possible I got the wrong impression," he then answered. "The only women I come into contact with are hookers. I pay them to do as I please, and later I can forget about them just as easily."

"I gather you reckon me amongst them," she replied, stung by his words.

Her words hurt him, although he could not understand why. He fought back some anger and then felt prepared to give it another try. "You are wrong, Duchesse," he said. "I don't look down on you. I just … damn, I don't know what to think anymore! Can't we at least try to be friends?"

For the first time since they were together, his eyes had a tender glow and unconsciously she responded to it. She appreciated his attempts in trying to mend their relationship. Thus she allowed him to come nearer and offered him her lips for a kiss. For a short while she enjoyed it, but then a little devil deep down compelled her to make him pay for the humiliation of the past week. She still could not explain why she felt so bad about him leaving her after he took her virginity. She had expected him to value it and show adequate affection.

When he finally finished the kiss and leaned back, she hauled out fast and hit him hard in the face.

He rubbed the painful spot on his cheek, wondering what in heaven's name he had done wrong this time. Then he saw how her lips curled into a triumphant smile. It slowly dawned on him she was playing with his feelings. Because he found not adequate defense against this, his anger returned. "Right, if it's war you want, it's war you'll get," he said. At the same time he thrust himself forward and grabbed her wrists to avoid getting hit again.

Marguerite was not able to do anything. At that moment, she realized she had been wrong in challenging him to the point of rage. For a brief time she considered if she would offer him her apologies. But no, it was too late for them. He would not believe her anymore. The only thing she could do was to continue on the road she had chosen. She would not give him the satisfaction of hurting her, sexually or psychologically.

She looked him straight in the eyes and gave him a disdainful sneer. "Go ahead," she said. "Go ahead and do it."

He cursed then let go of her. Quickly he rolled off the bed and ran out of the room. The bang with which he closed the door reflected his state of mind.

"Yes, just run away again," he heard her yell after him. "Such an easy way to solve problems!"

Eleven

"So you know what is expected of you?"

"Very well."

There was no trace of warmth and tenderness in Marguerite's words. She only felt contempt for the man who now, leaning comfortably against the back of his chair, pretended nothing had happened and was only briefing her about the tasks she had to perform at the club. Her fingers itched, as she wanted to slap him in the face for a second time. That would certainly swipe away that self-sufficient grin!

She was wearing the gown he had chosen. Madame Dumoulin had told her, an hour ago, that she should come to the library in the gold-and-white dress that had been brought.

He looked her over. "I must say, that gold brocade does your complexion every right," he concluded. "Now we only have to decide which disguise you'll be wearing."

He searched around for a while and finally handed over a black mask. "Here, put this on. See how it fits."

She did as he asked. The mask only partially covered her face and was ill fitted.

The Chevalier kept on staring at her. "No, that won't do," he said after a while. "I need something special."

She did not dare to move, although she was not pleased with his behavior. How strange this man could act! She watched him jump to his feet and walk out of the room. It took some time before he returned with a tin veil in Valencienne-lace and a couple of hairpins.

"Put up your hair," he suggested.

"I'll need help for that," she answered. "Otherwise I don't see what I'm doing."

"I'll help you," he said. "Just tell me what to do."

Guided by Marguerite, the Chevalier pinned up the hair then began to fuss with the veil. At last he seemed satisfied with his creation. The longest part of the veil now fell over the young woman's shoulders, while the shorter end covered her face to the mouth. "Perfect!" he exclaimed. "This is what I had in mind. Now you only need to put some rouge on your lips, and of course you'll do me the pleasure of wearing your diamond necklace," he added. "You will look more adult and mysterious that way."

~ * ~

With acquired ease, Marguerite mingled among the select public which attended the Domino Club by night. During the previous evenings, she had gained experience in how to endure the long hours of welcoming and chatting. None of her gestures or expressions betrayed she would rather spend these late hours in her cozy bed; not a sign told she was tired and gambling would never interest her.

"*Bonsoir*, Monsieur Jauvert," she greeted a new arrival. "What a pleasure of seeing you again! Come, let me show you where your friends are."

Returning to the main salon, she ordered one of the servants to light more candles and to provide more cooled wine. "Have you put the bottles on ice?" she asked, knowing the answer would be positive. She let her glance linger through the room. Her eyes sought out the Chevalier, who was at one of the gambling tables and was chatting the time away with some long-time customers.

Every night, she kept his advice in mind: *Don't say too much to guard the mystery around you. Only laugh when an indecent proposal is made to you. Never give in to the plea of customers to join them in a card game. I'll tell you when it's allowed. Always keep in control of yourself and don't lose your temper.*

She did not have the faintest idea the undisturbed smile on her pink lips, made more mysterious by the veil, soon became one of the outstanding attractions at the club.

The salon was quite warm, and she used her ivory fan to waver some cool air into her face and neck. Only midnight--God, how she was bored! She discretely hid a yawn and wished that, for once, she could retire to her bed early. The club remained open until the early hours, night after night, and her feeling of exhaustion did not seem to go away, no matter how long she stayed in bed.

Sylvain let in three gentlemen. She pulled herself together and went to greet them. "Good evening, Messieurs. May I bid you welcome in the Domino Club?" she smiled.

The men returned her greeting and kissed her hand.

"I believe you are here for the first time?" she said, as the last of the men bowed over her hand.

"Indeed, Madame. My pleasure," he answered.

Her chin lifted in surprise. Where had she heard that voice before? The masked man was tall, had reddish-blond hair--which would normally be covered by a wig--and dark blue eyes. She did not learn much by just looking. Because she had no time for further considerations--more guests were coming in--she put the thought of knowing him aside for the moment and returned to her duties.

The tall man remained standing in a corner and his eyes kept following her for a while. With studied nonchalance he took out his snuffbox, held the tobacco under his nose then curled his lips into an evil grin.

"My dear Duchesse," the loud voice of the Marquis de Troismart, one of their regular guests, boomed through the space of the room. Marguerite hurried to the table where he was sitting.

"My dear girl, won't you relieve me of these cards?" the marquis begged her. "I've met this lovely brunette and I'd like to spend some time with her."

"Of course, Monsieur," she agreed. The marquis spent great deals of money at the club and losing him as a guest would be a disaster. He was one of the men whose every wish should be granted the Chevalier had told her. So she took his place at the table and began to deal the cards. She was an accomplished player by now, who seldom lost to the bank.

While playing, she caught sight of the reddish-blond man once more. He casually walked towards the playing tables and found a seat at the table behind hers. She sensed his piercing looks and began to feel uncomfortable after a while.

This is strange. Normally I don't mind that others are watching me.

When the occasion arose, she put down her cards and excused herself to the other players. "I can't stay away for too long," she smiled and they all could understand her reasons.

When she walked to the table where the wine was set aside, the tall man suddenly appeared at her side, unasked for.

"You play cleverly, Madame," he complimented her. "May I offer you a refreshment?"

He smiled and normally she would have found this rather sympathetic. She just could not explain her aversion towards this man.

"Madame?"

His voice had a special timbre, somewhat hoarse and sensual at the same time. Who talked this way? One of the men she used to meet at the soirees of Comtesse d'Arcourt?

"Forgive me, Monsieur," she answered, trying to remain polite. "I was not paying attention."

She was forced to except his arm and had to allow him to accompany her to one of the salons. The Chevalier had warned her never to spend too much time on a single customer, but she could hardly offend this man either. However, when he ushered her into a niche--aptly called 'Cupid's Cave' by the other guests--she began to utter some protest. "Monsieur, my duties don't allow me..."

214

The niche was protected from curious looks by heavy velvet draperies and only a single candle shed its light into it. A quick survey of the space told her Chevalier was not in the proximity.

"Madame, I want to talk to you about an important matter," the stranger told her, while his hands exercised some pressure and pushed her down in a sitting position. Once he had her on the love seat, he closed the draperies with care. "This way we won't be disturbed," he said, with a fine smile.

A shiver ran over her spine. "Why are you afraid to be disturbed?"

He did not answer that question. "I need to ask you something about your necklace."

At first she thought he was out to ravish her, but she now feared his intentions were more evil. Why was he interested in the necklace? "What's so special about it?"

"It surely is a unique piece. May I ask, Madame, how you came by it?"

She shrugged her shoulders. "It was given to me by a friend. It was a birthday present," she said.

The expression of the eyes that watched her through the slits of the mask was one of pure contempt. More gooseflesh crept up her neck. Second by second she was feeling less comfortable.

"Please, Madame? Do you take me for a fool? You must know the Medici Diamonds are unique in the world!"

Instantly her hand went to her mouth to hide her shock. The Medici Diamonds? Even in Vallencieux they had heard the myths that were spun around the possession of this infamous necklace. Years ago, Catherine de Medici was offered a collection of brilliants, of almost equal size and cutting. The Jewish vendor had asked an exorbitant price for them. Although the Italian princess was known for her prodigality, this sum was too high even for her. But not long afterwards, the Jew had been found dead…and his son sold the necklace for a much lower price.

This did not end the bloody history of the diamonds. Catherine gave them to her daughter, Marguerite de Valois, who wore them at her wedding with the Huguenot prince Henri de Navarre. And everybody knew how that wedding night had ended.

Marguerite felt sweat run down her armpits. No, this could not be true! For sure Cartouche would not give her a necklace with such notorious history. And if so, where did he get it in the first place?

While she was still assimilating these thoughts, another one popped up. She could not explain how she came by the notion, but she suddenly feared these diamonds were much more important than she had imagined. She remembered how the Chevalier explicitly requested she wore the necklace when she worked in the club. And going back in the past, she remembered she had the necklace around her neck on the night he offered for her hand.

"Why are you so sure my necklace is the Medici one?" she protested, although she knew better. "I am sure you must be mistaken, Monsieur."

"Mistaken?" he sneered. "No, Madame, I know a lot about jewelry and I definitely recognize this string of diamonds for what it is."

"Perhaps you are right," she said on a reconciling tone, keeping in mind he was a guest of the club. "If so, where's the importance to you? As I said, this necklace was given to me as a present."

He did not speak for a while, but remained blocking the exit to the bigger salon. He seemed lost in thought. "That necklace is stolen property," he finally said.

She felt the coldness of these words, and she could not withhold the feeling she was being caught up in an invisible web of intrigue.

"I know the rightful owner," the stranger told her. "He is a friend of mine. He doesn't expect ever to retrieve it, but I want to return his property. Are you aware, Madame, that I can bring the law down on you?"

She shook her head. "Monsieur, you speak nonsense. Enough people can vow the necklace is mine."

He smiled. "Of course, I won't be so cruel. I have a much better proposition. Let me offer to buy the necklace for…let's say five hundred *livres*. You can obtain at least three other necklaces for such an amount of money and for you it can surely not make that much of a difference!"

How dare he threaten her? Despite the Chevalier's advice, she let go of her anger. "Never," she told him plain. "I won't sell my necklace. Nothing you can say will persuade me."

The smile on his lips did not go away. His calmness frightened her more than his words. "In that case, Madame," he said softly, "I will feel obliged to simply take it." His fingers crawled for the necklace and, pulling at it, he managed to unlock it.

Marguerite screamed her heart out and at the same time fought back. She managed to grab hold of the necklace and clenched it in her hand. A fist hit her hard in the face and she almost lost consciousness. She fell slowly to the ground and sensed how his fingers tried to pull the necklace out of her grip.

Suddenly the stranger paused then jumped from his kneeled position. Someone was coming! Running feet came closer, so he turned on his heels and disappeared.

~ * ~

The first thing Marguerite heard when she opened her eyes were whispering voices. She shifted her head on the pillow and tried to understand what was being said.

A woman--Madame Dumoulin--was telling the master what she thought about things. "That poor girl," Marguerite heard her say. "You shouldn't have gotten her involved in your dangerous games, master."

"This time I must agree with you, Marthe," another voice answered.

Did she spot guilt in those words? If so, she thought it very strange. She tried to lift her head, but a wave of nausea came over her. Pearls of sweat appeared on her forehead and her armpits felt wet. What was wrong with her?

Her faint movements caught Madame Dumoulin's attention. She hurried to the bedside of the young girl. "Now you keep still, Duchesse," she told her in a firm voice, which surprisingly sounded warm and compassionate.

"What's wrong with me?" Marguerite asked.

"Don't you remember? You were knocked unconscious and most likely you have a light concussion. The only remedy for that is to stay in bed and rest for a while."

Marguerite closed her eyes again and drifted back into sleep. When she woke up for a second time, the feeling of nausea was less and she was able to move her head. And now the memories came back.

"The diamonds!" she suddenly uttered. "Did that villain get the diamonds?"

Now the Chevalier appeared in her viewpoint. "He did not get them," he told her. "They were on the ground. You must have held on to them while you fell. We've put them in a safe place so you can be at rest."

Madame Dumoulin, who had momentarily left the bedroom to make some tea, returned and offered her a cup. "Here my girl, drink this. The herbs in the tea will do you good."

Marguerite accepted the cup feeling stunned. The sudden friendliness of the housekeeper and the warmth in her voice were quite new to her. She gave her a strange look, but the woman did not seem to notice.

"Don't tire the child too much," she advised her master. "She has suffered a shock and needs a lot of rest." Then she left the room to give them more privacy.

The Chevalier took out a handkerchief and carefully wiped away the sweat on Marguerite's face. His gestures were extremely tender. His ordinary show of arrogance seemed completely gone. "It was irresponsible of me to send you blindfolded into the arena," he confessed.

His words were spoken in a clear voice, from which she understood he expected to be blamed for it.

"I'll understand if you say you hate me for it," he added. Then he waited for her answer.

She did not say anything at first. She had to think.

He tried to remain calm, but inside he felt unsure. So many things had gone wrong, so many misunderstandings had popped up--and all of them because he could not forget Isabelle's betrayal.

Marguerite took her time in answering. There were too many questions whirling around in her head. "What is the importance of the diamonds? You made me work in the club because of them, didn't you?"

He did not avoid her piercing gaze. "Yes," he admitted. "I knew the murderer would react when he saw you wearing the necklace. I thought I'd be able to keep a thorough eye on you, but still I almost came too late."

There was a lot of remorse in this statement. He clearly blamed himself. She put her hand on his arm. "The murderer, you say… But the man did not want to kill me. He only wanted the necklace. He became afraid when I called out."

"He would have killed you if he'd had more time," the Chevalier said with certainty. "That man is dangerous beyond your imagination. He has committed one other crime and perhaps more of which I have no knowledge."

"You know him?" she whispered, absorbing the meaning of what he was saying. Murder! Indeed she was caught in a dangerous web.

He shook his head. "I wish I did. For years I have been trying to get track of that man and punish him for the death of my wife and my consequent conviction for murder."

New facts on top of it! This was all very confusing to her yet she sensed an urge to participate in solving the mystery. She was in too deep now to leave it alone. "Maybe I can help you," she offered spontaneously. "I am sure I have met this man before. I can't recall where, but one of these days it'll come to me for sure. Then you will have his identity."

"Don't strain yourself," he refused her offer. "I have already asked too much of you, Duchesse. Now you go to sleep and forget everything."

He gave her a furtive kiss on the cheek and planned to walk away. She could not tolerate him leaving. She suddenly longed for his presence and to obtain it she wrapped her arms tightly around his neck. He could not go away, she needed him.

"Duchesse, what are you doing?" he protested, but not very convincingly.

"Don't you think I have every right to know all the facts?" she asked, to divert his attention from the true reason she wanted him to stay. "Please?"

He remained silent, but his body melted against hers and his fingers began to weave through her hair. It had not taken much for her to win the battle. "You are right," he agreed. "You will understand everything much better once you know all the facts. And perhaps you will also come closer to understanding my motives. But it's a long story."

"It doesn't matter," she answered. ""I'm too stressed to sleep anyway."

She padded on the mattress and made room for him. He took her in his arms and felt how she rested her head on his shoulder.

Twelve

"I suppose I should start with my father," the Chevalier said, his mouth almost into Marguerite's hair.

She quite enjoyed this closeness and snuggled closer to him. "Yes, tell me," she said and hoped the story would be a truly long one. She really liked to be held this way.

"My father, Gerald St. Lawrence, was the second son of the Duke of Shrevenport who owns a large estate somewhere in the south of England. The duke arranged a military career for him and that is where the problems originated. My father became a member of the personal guard of the king and quite liked his sovereign. But my grandfather was among those who wanted James the Second out of the country because he was a catholic. Father and son got into a big dispute, and as a result of this, the duke forbade his youngest son entrance to his castle. My father, his wife and their little son--myself--followed the king into exile to France."

"Looks like all the men in your family have a stubborn trait in their character," she whispered.

He smiled. "Not much later my father died of influenza. My mother, who had no family left in England, remained in France where she mourned for a short while then remarried. Her new husband was also a widower with a little daughter of five."

"She was very practical, I guess."

221

"Yes, she was. And theirs was a good marriage. Monsieur de Montfort did love her, and she was devoted to him. Simon became like a father to me. He considered me as the son he'd never had and cherished the hope I and his daughter would become a couple and take over his estate."

"Aw," she said, "that was not very clever"

He agreed. "Yes, afterwards I can see your point. But as a young lad, I absolutely adored Isabelle and wanted her for my wife."

So now at least she knew who Isabelle was--and she could understand his past behavior. A first love is always special, and you will not soon forget about it.

"We married when I was eighteen and she was sixteen. At first everything went fine. I tried to fulfill her every wish and she was proud to be called Madame de Saint-Laurent."

He fell quiet for a while, his thoughts racing back to those days when he and Isabelle had been lovers. "The trouble started when my wife's uncle, Monsieur de Longchamps, came for a visit. He was a rake of the worst sort and his only divertissement was Isabelle. He whispered into her ear how beautiful she was and how this beauty would win over numerous hearts in Paris. When he returned home, Isabelle began to nag about making a trip to the capital."

Marguerite did not say anything to that. She just nodded, realizing her first impressions of the woman had been correct. She thought she was foolish to look for something better than the Chevalier--for despite all his shortcomings, she did recognize that at heart he was honest and strong. "What is your real name?" she asked.

"It's Anthony, didn't I mention that before?"

"No."

"Well, I could not bear Isabelle's complaining anymore, so I agreed to take her to Paris for a stay at her uncle's. She began to change. Monsieur de Longchamps arranged for her to have a set of new clothes, and he took her to various balls and soirées. I did not always go along, as those occasions bored me to death. Now I know I did wrong there. If I had been present, perhaps I could have prevented her meeting that other man."

"No," Marguerite knew, "nothing you could do would have made any change."

"They became lovers, quite shamelessly. Even her uncle--not a puritan either--began to feel embarrassed by her behavior and urged her to be more careful. She just answered the role of moralist didn't fit him and a woman needed a real man. Can you imagine how I felt at that moment?"

Marguerite kissed his cheek. "You're more than man enough for me."

He smiled once more and absently squeezed her ear. "Sometimes she stayed away for days. Then, weeks later, she would come to her uncle's house to show off a string of diamonds her lover allowed her to wear. According to her, they belonged to his family heirloom. She believed he'd make a wedding present out of them."

"So she did not want to be your wife any longer?"

"No, she hoped I would give her a divorce. And she continued to taunt me by wearing it every time she deigned us worthy of a visit. She continuously said cruel things to me and one night I lost my temper. I threatened to kill her-- which of course everybody bore witness to."

"But you didn't, right?"

"No, I didn't. Somebody else--most likely that mysterious lover of hers-- had her killed because she refused to return his necklace. And the next morning, her dead body was found at the bottom of our staircase."

She felt how his muscles tensed and realized this was an extremely difficult passage for him to tell.

"I was blamed and I was arrested. I denied the accusations, alas to no avail. The judges sentenced me to death. My stepfather and Monsieur de Longchamps both made an appeal for mercy with the king. Louis the Fifteenth gave the matter his careful consideration, and as a result of this, my sentence was changed into lifelong banishment from France. I had to leave immediately and was not even allowed to say goodbye to my parents. I wandered through the Netherlands and the German countries, a banished man who could not call one place his own. Because I needed money, I sold my services as a hireling to one or other warlord. I was wounded in a skirmish in Poland. There I discovered I still had friends. One of my mates, a former card-shark who escaped the gallows, looked after me and became a new father to me. Michel Chatelain taught me a lot. It was he who advised me to return secretly to France and try to find out who did kill my wife."

"When was that?"

"About two years ago. I used the references Michel gave me and found a place to hide in Saint-Denis where I became the Chevalier. I set up some card tables and soon began to earn money. When the profits became bigger, I bought this house in the Rue Quincampoix and created the Domino Club."

"And what about Madame Dumoulin? Where do you know her from?"

"Marthe used to be the housekeeper of Simon de Montfort. After my banishment, my mother and stepfather pined away and died shortly afterwards. Marthe had saved up some money by then and she waited for my return, along with my father's former aide, Robert McFarlane. I can totally trust those two."

"They are your faithful servants."

"Yes, and they are worth their weight in gold."

"Did you find any trace of the real killer?"

"No, not yet," he said. "The first important lead came when I sat drinking with Louison and Jaquot one night. We all had a bit too much. Deep into his cups, Jaquot mentioned the necklace. He told me they had once broken into a house in Saint-Germain and found not only the necklace but also the corpse of a young woman. From their description, I realized they were talking about Isabelle and went to the house. Neighbors told me the new owner was a far cousin of the old man. One man remembered the house had been rented out for a while and a young woman had taken up residence there. And one night, when he was not able to sleep, he'd heard a lot of noise coming from the building. To me, it was clear that somebody was looking for the necklace. So you can imagine my surprise when you showed up, wearing that damned piece around your neck!"

"I got it from Cartouche," she told him. "He said the necklace had been in his pockets for quite some time. Of course, I don't know where he got it."

"Oh, I can answer that," Anthony returned. "He probably stole it from the gipsy girl who had robbed them on her turn from Scarron, the former leader of the gang."

He paused shortly to pour them both a glass of wine then decided to share more confidentialities with his companion. "I must admit it was a terrible shock to me when I first saw you wearing those damned diamonds. The last time I saw them they were around Isabelle's neck... I could only think how lucky I was to have been handed a weapon in my search for the murderer. You'd be my instrument of revenge. Isabelle's lover--the man who must have ordered her death--is still living; we know that now as we got the proof tonight."

"You could have warned me in advance," she softly chided him. "But as always you wanted to have your own way." She looked up to watch how he would respond to her faint attempt at sarcasm. To her satisfaction, she noticed a treacherous blush creeping up to color his cheeks. She had to hide away her triumphant smile. That man! How delicately he had to be handled!

"I already apologized for that," he hastened to say. Making apologies was not his strongpoint. It had already cost him a lot to admit he had been wrong in sending her into danger without any warning. "But I agree," he said despite himself. "I should have been honest with you from the start."

"Let's not talk about it anymore," she said. "You came to my rescue, and that means a lot to me." Slowly and deliberately, her fingers caressed the worried lines around his mouth.

She succeeded in catching his attention. His own hand began to explore the line of her neck and came to rest on the buds of her breast. After a while, he pressed his lips on them and almost made her crazy with desire.

Marguerite desperately tried to keep her senses together. There was still so much that needed to be said, so she gently pushed his head aside and made him sit up again. "I'm a stubborn brat," she said to him. "No doubt you'll have noticed that, Anthony--do you mind me using your given name?" He did not answer, which she took for approval. "Sometimes I behave badly and I never seem to find the courage to admit to that. A couple of weeks ago you came to my room and…"

He put a hand over her mouth. "Don't say anything more, "he whispered. "These things are in the past."

"Still," she insisted, "this needs to be said, if we intend to become friends of sorts. Otherwise the opportunity will be gone forever. You wanted a sort of…truce, did you not? More understanding and at least respect for one another. I think I'm ready for that now."

He shook his head, not daring to believe her. "Now you speak like this, Duchesse. Don't forget you had a nasty shock tonight. Perhaps tomorrow you will reconsider. I think I can better leave you to rest now."

Of course he did not actually mean that. He *did* long for more intimacy between them, as he had grown quite fond of the girl. It was his male pride that made him speak those words. He found it hard to accept she should feel obliged to him.

Marguerite looked hurt and her eyes became darker. He was going to abandon her, let her sleep on her own! No, she did not want that. She grabbed hold of his shirt. "Don't go," she hastened to say. "I never change my mind, however it may turn out. What I want right now are your arms around me, to feel your lips on mine. I have missed you so much all these lonely nights, Anthony…"

He no longer tried to resist. Her pink lips irresistibly drew him nearer and with a groan he covered her mouth with his. His hot breath stroked her skin.

He did not see her small smile of triumph--anyway, it was soon gone as she too became overpowered with desire.

Thirteen

Three weeks later, Marguerite woke up feeling nauseous. She had to hurry out of the bed, unless the contents of her stomach would be emptied right there. As she did, she also felt somewhat dizzy. She blamed it on the meal of fish they had the previous night. *Probably not quite fresh anymore.* She felt alright during the rest of the day and thought nothing of it.

The next morning, however, she had the same problem. And now she could not blame it on the food. What was wrong with her? Was she too tired? She had begged Anthony to let her return to the Club, as she was the only one who could identify the killer. "I'm not afraid of being down there," she had told him. "I know you'll be there to watch over me." So night after night she played her role as Duchesse. Yes, these nights were long and tiresome; that must be the explanation.

That evening, while watching the guests take their bets and hoping for the stranger to return, she remained in a reflective mood. Once the killer was exposed--and that would happen, she felt sure of it--Anthony's name would be cleared. What would happen then? When he could return to his former life, free of blame, would he still care for her? *I'm honest about my feelings*, she meditated. *I can no longer deny my indifference towards the man who has taken me into his* house *and his* bed. *Now he no longer has the sole use of my body, he also has my heart.*

Not much later, Madame Dumoulin opened her eyes to another truth. By now they had become friends. While they were having tea--a habit that the

St. Lawrence's had brought along to France--the housekeeper carefully steered the conversation towards what was on her mind.

"Mademoiselle Marguerite," she began, "I must admit I'm somewhat worried about you."

Marguerite smiled. "Surely, Marthe…"

"Yes, dear. You always look so pale and sometimes you definitely look ill."

"Oh well, I need to rest once this quest for truth is over," she shrugged. "I feel tired all the time."

Marthe shook her head. "No, dear," she answered. "You suffer from something else. Tell me, do you feel sick in the mornings?"

Marguerite put down her cup of tea and gave her a quizzical look. "Every now and then. Is that serious?"

"If I'm right with my suspicions, you will in time have to take out the seams of your gowns, dear. I think you are with child."

Marguerite's mouth dropped open. A baby? Was she really this naïve? For months now she had been sleeping with Anthony and not once had she thought of the possibility of getting pregnant.

"When did you have your last monthly period?" the housekeeper urged her to consider.

"Almost two months ago," Marguerite had to admit. She simply had not given this any thought with everything happening.

Marthe was completely sure now "You are going to be a mother, Marguerite. I did witness many a pregnancy during my time at Montfort, and all the signs are there. A woman carrying a child behaves differently and there is that certain look in the face. Well, dear, aren't you thrilled?"

The young woman could not answer that question straight away. The idea was so new to her, so completely overwhelming. It frightened her and at the same time it made her happy. She was having Anthony's child.

Marthe's next words shook her out of her reflections. "An heir to Montfort! I'm sure that will make the master extremely happy."

A wave of panic came over her. Her love for the man was still vulnerable and she knew that having the baby would put her in an even weaker position. She was not yet ready to deal with this. "I don't want him to know-- not now, anyway!" she exclaimed. Thick tears rolled down her cheek and automatically she turned to the older woman for support.

Marthe tenderly put her arms around the frail shoulders of the girl and patted her back until the shaking of the body stopped. "Hush dear, don't get upset," she murmured in a soothing tone. "My lips are sealed, I promise you. I understand perfectly well what you are going through. You're afraid, aren't you?"

Marguerite nodded numbly. She realized that Marthe had guessed how she felt about Anthony and that her reactions were no secret to her.

"You shouldn't be," Mathe continued. "Not anymore, that is. He has accepted you in his life now, and he knows his duty." She wiped off the tears on the young woman's face, like a mother would do. "I have been very worried," she then confessed. "When he came back to France, he was so totally different from the caring boy I remembered. He acted like a man without a soul, without feelings. While he used to show compassion and respect for every living creature! He treated the occasional women like dirt, like something you pick up from the gutter then throw back. His precious Club became an obsession, finding the murderer of Isabelle his goal. Some days he locked himself away and sat brooding over dark plans."

Marthe drew a deep breath and remained silent for some time. Her thoughts returned to the day when she had entered the library and had caught her master with the portrait of his murdered wife. She had not been able to bear the sight. His face showed so much torture, so much pain.

Then she looked at Marguerite and her face cleared up again. "I believe you have chased away the ghost of Isabelle, my dear," she said with calm certainty. "He needed someone like you."

"I think he loved her a lot," Marguerite sighed. "Do you think he'll be able to love another woman just as fiercely?"

"But he never loved Isabelle," Marthe stated as a fact. "What he felt for her was just infatuation, which he took for love. She could be so charming, our Mademoiselle, and she had put it into her mind young master Anthony had to become her husband She used all her cunning tricks on him. The poor fellow didn't know what was happening. I doubt he'll ever fall for such tricks a second time. He's much wiser now. A pretty face and vain manners don't impress him. So I think you'll make him a much better wife than Isabelle. You are what he needs--and he's a fool if he doesn't realize that."

With these comforting words she left Marguerite on her own.

~ * ~

As soon as Marguerite opened her eyes, the familiar feeling of nausea came over her. Carefully, as not to disturb Anthony, she climbed out of bed and hurried to the toilet pot which was hidden in a closet, adjoining the bedroom. This time she was not very lucky. Her stomach acted so nervously she had to grab for the wash-basin. She sunk to her knees and vomited.

"Duchesse, what is wrong?"

With a start she turned her head, still wiping her mouth. Anthony sat upright in the bed and watched her with a worried look on his face. She tried to think. The best thing was to pay no attention to him. So she calmly picked up the basin, went to the toilet to dispose of its contents, and cleaned her face and hands with water before returning to bed. "There's nothing wrong with me," she told her lover. "Perhaps something I ate yesterday evening"

"Are you sure?" he insisted. "There is nothing wrong with your health?"

She did not feel all too comfortable under his genuine concern. Did he suspect anything?

"Duchesse, come here"

She could not neglect the note of command in his voice and hesitatingly did as he requested, allowing herself to be embraced. Ill at ease she cast down her eyes and began to fumble with the ribbons of her nightdress.

"Why are you lying?" he demanded. He had to hear her answer, although he knew what she tried to hide. He did not have his eyes in his pocket! She was having a child--something he was thrilled about. And if the baby was anything like its mother, it would be a handful too.

Marguerite did not say anything. Her head sunk lower when she realized he *had* guessed. What could she say?

"Why don't you want to tell me that you are carrying my child?" he asked.

Deep blushes colored her cheeks. Still she was not able to face him "I would have told you in due time," she offered as defense. "I wanted to wait for a better moment."

"And when would that be?"

Her head sunk deeper to her chest. "Perhaps after we've exposed the murderer," she whispered. "Surely that is only a matter of time. Only yesterday I came close to remembering that fellow's name. Then you can go to the king and apply for grace."

He did not give her the opportunity of saying anything more. "Then you'd disappear and I would never know you gave birth to my child," he said knowingly. He put his hand under her chin so she no longer could evade his quizzical look. "Do you trust me that little, Duchesse? Where, for heaven's sake, would you go?"

"Home," she murmured. "If they'll still want me there, that is."

She had planned it that way. She did not want to be a burden to him. Nothing in his behavior seemed to verify Marthe's conviction he felt something more than desire for her. So she intended to help him find the man who was responsible for Isabelle's death then she would--finally--return to Vallencieux. She knew life there would be hard for her just as well, but anything was better than staying in Paris.

"I won't allow you,'" he told her, his voice hoarse with emotion. "We find ourselves in strange circumstances, I admit, but you can't deny me my child. You can't understand how a man feels when he knows he is going to have a son. I wish that he shall carry my name and therefore, *chérie*, I have decided we shall be married as soon as possible."

She shrank away when she heard him say that. How humiliating those words were. He did not marry her because he loved her, but because he wanted to have an heir. That damned male pride. She doubted very much she would be strong enough to accept that she would be his wife because he felt obliged to. She wished she had been able to conceal her condition a while longer.

"Maybe the baby is going to be a girl," she argued. "A daughter cannot inherit your title and you wouldn't need to marry me."

He laughed. He just loved it when she tried to argue with him. "I won't risk that. Besides, what are you worrying about? If it's girl, we'll have a boy afterwards."

He did not give her any more opportunity to bicker and smothered her protests in a burning kiss. Heavens, how long would it take him to tame this soaring spirit?

~ * ~

Exactly one week later Anthony and Marguerite stood before the priest of a shaggy and ill-lit parish church. The clergyman murmured the trusted words of the wedding service, while his eyes shot nervously from the couple before him to the attendants of this happy occasion. They really looked a rabble. *Even priests are no longer safe in the streets of Paris*, he thought, thinking of that afternoon.

Here I am, doing my duty in attending a sick parishioner, walking back to the church. Suddenly there are two men standing before me, both dressed in dark capes and their faces barely visible. They ask me if I can perform a wedding? I'm sure they'd hurt me if I said 'no'... So I agreed and for that they give me this big purse. Thank God! I'm not asking where the money comes from, but I can do so much good with it.

"... and so I pronounce you husband and wife," he ended his speech and turned to the bridegroom. "You may now kiss the bride."

Anthony complied willingly. His arms slid around Marguerite's waist and his mouth sought hers for a burning kiss.

In the meanwhile, the priest shut his missal and hurried to the sacristy. The wedded couple followed him some time later. On a table was the register, and the priest entered the date of the wedding. He then invited the couple to sign.

For Marguerite this was the moment of truth. Her family pride would not allow her to sign under false pretenses, so she took the pen between her trembling fingers and wrote: "Marguerite St. Lawrence, *née de Vallencieux*".

With no apparent emotion Anthony took the pen out of her hand and wrote down his name.

~ * ~

Only late in the evening, after the excessive meal the members of the brotherhood at L'Ange Noir offered the newly-weds, did he gave away something of his astonishment. They were lying close together in the big bed after an hour of passionate lovemaking. "When will you stop being a mystery to me, My Lady?" he softly said. "When will I really get to know you? I should have suspected you had noble blood, judging by your fighter's nature."

"Why should I care to tell?" she answered. "I ran away from home. My father probably has disinherited me. Not that I'd receive much anyway."

Suddenly he gave her a teasing smile. "Shall we announce our wedding to him?"

His words were not quite cold when he noticed the fear in her eyes. He gave himself an imaginary kick in the butt. She did not wholly trust him yet. He wondered if that moment would ever come. "I was only joking, dear," he hastened to ease her worries. "It doesn't interest me who you were. I have only known the woman you are now, Marguerite. By the way, don't you agree that name sounds so formal? I think I'm going to call you Margie, after Margaret. Do you like that name?"

She nodded. The name sounded cozy, even tender.

"My Margie," he repeated. "Mine forever."

233

Fourteen

In a tavern near Saint-Cloud a well-dressed young gentleman sat at a table near the window, sipping his wine. He had an appointment with a lady and for that reason he paid little attention to the group of junior officers of the royal guard who stormed in with all possible *élan* and claimed the best places in the taproom.

When he was about to fill his glass once more, a hand landed heavily on his shoulder.

"De Bassy, dear chap!" a voice boomed.

Claude looked up in surprise then recognized the man who treated him in such a boyish way. With a grin he leaned back in his chair. "Armand, it's been a long while!"

His hand went up in the air. "*Patron*, another bottle for me and my friend!"

Forgotten was the woman he had been waiting for. Claude longed to renew his friendship with the young count. Armand and he had gotten along fine when he was staying at Vallencieux, last summer. As far as he knew the young man who now sat opposite him had no idea at all he had taken his sister to Paris, otherwise he would not behave so friendly. And although the Vallencieux's were not well off, they probably had more money than he had left in his pockets.

"*Mon vieux*, it is truly a pleasure of seeing you here," he said, toasting to Armand. "How are you doing?"

"I'm well enough," Armand answered. "I have finished my training to become an officer and now I'm waiting for a new commission in the Deux-Ponts regiment. A little bit of time to do nothing but enjoy myself."

"Knowing you, that won't be a problem," Claude smiled. "And how fares your family, if I'm allowed to ask?"

Armand's face got a wry expression. "My father is dead," he said curtly. A condition of the heart, according to the doctor. All because of that stupid affair with my sister"

Claude pretended ignorance. "Wasn't she called Marguerite? What has she done then? When I left your castle she was engaged to be married to my cousin Laneuil"

"She ran off," his friend stated sourly. "She chose her moment well, I must say. Only a few days after the engagement! When my father learned of this, he flew into such a fit of anger we had to call for the doctor. A couple of days later he was dead."

"I'm deeply sorry," Claude said, putting a tone of sincerity into his voice. "Please accept my condolences"

"Thank you."

"And have you heard from Marguerite in the meantime?" he dared to remark. He wanted to find out if she had returned to Burgundy. Meeting her would be somewhat awkward, he reckoned.

"The darned girl hasn't returned," Armand said, to his relief. "If she does, I'm going to have a word with her!" He made a gesture that did not need more explanation. Then he laughed amiably once more. "I must say though, your cousin is a decent chap He assured me he still wants to marry Marguerite, should she choose to return."

"How charming," Claude smiled, making fun of his cousin's honest feelings. "Well, we can't do much about it, can we? So what do you say if I propose to celebrate our meeting with a night out one of the coming days? I know a few addresses in the old town which are certainly worth a visit"

"Sounds interesting," the young count responded enthusiastically. "When and where shall we meet?"

"Are you familiar with that inn near the Pont Neuf? I'll see you there tomorrow evening."

At that moment a masked woman entered the establishment and looked around the room searchingly. Claude excused himself with Armand and went to greet her.

~ * ~

A lackey showed two young men into the salons of the Domino Club. The hour was close to midnight and the rooms were crowded with people.

The new arrivals escaped Marguerite's attention. She was deeply involved in a conversation with Marquis de Troismart, who was a master at describing funny situations. This evening he was telling her about a game of hoca in which he had been extremely lucky.

"*Et voilà, Madame*, there I had a king and a queen in my hand! Poor Duchateau had to put down his cards and thus I became the owner of a merchant ship. Now I thought it would not be too difficult to get rid of it, perhaps the ship would wreck itself in a storm or pirates would capsize it. But no, that wicked vessel always returns safely to port and makes me a merchant in my old age!" He told this with an even face but his eyes were twinkling.,

Marguerite laughed aloud. How thankful she was for the marquis' jokes, which broke the monotony of these awful long nights. She felt a little annoyed when Sylvain announced the presence of another important guest. "*Mon cher marquis*, will you excuse me for a moment?" she said. "Duty calls, unfortunately."

"But of course, my dear lady. Remind me to tell you the rest of the story later."

With a last sorry smile, she turned away from the marquis and quickly moved to the hall where she normally welcomed visitors. She gave the last entry a proper greeting and showed the man around, introducing him to some of the guests who often visited. When she thought he would be alright, she left him in the capable hands of the card dealer and slowly walked off.

She listened in on some conversations, offered advice here and there and ordered a lackey to light more candles. She was about to get a drink when she happened to overhear part of a conversation.

"… in Dijon."

"Yes, that was…"

She froze in her paces and listened more carefully. She recognized these voices! She bit her lip and a feeling of panic came over her. No, this could not be possible. Under her veil her face turned white and her eyes betrayed her nervousness. She wanted to run away, but the acquired discipline kept her from giving in to the panic. She remained calm on the outside and went looking for Anthony.

She found him in one of the card rooms where he was the uninterested onlooker at a game of poker. He seemed to be thankful when she discretely called him away.

"Dearest, would you mind taking over my duties for a while?" she begged of him. "I have developed a nasty headache and I'd like to lie down."

She was not given away by the tone of her voice but by the cramped fingers that held her fan. Anthony at once realized something was extremely wrong and his brows drew together. "Only a headache?" he inquired. "Are you certain nothing else is bothering you?"

In all her misery Marguerite thought he was referring to the baby, which made her feel worse. It was obvious he only cared for the child, and her welfare was unimportant to him. "I am quite fine," she assured him evenly. "I just need to get out of these smoky rooms with their humid atmosphere."

"By all means, go to your bed," he sighed in exasperation. "There's no need to come back," he added. "I'll kindly ask our guests to leave early, so we all can have a decent night's sleep."

She mounted the stairs to their apartment, hurried to the bedroom and hurled herself onto the bed, thankful for the peace and quiet.

Armand and Claude de Bassy! Images of the past swept through her mind. Was it possible they had discovered her whereabouts, or was their visit a mere coincidence?

Whatever the answer, she felt uneasy about it. Did the veil really cover up the features of her face? Suppose one of them had recognized her? She pressed her body into the mattress to stifle the trembling in her limbs and whispered a desperate prayer to ward off possible danger.

~ * ~

Armand de Vallencieux gave his companion a teasing wink. "Well, *mon vieux*, I admit this is an excellent place, but where in the hell is your mysterious hostess? Did we frighten the lady away?"

Claude grinned somewhat sheepishly. "There you say something. Come to think of it, I haven't seen her since we entered the place. That's not normal. Usually she remains here until closing time."

The count ticked off a bit of fluff from his sleeve and yawned discretely. "A real shame. I suppose we'd better leave then--although I must say I'd liked to meet this woman in person. I love solving mysteries."

De Bassy had to swallow the little bit of decency that still remained inside his being. He could not spoil the unexpected opportunity Armand provided him with. His thoughts shot back to a certain evening, not so long ago, when he was playing at cards with old acquaintances and Lady Luck seemed to abandon him. In a last attempt he had put everything on one card. Of course he lost the bet, but that was not the worst of it. His opponent, the son of a bitch, had him cornered. He needed a chore to be done, to relinquish the debt De Bassy owed him. Claude had to accept this offer, but now despised himself for his lack of character. "If you insist, there is always a possibility," he managed to say, pretending to be as light-hearted as the count. "I happen to know that Duchesse has an apartment above these rooms. I suppose she can be found there."

"Are you serious?" Armand laughed. "Although, it's a nice idea--moving into her territory, so to say..."

They watched Sylvain and took opportunity of a moment of inattention to slip through the hall and mount the stairs to the upper floors. Darkness surrounded them and they had to search their way carefully.

At last they reached the corridor to which Marguerite's bedroom door opened.

Fifteen

Marguerite heard footsteps on the stairway and wrongly interpreted them to be Anthony's. So he had kept his promise and come to bed early. She straightened her shoulders, wiped away every trace of wetness on her face with a lace handkerchief and pinched her cheeks to bring back some color. She finally shook out her skirts then walked to the door.

"Anthony? What…?"

The words ended in a shrill pitch as she froze stiff in the doorway. Her eyes opened wide as she stared at the two men who stood before her like demons.

Their faces equally gave way to their surprise. None of them had counted on this. Armand was the first to return to reality. He set one step forward and grabbed his sister's arm in a not too friendly way. "Marguerite! For heaven's sake, what are you doing in such a place?" he yelled at her, and when she remained speechless and numb, he completely lost his temper and shouted even harder. "Damn you! Open your mouth, you slut!"

He was white with anger. To find his sister, a born countess, in a place of ill repute shook everything he strived to live for. Their reputation as a family would be damaged beyond repair when this would become public knowledge. Marguerite deserved the most sever punishment he could think of. He began to shake her.

Finally the numbness left her and she felt the painful pressure of his fingers in her flesh. It made her angry and ready to fight again. "Let go of me,

Armand! Don't you dare interfere in my business," she yelled back. Simultaneously, she kicked his shins and tried to scratch his face with her sharp nails.

The swiftness of her attack surprised the count at first, but then he managed to get hold of both her hands and kept them in an iron grip. With his free hand he slapped her hard in the face.

The noise in the corridor alarmed Marthe who, making use of the commotion, managed to hurry down the stairs unseen. Putting aside the contempt she felt for such places, she did not hesitate to enter and went looking for Anthony, blind to the stares she drew. When she at last located him, she pulled him by the sleeve and did not care he was speaking to a real duchess. "Master, you have to come immediately," she whispered urgently. "Two men are harassing the mistress!"

Anthony did not give her the opportunity to say more. He left her and the duchess standing, ran through the rooms and mounted the stairs two steps at a time. His arrival, which was so sudden, surprised Marguerite's aggressors.

Armand loosened his grip for a fraction of a second, but it offered opportunity for Marguerite to free herself from his hold and run for the safety of Anthony's embrace. With a sigh of relief she fell into his arms.

He immediately pressed her against his body in a protective manner. Then he addressed the two unknown men with a haughty air. "Messieurs, may I ask what you are doing in my private quarters?"

His words cut through the building tension. However, they failed to impress Armand. Showing the same hauteur in behavior he slowly studied the Chevalier's face. "Our host, I presume?" he said, giving Claude a wide grin. "My dear sir, forgive me for not announcing our visit, but I have to settle some urgent affairs with the lady." His chin pointed at Marguerite with a disdainful gesture.

Marguerite's eyes shot fire. "Make them leave, sweetheart," she urged Anthony, forgetting she had never shown her affection in such a way. "I have no need to entertain these men. Why could they not remain in Burgundy?"

Anthony still did not fully comprehend what was going on, but he caught the urgency in her voice. He took her hand and pressed it encouragingly. "Oh, but they are leaving, my love," he reassured her. "Gentlemen, you heard the lady. Your presence is not required anymore. So may I ask you…" He made a broad gesture while the irony dripped off his words.

Armand was a worthy opponent, though. "I refuse to leave," he stated firmly. "I am not sure, Monsieur, that you are aware of the fact this lady is my sister."

The only sign of Anthony's surprise was the tightening of his grip. His expression remained even. "And still you have to leave my house," he spoke softly, in a menacing tone.

Marguerite felt how his muscles tightened under the touch of her fingers and she assumed he must be very angry to find out about her brother.

"Marguerite may be your sister," Anthony continued, "but I can assure you are no longer her guardian. She happens to be my wife, you know."

Armand heard that last remark and went white. His blood boiled with the insult done to him. He swore to make Marguerite pay dearly.

Next to him, Claude watched the scene with opened mouth. He did not fully understand all that was going on.

"Very well," Armand managed to say at last. "It may be the truth." Then he addressed Marguerite. "Is this your latest game, dear sister? Have you by now forgotten the husband you left behind at home?"

Anthony suddenly let go of her hand. This reaction shook Marguerite most of all. The bastard! What if the Chevalier believed him? "Armand is just making this up," she hurried to state with righteous anger. The sheer strength of it made Anthony look up to her. "I know what he tries to do," she explained. "He wants to split us up. I swear to God I have not married before. My father wanted me to marry a cousin of Claude's, who is also present, but I ran away from home after the engagement. I didn't want an old man for a husband. Please, say you believe me." She watched his reaction.

At first Anthony was doubtful. He whispered, "I know so little of you, *petite*," and thought of her unpredictable deeds and actions. What finally convinced him was the triumphant gleam in Armand's eyes. Yes, she spoke truth. He then gave her an encouraging smile, which however failed to convince her completely. "I believe you, my dear. Your brother won't separate us."

Armand laughed. "That is fine with me. If my words don't succeed, I'll have to try another way. We'll settle this affair by the sword. I am determined to bring my sister home with me to Burgundy and marry her off to Etienne Laneuil." While speaking, he drew his sword and positioned himself for the fight. "*En garde*, dear brother-in-law!" Without further warning, he leaped forward in a fluent move and the point of his sword cut a shallow wound in the arm of his opponent.

Anthony was not able to defend himself immediately. His first concern was the safety of his wife and their baby. He tried to maneuver her out of the reach of Armand's sword but was not fast enough. Marguerite almost got hurt when her brother attacked again. He could only prevent a mortal wound by throwing himself before her, which resulted in a deep gash across his face. Blood dripped into his eyes.

At last he was able to push his precious charge into the still open entrance to the bedroom where she would be safe. Then he jumped away, to create a distance between him and his opponent. With acquired ease, he also drew his sword and wiped off the blood with an impatient movement. He did not yet feel the intense pain this wound caused. "Between us now, count!"

Soon the fight exploded in full fierceness. Armand came to the conclusion--and not a pleasant one, for the part--that the other man was a master at handling the sword and he had greatly underestimated him. The Chevalier showed a fluency in striking and withdrawing which far surpassed his own skills and only thanks to the routine he had acquired in his army practice he managed to ward off the terrible blows and sometimes even attack.

While the fight went on, Marguerite sought comfort in the arms of Marthe. Huddled together, the two women watched the movements of the fighters with frightened eyes.

None of them took notice of Claude de Bassy, who chose exactly this moment of confusion to sneak away and enter the rooms, one by one. It did not take him long to find what he was looking for. With a sigh of relief, he took the Medici necklace out of its case and let it disappear into his coat pocket. At last! With this single gesture he could pay off his debt to that nasty man.

Anthony's blows became fiercer and clearly showed his intention to strike down his opponent. The point of his weapon pierced through the flesh of Armand's arm, enraging that one even further.

The count knew he was losing the duel. He realized he could not last five more minutes and this increased his intention to end the fight. His only chance lay in applying a trick a tough veteran of three wars had once shown him. He maneuvered in such a way to cause the hilts of the swords to clinch together and he came breast to breast with the Chevalier. Both men were panting hard. Seconds slowly ticked away. Then Armand delivered his opponent a harsh kick against the shinbone.

Anthony lost his balance for a fraction of a second. The action gave Armand just enough time. He eagerly and expertly put one step backwards and thrust his weapon into the Chevalier's breast, with deadly precision.

A cutting cry escaped Marguerite's throat. Her eyes became dark pools of grief when she watched her husband go down with a look of surprise still on his face. A stream of dark red blood gushed down from the wound, forming a puddle on the floor.

"Darling!" she breathed, letting herself fall down beside his body. Her fingers sought frantically for the vein in his neck, hoping to feel a heartbeat. A beating would mean he was still alive. But she felt nothing. His bloodless lips did not quiver and she could not trace any pulsing of blood. Losing control now and whining like an animal caught in a trap, she stood up, her skirts reddened by the blood. Nails outstretched, she threw herself on Armand to seek revenge. "You killed him!" she yelled. "I hate you, I hate you…"

Her fists battered away at his chest and Armand had all the trouble in the world to ward her off.

Marguerite suddenly became aware of darkness. Everything turned black before her eyes. She did register how her limbs became weak and how at last she lost the power over her legs. With a deep sigh, she closed her eyes.

~ * ~

Armand felt his sister's resistance suddenly fall away. Looking down at her, he noticed she had lost consciousness. He did not make a single attempt to prevent her from falling as she sunk against his legs.

With a last look of contempt for the dying man and the housekeeper, who stood paralyzed with fear and was not able to react, he stooped to pick up his sister's limp body and carried her down the stairs, into the dark night.

1721
One

In the present, Marguerite did not realize she had sunk down on her knees and was now half-lying on the cold pavement.

The boy Jeanot heard her moan and tried to shake her back to consciousness. "Madame Marguerite, wake up please!"

She vaguely heard a voice calling. At first she did not know whose voice it was. Marthe's? Claude's? The sound became more persistent and reluctantly her mind returned to the existing situation. When she finally opened her eyes, she did not realize where she was. The Chevalier and Armand were dueling and she crouched away, sought shelter in Marthe's arms. She still heard the swords clashing.

Then she became aware of the frosty night air and reality set in. This was not Anthony's house in the Rue Quincampoix--but Hilaire's mansion in Saint-Cloud. She was not seventeen anymore, but a woman of twenty-seven. Only the sounds of the fight remained the same.

The seventeen lost years of her youth melted together with her experiences from the present and made her see the horrible truth. She now knew with certainty who had killed Isabelle--the same man who was responsible for the attempts on her life. She even knew his motive--nothing more than vile greed.

So many years ago, at the Domino Club, she met the murderer for the first time--or at least she thought so at the moment. Back then, she tried to remember whose eyes were behind the mask. Now she succeeded without effort.

It was easy to put all the missing pieces together. She realized Isabelle's desire to have the Medici Diamonds had killed her. Obviously, the intention was that the necklace should be returned to its rightful owner, but Louison and Jaquot prevented this. Afterwards, the damned necklace found its way into Cartouche's pockets. It was her bad luck he chose to present it as a birthday present to her--from the moment she showed it off, her fate was equally decided. She had to die too. The hired villains wrongly assumed she would be in the coach with Etienne. Then they tried poison, but she refused the cacao and let Rosette drink it. More attempts followed, and each time it became more important she should not be given the chance to remember... For that reason others had to die as well.

Jeanot shook her once more. "Madame! Please!"

She rose and shook her skirts. The fight was still going on and became crueler every second. What use was thinking of the past? She had to act, and had to do it immediately. Gently, she got rid of Jeanot's hands. "Don't worry about me," she told him in a reassuring way. "I'll be fine. But I have to do something."

Determinedly, she pushed the boy aside and worked her way through the ring of servants that had formed around the duelists. Most of them were still in their nightclothes.

Finally, she managed to enter the house, which was now quiet as a tomb. The heels of her slippers made a thundering noise as she hurried up the stairs to her room. Three hours ago she felt sick for killing a hired villain. Now she was more than prepared to commit murder in cold blood. She loaded her pistol and keeping a firm grip around it, ran down the stairs once more.

The duel still was not decided in favor of one or other party. Both men wore unimportant wounds which only enflamed their will to end the fight. The surrounding crowd of servants watched their movements with no sign of emotion--they did not particularly like their master and the other man was a stranger. The still of the night was only broken by the sound of shuffling feet, the forceful breathing of the men and the clatter of steel onto steel.

When the servants saw her approach with the pointed gun, they drew back in awe but remained standing before the house. Marguerite advanced until she was close to the men. Sharp as glass, her voice rang out. "Hilaire, stop the fight!" she commanded. "You are under fire."

The duelists froze in their movements. A muffled rumor gulfed through the crowd of spectators. The marquis slowly lowered his sword and directed a disdainful look of contempt towards Marguerite--the only one of those present who also knew the truth.

~ * ~

Stupid bitch, he thought. *Did she really think she'd get a chance to reveal her story to the world? Yes, he had to admit she'd been extremely lucky. Her maid drank the poisoned cacao, not she. The hold-up of the carriage was a disaster and Newton came between her and her destiny twice.*

When he'd unexpectedly paid a visit to a new club, he had been astonished to see his stolen diamonds around the neck of the club's hostess-- whom he also recognized as the girl who once had turned a nasty trick on him. Of course he then sought a way to seek revenge. Young Claude de Bassy was indebted to him and with some 'friendly' persuasion he convinced him to enter the private quarters of the club and take the necklace away.

De Bassy returned with a story of a bloody duel, but in the course of the years he forgot about that. Who could foretell his surprise when, so many years later, he stood eye to eye with a woman who resembled Duchesse like two drops of water? It took some time before he realized this Madame de Laneuil was the same girl Claude had talked about. Luckily for him, she appeared to have lost all memory of the events nine years ago. He decided to win her faith, to give him the opportunity to get rid of her.

Unfortunately, it had not worked out as he planned. She fought all the way and reluctantly he had to admit she showed courage. She was a woman of character and in other circumstances he would have admired her for that. He could have loved her had she not been the only witness to his vile deeds.

He gave her a last, calculating glance. She would not shoot, not the Marguerite he remembered.

Their looks met, and suddenly he didn't feel so sure. Her green eyes had never before shown this iron determination and the hand in which she held the pistol did not quiver. Slowly, her index finger curled around the trigger. A muscle in her cheek trembled lightly.

At this moment, Anthony chose to intervene. "Margie, what is the meaning of this?"

He clearly was at a loss and involuntarily she had to smile. "It means, my one and only love, that Hilaire is the murderer of Isabelle," she explained, keeping her gun steady. "He also tried to have me killed. Don't I have the right to be his executioner?"

Anthony had to swallow his surprise. "No, Margie, that's a right I demand for myself. I won't tolerate your being branded as a murderess. I shall defeat the marquis in a straightforward duel. Put down that pistol, love, and let the swords decide."

He turned to Hilaire. "*En garde, Monsieur!*" In one fluent movement the point of his sword described a circle in the air and touched Hilaire's shoulder, leaving behind a torn shirt and a shallow gash in the flesh.

The marquis bit his lips and returned to his defensive position. He managed to administer an almost identical wound to Newton's leg.

"You'd better believe me, d'Aubervilliers," Anthony breathed in deadly earnest. "I shall kill you for what you have done to my first wife and then to Marguerite!"

"Isabelle deserved her fate," Hilaire sneered. "She was greedy."

"Perhaps. But you were the one who stirred up this greed. She only turned vicious after she'd met you. Still, I hate you most for the perils you let come down on Margie."

"She was the only one who could recognize me. I could not risk her memory to return, although it certainly was funny. I could tell her anything."

Each time one of the duelists was hit, a sympathetic groan went through the crowd. Jeanot clung to Marguerite's side and pressed her hand encouragingly. "Our lord will win," he said with conviction. "You must have faith, Madame!"

~ * ~

Marguerite never let her husband out of her sight. As far as she could judge, he was only bleeding from superficial wounds, but she had doubts he could continue the fight in the current ferocity. How long would he be able to withstand Hilaire's blows? There had to come a decision soon, especially because her nerves threatened to give up on her.

How could she help him? She forced her brain to scan every possibility and finally came up with the answer. The fight between Anthony and Armand, the hilts of the swords touching then Armand's foot which shot forward; his sword piercing through Anthony's chest and blood flowing freely. Rich streams of blood. "Darling!" she cried out in relief. "Kill him the same way my brother struck you down. He doesn't deserve any better. Make an end to this duel!"

Anthony understood her words but could not lower himself to do a deed so shameful. He hated d'Aubervilliers with every inch of his being yet he would give him a fair chance. He knew his strength. He could win this fight--for Marguerite, not for Isabelle. His love for his first wife had died a long time ago, even before she was rudely taken from him. Margie loved him with all of her heart. Only now, however, he felt certain she fully answered his own feelings. Had she not agreed to give up everything and accompany him to England, even before her memory had so miraculously returned? Had she not been prepared to become a social outcast in order to be with him? Yes, she did love him.

Thick drops of sweat troubled Hilaire's sight and he missed his aim a second time. He felt a fierce pain when Anthony's sword pierced through his upper right arm. It was his fighting arm and he was now forced to change his position. Left was his weak side. His breathing came harder and harder. What did Marguerite yell a couple of minutes ago? Armand's trick? His brain slowly rendered a search of his memory. Once Armand had bragged about the way he dealt with difficult opponents. He now remembered the trick and realized it could come in handy. He let go of a triumphant sound, deep in his throat, and threw himself onto Newton, ready to move.

"Anthony, watch out!"

Marguerite's cry warned Anthony just in time. He dodged out of d'Aubervillier's reach, and used the second his opponent was out of balance to drive his own sword into the body nearby. At first the tip touched the breastbone, but then it slid off and entered deeply, piercing the lungs of the marquis.

A look of intense wonder appeared on Hilaire's face as he sank on his knees and slowly tumbled to the ground. A thin stream of blood ran out of his mouth's corner and his eyes turned glazy.

Outwardly unmoved, Anthony withdrew his sword and flung it away. Justice had been done.

Marguerite and he exchanged a wordless conversation. His smoky gray eyes looked straight into her emerald ones and told her of his love.

Unconsciously, she moved a few steps forward until she was close to him. She neglected the bloodstains on his skin and clothing and pressed herself against his body. Automatically, his arms enclosed her and held her tight. Only then she let go of her emotions and allowed the tears to run freely. They only stopped when he kissed her.

Slowly, somebody in the crowd began to shout his appreciation. The rest of the onlookers joined him after a few seconds. The scene began to lose every bit of reality.

~ * ~

"Make way in the name of the Regent!"

The razor-sharp command cut through the night and worked as a shower of rain. Everybody returned to the present.

The servants reluctantly stepped aside and cleared the way for the detachment of the royal guard. Anthony let go of Marguerite. He immediately understood the soldiers were not there by accident. Someone of the household must have warned them.

The horses came to a snorting standstill. The officer in charge overlooked the scene. His face remained blank of expression as he greeted the count and the marchioness in a polite way--after all, they were no strangers to one another. He was one of those younger sons who started their career in the army and moved frequently at the court.

"You know the law, Monsieur?" he asked courteously, addressing Newton.

This one nodded, suddenly feeling the tiredness after this trying experience. He knew what was coming to him.

"Then I see myself obliged to arrest you. You may follow us in your carriage, m'lord Newton."

Marguerite turned pale, paler than she had been before. "You can't arrest him!" she cried out, getting hold of the officer's sleeve to attract his attention. "Please let me explain what happened. They were not just dueling, it was…"

"However I regret it, Madame," he interrupted her kindly, but firm in his denial, "I have to follow my orders. His Royal Highness, the Regent, has personally demanded that the winner of this duel should be arrested."

"It is not right! You can't arrest this man," she exclaimed.

"Leave it, Margie," Anthony intervened quietly. "This poor man is only doing his duty. We'll sort things out, don't you worry."

251

He gave her an encouraging smile then mounted his carriage which was still waiting in the street. The officer gave the signal to move on. As the coach pulled out, she lifted her skirts and hurried after it. "I'll go to the regent," she yelled into the night. "I won't settle until you're released and free of blame."

Her mouth set in a determined line as she stared into the darkness. She remained in the middle of the road until the last sound of the hooves and the wheels died down. Only then she turned slowly and headed back to the house where the servants still crowded together.

"Well, what are you all waiting for?" she asked angrily, showing no patience with them. "The body of your master has to be brought inside and somebody had better throw some water over those cobbles!"

Without a second glance to make sure her orders were followed, she disappeared into the house. Impressed by her regal bearing, the servants set to work.

By then it was almost morning. In the neighboring houses the first lights were lit. Some merchants appeared on the streets. Soon the story of the fight spread all over Paris.

Two

Marguerite was good for her word. After a few hours of sleep, she got up and bathed. Then she ordered Pauline to fetch a soft gray gown, laced with purple frills. The maid helped her in it and afterwards held up a cape, in the same purple hue as the trimmings of the gown.

By then the coach was waiting. Accompanied by her faithful page, Jeanot, she stepped in and ordered the coacher to ride to the palace. For the first time ever, she had used some tricks to soften the lines of fatigue on her face and to brighten up the color of her eyes. She had also discretely applied some soft pink to her lips and had sprayed some perfume over her wrists. She now felt ready to face the world.

Once arrived at the palace, she stated her business to one of the court's dignitaries and was shown into a small study. She sat down and prepared mentally for the words she was about to deliver.

The waiting took unnecessarily long. Only by calling upon her common sense, she managed to keep her calm. She convinced herself and Jeanot it would not help Anthony's cause if she burst out in a fury or started to show nervous shivers. She clenched her hands together and succeeded in preserving an unrevealing expression.

After what appeared an eternity, Philippe d'Orléans entered the room. She rose from her seat and sank down into a deep curtsy. The regent signaled her to rise. In the meantime, the boy Jeanot kept a respectful distance.

"I was told you urgently needed to speak to me, Madame," Philippe spoke. His tone suggested he did not quite agree with this intention.

She straightened her shoulders and answered his studying glance with an equal candid look. "I came to see you about Lord Newton, Your Highness."

The prince walked to the other side of the study, placed himself behind an elegant bureau and picked up some documents one of his secretaries had put there. He remained silent--the only sound Marguerite heard was the rustle of sheets being lifted and put down again.

"Have a seat, Madame," Philippe said at last, not even looking up from the papers. "I must admit, this looks quite serious--a duel in the middle of the street, a man dead--a personal friend of ours, by the way. Given the previous conviction of the prisoner this must be a capital offence."

Only then he looked up and eyed Marguerite interrogatively. "What interests me though, Madame d'Aubervilliers, is that you come to me in favor of your husband's murderer. Can you please explain why you are doing this?"

A faint smile appeared at the corners of her mouth. She thought his curiosity was typical. "Your Highness has heard the gossip too. Well then, I swear by the Holy Bible that I am not Lord Newton's mistress. I am his lawful wife."

Nobody could have acted more surprised than the man before her. To hide his astonishment, the prince adverted his face and coughed lightly. When he had resumed his composure, he addressed Marguerite again. "If this be true, it puts an entirely different light on the matter," he concluded. "Please give me more details, Madame."

His tone had softened noticeably. Marguerite acknowledged it by a graceful inclining of her head. She knew exactly how she would go on--she had spent the hours in bed to come up with a story which had a true ring to it.

"Your Highness, I'll try to make this as short as possible. You probably do know I suffered from loss of memory?"

The prince nodded. Her unfortunate circumstances were widely known in their circles.

"Because I did not remember what happened in the past, I trusted my brother Armand. He kept hidden from me that I married a man called Anthony St. Lawrence in 1711. I can only fathom his reasons for it. And so I allowed myself to become the bride of Etienne de Laneuil. And later on, when my dear Etienne died, I became the wife of marquis d'Aubervilliers." She stopped to breathe for a moment and noticed the prince listened attentively.

"During the festivities in honor of my birthday, I met Lord Newton. And believe it or not, that meeting triggered some memories and finally brought back my lost past. Can you understand my dilemma, Your Highness? All at once I found out I was a bigamist! I could not bring myself to admit everything to Hilaire straight away. Whatever I did, I knew I'd hurt one or the other."

"Indeed, you were in a difficult position," the prince had to admit. "But I fail to understand is how it came to yesterday's duel? Marquis d'Aubervilliers is--was--a reasonable man. Killing him was hardly necessary."

"That's what I thought myself," she agreed softly. "I knew the marquis as an attentive and understanding man."

She did not even blink her eyes. Sometimes the truth in itself is not enough, and needs some half-truths which sound more convincing. If she was to rescue Anthony and bring him home with her, it was imperative she told a colored image of yesterday's events.

She continued: "Recently, however, strange things began to happen. My chambermaid died, poisoned by a drink meant for me. And only last night cutthroats pursued me. If it had not been for Lord Newton's interference, I would not have reached my house alive. I had not yet put this frightful experience behind me when Hilaire arrived home and literally confessed he was behind these attempts. Evidently, Anthony challenged him to a duel. It was fought openly, with myself and our servants as witnesses. I thank God the one to die was Hilaire--after all, he was nothing but a vile murderer!"

Philippe d'Orléans looked clearly shaken. His nervousness showed in the way he played with the ring around his index finger. "That is a daring remark, Madame. And have you proof of this?"

Marguerite's cheeks unexpectedly turned red and her eyes sparkled fire. She stood up from the chair so abruptly it smashed to the ground. She leaned over the bureau.

She brought her face so close to the prince he drew back in his seat.

"Proof!" she sneered. "Do you doubt my word, *Monsieur le prince?* May I remind you then I am equally one of King Henri the Fourth's descendants? I was born a Vallencieux."

The prince was still so much impressed by her behavior he could only shake his head in denial. At the same time his admiration for this formidable woman grew. It took courage, he knew, to withstand even the highest authorities. "I would not dare to doubt your word, *ma chère dame*--or should I say dear lady?" he whispered.

She had the decency to blush. "Your Highness, I beg your forgiveness," she stammered. "My emotions run away with me. Of course I have proof."

Philippe d'Orléans smiled. "Now that we agree on d'Aubervillier's guilt, I would not mind hearing the entire story, lady Newton."

She nodded her consent and started talking, keeping carefully to the story she had made up, and which linked the current events to the old murder of Isabelle de Saint-Laurent. It was already past noon when the regent finally signed a release form that would permit Anthony to leave the Bastille as a free man. He also promised her he would do everything in his might to grant the count a full rehabilitation.

~ * ~

When dusk came, Marguerite welcomed her husband home. Apart from the state in which his dress appeared--his shirt was still stained with blood--he looked well and rested. His wounds had been looked after and had been dressed. The tired lines around his mouth were gone.

When he caught sight of her, he donned her a loving smile and suddenly seemed a lot younger than his thirty-nine years. He opened his arms and wrapped her up in a tender embrace. "I assume you are responsible for my release?" he asked, although he knew the answer. While talking, he walked her to a sofa and put his arm around her shoulders.

"I had a thorough conversation with the regent," she told him. "When I finished, he immediately signed your release form and promised me everything will be set to right. Hilaire's properties will be confiscated by the crown but should be given to you as a kind of retribution. His guilt to Isabelle's murder will be announced publicly. Concerning my situation, I'm permitted to keep Etienne's inheritance because I did not commit bigamy knowingly."

He cut her short by covering her mouth with his.
"Let that wait until tomorrow, my love," he whispered into her ear. "Right now my mind is not set on talking."

Three

One month passed. Cuddled up in their bed, Marguerite grabbed Anthony's hand. "There's something I have to tell you, my love," she said softly.

He smiled tenderly, never bored to hear her witness how much she loved him. "You did not have another conversation with the Regent, I presume?" he answered, trying to tease her. Philippe d'Orléans often sought Marguerite's presence nowadays, even called her '*ma chère cousine*'. And for once he was true to his word. Only one week after his release from the Bastille, he and Marguerite were invited to the Louvre, where young King Louis officially granted him rehabilitation. Afterwards, the regent had handed him the deeds to the possessions of his stepfather, Monsieur de Montfort and to those of Hilaire d'Aubervilliers.

These donations made him a very rich man. And there was something else as well.

"I have some news for you, too," he confided. "Who goes first?"

"You do," she said. "I can see you are a bit worried."

He nodded. "I received another letter from the Duke of Shrevenport's physician," he said. "Apparently, the old man is not too well and he urgently wants to see me. I have to travel to Marsden Castle as soon as possible."

"Of course you must go," she agreed. "He is your grandfather after all. But you'll have to go on your own."

Her words surprised him. "Don't you want to accompany me? What do you have against England?"

"Nothing," she assured him. "Comes the time, I'll gladly live there, as long as you are with me. But right now, I like to stay here where I have a family to help me."

"Help with what?"

She squeezed his hand rather tightly. "Because we are going to have a child," she whispered. So many years she had thought herself to be infertile. All through her long marriage to Etienne, and afterwards while being with Hilaire, she had been unable to conceive. When the miracle happened, she could not believe it at first. She had waited another month just to make sure. Tears sprung in her eyes when she watched her husband's face.

A light sprang up in Anthony's eyes when he heard her news and a slow smile curled around his lips. Then he hugged her oh so tenderly. "My love," he breathed. "That is the best news ever! I love you and will cherish you and our child for as long as I live."

"I know that," she responded. "I love you too. I can't wait for the moment when I can hold the little one in my arms."

"Are you feeling well?" he wanted to know, suddenly realizing there were risks when a woman her age conceived a baby.

She nodded. "I went to see a midwife last week--the one my cousin Chantale used to deliver her babies. Madame Gentier told me I should not worry, all is going well."

"No problems with morning sickness?"

She smiled. "No, not yet. And Madame told me this sickness normally occurs during the first three months of the pregnancy. Some women never feel sick, apparently."

He kissed her another time, more ardently this time. "You are wise not to go to England right now. Just stay here or go visit your cousin. I'm sure you ladies will be happy enough to talk about babies and confinements."

"I've heard a lot of these stories already," she said.

"I shall make the journey as short. I'll see my grandfather, but I'll return to you as soon as possible."

~ * ~

When Anthony returned to France in June, six weeks later, it was as the Ninth Duke of Shrevenport. Marguerite was glad to see him, because she was bored with life in Paris. Although she liked her cousin very much, she hated the fact that her house became the place to be. Day after day, visitors called and were dying to meet the new duchess. It had not taken long for all of Paris to learn about the events and now everyone wanted to befriend them.

Marguerite categorically refused to see anyone apart from her old friends. She felt only hatred for all those who had once denied her husband entrance to their homes and had made him a social outcast. Now their fortune had changed, they chose to forget this. But not she! She used her pregnancy as an excuse to keep to her rooms and not entertain visitors.

"I'm done with Paris," she told Anthony after he had taken a bath and was sitting down to the evening meal they took in their private room.

He gave her a sharp look, understanding what she meant. "We can go somewhere else," he agreed. "Didn't Etienne leave you a house in the country?"

"He did," she said. "But I have an even better suggestion. Why not go to Vallencieux and spend the summer there?"

"Vallencieux? That's your old home," he responded. "Why now, my dear?"

She stood up and went to her desk. "Because I got this letter." She handed it over to him. "It is from my brother René. You remember I told you he immigrated to Canada? When Armand died, our solicitor wrote to him, telling him he'd become the next count. We had to wait very long for an answer. But finally it arrived."

Anthony studied the contents. "Your brother married Blanche, the daughter of a surgeon from Montréal, and he has a son who's named after your father."

"More importantly," she added, "he plans on returning to France. When all goes well, the ship should arrive by August."

"You were quite fond of that younger brother, I remember."

"Yes, we were the best of friends. And that is why I'd like to discuss something else with you."

He could see the determination in her eyes and knew already no argument of his would stop her. He smiled. "What do you want to tell me, my love?"

"The old castle is in ruins, you must have noticed when we visited a couple of months ago. Now that we are so wealthy, I thought I could use the money Etienne left me to make Vallencieux as prosperous as it once used to be."

He nodded and it was obvious his respect for her grew. "So good of you, my dear. I'm sure your brother will appreciate your generosity."

"You'll need to oversee the work," she told him. "The roof is in dire need of renovation, as are most of the rooms in the castle. And the tenants and farmhands live in worn-down cottages. They also deserve new buildings."

And so was done. Not much later, the Shrevenports and their servants set off to Burgundy, where a big feast celebrated their arrival at the castle.

~ * ~

Marguerite lazily leaned out of the window in the sunny tower room she loved so much. Looking down, she smiled as she spotted Anthony, who rode over the fields in the company of the estate manager. How well he did look! Gone were the worried lines which aged his face. In fact, he looked much younger than his thirty-nine years.

In the distance she spotted another rider. Could that finally be a messenger to announce the arrival of her brother?

When the rider kept urging on his horse, as if the devil was at his feet, she studied him closer. There was something familiar about it. At last she was able to distinguish his face. It was Cartouche!

She left the tower room and hurried down the stairs, not paying attention to her condition. She reached the courtyard at the same time the gang leader reined his steaming horse to a standstill.

"You appear to be in a hurry, my friend," she joked, with a broad smile on her lips.

Cartouche threw a worried look over his shoulder. "They're closing in on me," he breathed. "Are you prepared to give refuge to an outlaw?"

She did not answer, simply took the reins of the spent horse. She led it to the stables and relieved it of its saddle then told the stable lad to rub the horse dry and give it water. She invited Cartouche to accompany her to the living quarters.

"You need a bath," she told him, after a look at his dusted clothes and face. "Then we'll decide what to do. I believe we can use an extra hand at the castle."

"The bath can wait. I'm dying of thirst!"

She laughed and poured him a drink. At her invitation, he let himself fall into an easy chair. She sat down herself, curious to learn what had happened to him. "How did you get into this tight situation?"

He grinned. ""A trap, of course. Yesterday morning we held up a coach, just outside Saint-Cloud. Before we knew it soldiers surrounded us. It was sheer luck I managed to break through their cordon--I don't even know if any of the others had the same luck. From Jeanot I knew you are spending the summer at Vallencieux, so I spurred on my mount and headed in that direction. Unfortunately, my path crossed with that of a military patrol. Those guys were much too curious to my taste, and again I had a narrow escape. How could I venture they would follow me this far?"

"Won't you ever change?" she sighed. Her voice sounded unhappy.

He shook his head, looking at once less worried. "Don't spend any pity on me, Marguerite. I have chosen this life and I am well aware of what will happen to me in the end. I don't see any reason for stopping my activities."

"In any case, you're welcome to stay here as long as you see fit. We won't turn you in."

"I know," he acknowledged, reaching out for her hand so he could kiss it. "I thank you from the bottom of my heart, Duchesse. By the way, if I may be so frank, you look radiant."

A light blush appeared on her cheeks because his admiring glances did not escape her notice. She still had not figured out exactly what her feelings towards the Parisian gang leader were. He was a friend, of course, but much more than that. She knew all too well he loved her in his own way and this knowledge had the unsettling capacity of making her nervous in some fashion. "I'm well, Dominique," she finally replied in response to his compliment.

"And are you happy?"

Now she could answer without hesitation. "As never before," she beamed. "I have a loving husband and this." Her hand made a gesture towards her swollen stomach. "I can't tell you how much I look forward to the arrival of this baby. I thought I'd never have the chance of holding my own in my arms."

"Aha," Cartouche responded.

His reaction surprised her but she did not give it a lot of attention. She picked up her embroidery frame--now she had to restrain from bodily efforts, she was finally becoming a lady who did all the right things--and did some needlework while the gang leader drank his wine. Then she sent him off to wash.

~ * ~

Later that afternoon Anthony returned from his inspection tour. He came looking for his wife and found her in the drawing room with their guest. A stroke of jealousy shot through his body. Old distrusts lead a wary life and it took him a fragment of a second to take control again, after which he was able to greet the visitor cordially. "Look who's here," he said. "Our old friend Cartouche in person!"

The two men exchanged glances. Cartouche's attitude told the older man he had accepted the situation. A slow smile spread around his lips. "Your

Grace," he exclaimed in a quasi-humble fashion. "Your wife was so kind as to offer hospitality to a weary traveler."

Marguerite hastened to explain the true reasons for Cartouche's visit to her husband, a little bit afraid of how he would treat him.

"You are welcome," she heard to her relief. "How could we refuse you shelter? After all, don't we all belong to the same brotherhood?"

"That is true, but I thank you both anyway."

"You can stay for as long as you want," Anthony stated. "And while you're here, you can perhaps assist us in a certain manner."

Cartouche appeared to be taken aback. "Why?" he asked. "I thought you'd be rich enough by now."

Anthony could not resist giving him a hard slap on the shoulder, while he laughed heartily. "Explanations, man! Margie and I are keen to hear some answers to questions we were unable to solve."

"Are you?" Cartouche responded, obvioulsy quick to understand only he could tell them how and why some things in the past had happened. He settled in his easy chair again and held up his glass. "Could I have some more wine, before you start to interrogate me?"

The duke obliged him personally and took a glass himself. A pensive look was on his face while he sipped his wine. It took some time before he offered his first question to Cartouche. "Why did you leave me thinking Marguerite had died?" He remembered too well how shocked he had been when he saw her at that ball in November--not a ghost returned from the dead, but a living woman. "You told me I wouldn't see her back in the world of the living," he continued. "I almost choked when I was invited to a ball last year and stood face to face with a woman who resembled Duchesse like two drops of water. It left me very unsure of myself."

Louis-Dominique nodded in agreement. "Probably you won't approve with my motives, *mon ami*," he said. "I honestly confess jealousy played an undeniable role in the whole of it. Duchesse was...is...very dear to me. I knew she was having a hard time while she shared your house, and when her brother took her along to Burgundy it looked like the best solution at that time. Better still, when I found out she had no recollection of the past, I congratulated myself. For you, she might as well have been dead. Don't forget in what state you were yourself. You were badly wounded and fighting for your life. You made a slow recovery. Your old housekeeper did not leave you out of her sight and the Scotsman could only be restrained with difficulty of going after Armand de Vallencieux. Those were troubled times indeed."

"Yet it would have been better had you told me," Anthony mused. "Her supposed death hit me harder than I could have imagined, and most certainly slowed down my recovery. When I could finally stand on my legs again, I didn't give a damn about anything anymore. And that was when I began to win lots of money with my cards. Enough money to pay my way back into society. I borrowed huge sums without interest to Philippe d'Orléans and obliged him to me. Then my uncle and two nephews died and I became the next Earl of Newton."

At last Marguerite saw fit to intervene. "I believe I can understand your motivation, Dominique," she said with a slow smile. "However, what is still not clear to me is the reason why you left *me* in the dark. You could have told me I was a married woman, so my marriage to Etienne need never have taken place."

Cartouche shook his head. "Be realistic, Marguerite," he told her. ""You suffered from amnesia. You did not even recognize your own brother! How would you have reacted when a shady figure did pop up at Vallencieux, claiming you used to live among the vagabonds of Paris and had become the wife of a professional gambler? Be honest and admit to the fact you would not have believed me. And your brother would have me thrown out."

Marguerite remained silent for a moment. "Perhaps you're right," she sighed then but her voice did not sound wholly convinced.

Cartouche sensed her reservations and added, "Moreover, do you forget that not long before those dreadful events, you confided in me and told me how unhappy your relationship with the Chevalier was? You were so sure he did not love you."

"But I did!" Anthony exclaimed, grasping his wife's hand. "Only, at that time I was afraid to admit to it."

"Yes, I was wrong in that aspect," Cartouche gave in. "I realized later on. But by then I had enough reasons to thank God for all my interferences."

"In the end, it all worked out," Margot acknowledged. "Ten years ago I was a stubborn and arrogant child. When I met Anthony for the second time, it was as a grown woman. I could recognize the love I began to feel for him as the true feeling, and I could believe him when he swore he loved me. From then on we really could trust each other."

"And you're living a happy and peaceful life now," her friend concluded. "No more assaults. By the way, did the necklace I gave you for your birthday indeed play such an important role in the line of events?"

"Indeed. The marquis was obsessed by it. He would do anything in order to possess it."

"You're still well-informed," Anthony remarked.

"Of course. Don't I have my private spy in your household? How is my nephew, by the way? Does he behave himself?"

"Jeanot is a dear child and he behaves impeccably," Margot hastened to say. "We are all quite fond of him. I hope you won't object if we take him along to England shortly? He has asked to accompany us there."

"Isn't that marvelous?" Cartouche said cheerfully. "The boy is looking forward to a grand future indeed."

While talking, he stood up from his chair and set down his empty glass. "And now, my dear friends, with your permission I wish to retire to my room. I haven't slept for two days."

Four

Three days later two carriages, heavily loaded with luggage and people and accompanied by a mounted escort, reached Vallencieux. The old castle had undergone a thorough change in the past year and now made a proud impression. The banner with the crest of the Vallencieux family flew proudly from the highest tower and the welcome committee stood waiting at the entrance.

Marie--now a well-respected gray haired housekeeper--scolded two young kitchen maids who were wiggling their skirts and giggling nervously. "Girls, behave!" she demanded of them.

Marguerite, who stood two steps higher, stretched her neck in order to be the first to spot a glimpse of the nearing coaches.

A spontaneous round of cheering went up as soon as the horses trotted down the lane. The first of the vehicles came to a standstill in the courtyard. Lackeys hurried to the carriage door in order to be of assistance to the new count and his wife. On opening the doors, they offered their hand so the passengers could easily step out.

Marguerite completely forgot her newly acquired dignity and flew forward to take her brother in her arms. "René, how good to see you well!"

René underwent this demonstration of sisterly love with a grin on his lips. Then he held her at arm's length and studied her appearance more closely.

The grin changed into a broad smile, which rendered his tanned face a boyish charm. "But you've become a beauty, *petite soeur*! Who could have imagined our wildcat would turn into an elegant lady? Marguerite, you amaze me."

Her laughter rang through the air. "Flatterer! *You* are the one who's changed. You're almost a head taller and you look--well, tougher. O René, I think it is so wonderful you've come home again! And now I would like to be introduced to your lovely wife."

"My pleasure," René hastened to say.

He let her loose and reached for the hand of the slender fair-haired young woman, who had stood by somewhat timidly and apparently taken aback by the grandeur of the reception.

"Marguerite, my dear, this is Blanche, my wonderful wife. *Chérie*, meet my sister, Madame la Marquise d'Aubervilliers."

Marguerite did not respond to this wrongful introduction immediately. She extended her hand to Blanche then kissed her warmly on the cheeks.

Blanche responded, but nevertheless the look of caution did not leave her eyes. Experience told her how deceptive appearances could be. Therefore she was always careful when meeting strangers.

"Welcome to Vallencieux, Blanche," Marguerite tried to break the light tension, quickly studing René's wife. Blanche was not a beauty in the real sense, but her big eyes betrayed intelligence, peace of mind and determination. She would certainly be a good companion to René, who needed a mind stronger than his to guide him. "I do sincerely hope this will become a real home to you, and you'll be able to have a merry life here," she continued. "When René and I were children, this was certainly the happiest place to grow up. We should try to become not only sisters but friends as well," she ended in the hope the Canadian would accept her offer.

"You are very kind, Madame," Blanche answered in a soft voice, still under the impression of her sister-in-law's impeccable appearance and elegant manners. *Une très grande dame*, she thought. *I hope she won't look down on me, as I'm only a country lass.* Her gaze fell on Marguerite's swollen middle. Her lips curled lightly. "I too wish we can become friends, Marguerite. At least we have one thing in common."

She dared to lay a hand on Marguerite's arm and leaned over. "I'm also expecting a child," she whispered into her ear. "I expect my *petit bébé* in the month of January."

"Mine is coming in November," a surprised Marguerite answered. "But *chérie*, how have you dared to undertake such a strenuous journey in your condition?"

"We *Canadiens* are used to hardships," Blanche responded, now with a proud attitude. "*Les Laurentides*, the region where we had our farm, is rough and primitive. I loved living there."

"This woman doesn't know the meaning of fear," René bragged. "She always accompanied her father on his rounds through the hills and wilderness, and sometimes they were gone for weeks on end. She mounts a horse like the best of men and handles the pistol with a skilled hand."

Marguerite smiled at the insinuation. Then she remembered her manners and insisted Blanche enter the castle. "Take command of your new realm, sister," she invited. "The *chateau* is all yours now. Inside chilled wine and fresh fruits are waiting, and the chambermaids have filled your bathtub with perfumed water. Don't worry about your little son; our trusted Marie has already taken care of him. Jaques will be in the best of hands with her. Come in and have a rest."

She hooked an arm through Blanche's and started to mount the stairs.

~ * ~

René hesitated shortly in following them, trying to figure out what had caused the obvious changes to the old ruins he remembered from his childhood.

Anthony, who had kept to the background, spotted his quizzical glances. "It's not quite the old castle anymore, is it?"" he remarked, stepping closer. "By the way, I think I'd better introduce myself, as my wife seems to have forgotten. I am your brother-in-law."

"Ah, the distinguished marquis," René smiled. "I wondered where you might be."

"Always in the vicinity, my dear chap," Anthony replied. "Only I must point out a small misunderstanding."

"Which is?"

"I am not the Marquis d'Aubervilliers. My name is Anthony St. Lawrence, and I am the Duke of Shrevenport."

A whistle escaped René's lips. "Well, I'll be damned. Has Marguerite been up to her old tricks again? When she sent word to me, she wrote about Etienne's death and her marriage to Hilaire d'Aubervilliers. That was in February. I must admit I find it difficult to apprehend how it is possible she became a widow for the second time so soon afterwards, and found a new husband in the course of seven month's time."

Anthony laughed. "When put like that, it sounds strange indeed," he agreed.

"I suppose you can explain?" René demanded, showing his brotherly concern.

"I can and I will, " Anthony said. "But it's a long story. Relating everything that took place will have to wait until you have freshened up and we sit down to dinner.

~ * ~

Marguerite had arranged an extensive welcome home dinner for the new count and his spouse. The family sat down to it, savoring the rich food and the seasoned wine.

When the servants cleared away the last of the empty plates, Anthony poured brandy for René and himself, while the two ladies had another glass of white wine.

"And now I'd like to hear your story," René said. "I've been dying to hear what happened here during my absence."

"I shall begin," Marguerite announced. "You most certainly remember the night when you helped me to escape the castle?"

René nodded.

"Well, I rode my horse to the next village where Claude de Bassy was waiting for me."

With the help of Anthony, she then went on to relate all the events leading to the death of marquis d'Aubervilliers.

Réné looked thoroughly stunned. Different emotions could be read on his face, varying from disbelief at first to wonder, anger and shame towards the end of the story.

~ * ~

"And so it all happened," Marguerite concluded. "As soon as our child is born, Anthony and I will board a ship to bring us to England and we'll settle at Marsden Castle. I realize it will be a big change for me, but I look forward to it."

Not only she, but the rest of the audience, were startled by René's reaction. He began to swear whole-heartedly. Anthony frowned and Marguerite stared at him.

"What's the matter, *chéri*?" Blanche hastened to ask.

René stopped cursing and looked at her, clearly unhappy. Only when he saw the encouragement in her eyes, he dared to address his sister once more. ""You'll never forgive me," he exclaimed, the words rolling out of his mouth like a waterfall. "My God, I always knew Armand was a villain, but right now I could kill him!"

"He's already dead," Anthony stated dryly.

"I wish he were alive, so I could challenge him to a duel," René insisted.

Marguerite shook her head. "You don't know what you're saying," she spoke. "You could never do that. After all, he was your brother."

271

"How can you speak so?" he went on. "After all he did to you! Don't tell me that you mourn him."

"But I do," she stated with firm conviction. " I can't pretend I was very fond of Armand, but hate is such a consuming feeling. The only thing it does is to destroy the one who cherishes it. I've put all that behind me. Now I am glad that at least, at the end of his life, he tried to make up with me. Who of us can really judge what went on in his head? Perhaps the things he did were, from his point of view, the right moves."

"I don't believe what I hear," her brother said. "Marguerite, he decided about your future. And not only your own, but also that of your child!"

These last three words rendered Marguerite speechless. How could she have forgotten the fact she was carrying Anthony's child when he and Armand fought their duel?

Her eyes desperately sought Anthony's. He knew it was time to speak up. "Of course I knew about the child," he told her. "Even though you did not mention it anymore. I assumed you lost the baby, due to the terrible events."

She nodded in agreement. "Of course, it must have been like that. In the other case, don't you think the good nuns of the convent would have told me I had a child?"

The tension rose as René thought over his words. He coughed.

"The child--a boy--came into the world alive," he finally declared, although hesitatingly. "I'm sorry, Marguerite. I'm not at all proud of myself. Armand intended to send your baby to an orphanage and I was too weak to protest against it. I tried, but he fenced with his rights as your guardian over both you and me. I was too afraid to go against his wishes. And so he carried out his plans. Immediately after the birth, the child was taken away from you. The nuns would provide a home for him. Not much later I left for Canada. Our brother graciously offered to pay my sea fare and gave me money to start me off. It was nothing but a bribe. Since then it has been a burden on my conscience."

For a while Marguerite was not able to speak. She swallowed hard and tears ran down her cheeks. Then finally she whispered. "My child... is alive." Her hand blindly searched for Anthony's presence.

He hurried to her side. "We'll get our son back," he stated firmly and reassuringly. "It cannot be very difficult. The convent surely will keep records of everything that goes on there, and one of the good sisters will be able to tell us to which orphanage the boy was brought."

"That won't be necessary."

Cartouche had discretely entered the drawing room some time ago, and had quietly listened to all that was said. Up to this point he had seen no reason to make his presence felt, but now the time had come.

The duke and duchess were not bothered by his presence, but the count of Vallencieux eyed him suspiciously. "And whom might you be?" he demanded.

Anthony was the first to answer. "Dominique is a long-time friend," he said. "Marguerite and I owe him a lot. He's the one who introduced her to the street life of Saint-Denis."

Recognition dawned on René's face. "You are Cartouche! The one our entire police force is hunting down!"

"And they will never find him here," Marguerite interrupted. "We have given our word."

The tone of these words was so firm René apparently forgot his urge to report the whereabouts of the gang leader to the officials of the province. His mouth opened and shut. Quietly he returned to his wife's side, where he found the comfort he needed.

"I believe you wanted to tell us something, Dominique?" Anthony changed the subject. "Do you have information on our lost son?"

Cartouche grinned, showing his perfect white teeth. "I can tell you where he is right now," he teased. "Didn't I tell you so? I've been following the course of your lives with keen interest. Did you really think the birth of your son and heir would have escaped my attention?"

Behind his back, he pulled the bell rope. Only a couple of seconds later the young page Jeanot entered the room, ready to serve his mistress. Like he had learned, he knelt down beside her.

Marguerite did not immediately notice the boy's presence. When she caught sight of him, she waved him off impatiently. "I haven't called for you, child. Please leave us alone," she told him. Without further notice, she turned to Cartouche again.

"Speak up, Dominique! Does it give you pleasure to have us in uncertainty?"

He shook his head and smiled at the nervousness which sounded through her words. At the same time he managed to get hold of Jeanot's sleeve, just before the boy tried to disappear. "Not so fast my boy. I have decided that at last the moment has come to introduce you to your parents."

Jeanot was clearly in distress. "But my parents died a long time ago," he stammered. "Anyway, you always told me so, uncle. My mother died when she gave birth to me and my father was just a soldier who lost his life in one or other battle."

Cartouche pulled the boy closer to his body and stroked the thick dark hair. "I lied to you," he said honestly. "So many years ago, you needn't know the truth because it would only have distressed you. Your parents are alive. Your mother is a courageous lady and your father is a noble man," he declared, softly pushing the boy in the direction of the duke and duchess. "These, my boy, are your parents: His Grace, the Duke of Shrevenport, and Her Grace, the Duchess."

More tears dripped out of Marguerite's eyes but she wiped them away with a hasty gesture. Why should she weep at such a time of joy? She still could not fathom how it had become possible, but she had her son back.

Mother and son kept staring at each other--one consuming glance which conveyed everything they longed to know. Then Marguerite spread her arms and the boy hurried to her embrace. The salt of her tears mingled with his as they hugged and kissed.

It was quite a moving scene to those who witnessed it, and it took some time before all consternation died away. Only then Cartouche could start his explanation.

"I'm sure you're dying to know how all of this came about. Well, my dear Duchesse, do you remember Angèle?"

Marguerite thought for a moment. "Wasn't she the redhead who belonged to Pierre's band of girls?"

"Correct. Well, not so long after you were brought to the convent in Dijon, the police arrested Angèle. She was sentenced to serve time in a convent. Because she happened to come from Burgundy, just like you, she was sent to the same convent in Dijon where you were staying."

"Speaking of a miracle," Marguerite smiled, because she knew this would have been arranged as well.

Cartouche returned her smile. "We needed someone inside that convent. Angèle could tell you everything that happened. She told us when the child was born and found out when and how it would be brought to the sister convent in Paris. What else could we do but wait for them in ambush? We grabbed the child from the old nun who guarded him then brought the boy to a friend of mine who could nurse the baby."

"But why did you keep quiet about it?" Anthony asked.

"I thought it best at that time," Cartouche said. "Duchesse had lost all memories of what happened, and nobody knew how long it would take for her to gain back recollection. And you, my friend, still were branded as a murderer. I thought that for a child, this would weigh heavier than having an uncle who earned his way by robbing people's pockets. Besides, then was not the right time for revelations. You were too busy trying to make a success of your gambling house and you wouldn't have had time to care for a baby. I truly believe I was able to provide Jeanot with a happy childhood. After all, he was everyone's darling."

"Yes," Jeanot piped up. "I never lacked anything."

~ * ~

Anthony slowly nodded his head. There was truth indeed in Cartouche's reasoning. Yet the old envy popped up once more. Everything the man had done, had been for Marguerite and not so much for him. Cartouche had wanted to protect his wife and had wanted to bring the boy to her. Thinking about it, he realized that having the boy around would have meant so much to him. Perhaps he would have ceased to seek revenge so feverishly, perhaps having a child around would have changed his life, would have brought some joy in this dark period.

"And further?" he asked.

"Marguerite married Monsieur de Laneuil, and when he obtained the post of Attorney-General, the couple moved to live in Paris. A happy household, people told me. Unfortunately the marriage remained childless. One of the maids, whom I befriended, told me Madame longed for a baby and not having one caused her deep sorrow. What else could I do but give Madame what she wanted? Well, not exactly a baby but a young boy by then. I succeeded in bringing Jeanot into her household. We even set up a little charade. I knew Marguerite would not stand by idly and have a child arrested. And our trick worked out nicely! She took Jeanot into her protection and allowed him to accompany her to her house. He'd become her little page. It did not take long to notice how fond of the boy she became. Surely that must have been the motherly instinct. Just think of the grand plans she had for her page."

Finally, Anthony's lips curled into a genuine smile. Cartouche was a rascal but he had directed their lives in a masterful manner. He could better forget his deeply-rooted distrust and foster the friendship that was building up between them. After all, the gang leader had proved to be a good loser. "I thank you, my friend," he said in all honesty. "You've taken care of your charge more than properly. Jeanot is a fine lad: brave, quick-witted and loyal. He's everything we could wish for."

He touched the curly head of his son and answered his inquiring look. A feeling of pride took possession of him when he realized the boy behaved remarkably well under these surprising circumstances. How strange that neither he or his wife had spotted the definite resemblance Jeanot bore with Marguerite's father. How could they have been so blind? The boy moved daily through the house yet they had thought nothing of it.

"Can you also see it, my dear?" he asked Marguerite. "Do you see how he takes after your father and René?"

"I can now," she answered. "Oh yes, he is definitely a Vallencieux!"

Anthony took another look at his son. How would the future develop for the four of them? How would Jeanot behave in the knowledge he was no longer an ordinary child, but the heir apparent of a duke?

It was as if Cartouche could read his mind. "Never worry, *mon ami*," he said. "The child is not spoilt by the place or the people he grew up with. And he longs to learn. He'll adapt to his new way of living without any problems."

"Jeanot's behavior is always impeccable," Marguerite intervened, taking her child into protection. "You can count on him in all circumstances."

The boy freed himself of her embrace and brushed away the tears that wetted his cheeks. He felt a bit ashamed for them. Tears were for little children. What did he have to do now? Would it not be best if he said something? His uncle--he would keep considering Cartouche as his uncle, even more so than count René--nodded his approval.

"I thank you for telling the whole story, uncle," he said, feeling more sure of himself already. "I also think Madame Marguerite is a sweet lady and I could not wish for a better mother. Next to that, I always felt admiration for Lord Newton--the duke. I suppose I'd want to become like you, father."

Anthony grinned. "I'd rather you stayed your old self. I don't want you to commit the same mistakes I once made. Remember what you learned in Saint-Denis and combine it with what you'll discover later. And never lose the respect for the man who raised you as his son."

"Never!" Jeanot swore passionately. "We all belong to the same brotherhood, don't we?"

Then, with the quick change of mood so typical for children, he became fascinated with another idea. "I am a lord now, am I not? Milor' Newton! I think I can better start taking up English."

"We'll do that together," Marguerite said when the laughter died away. "Isn't it grand? An English duchess and an earl who only speak French?"

Five

The great sails of the three-master Mermaid were set to the wind and graciously billowed westward. Slowly the vessel moved away from the quay. The wind blew rather fiercely, and soon the mainland was only a vague line of brown earth and green grass against the horizons. From then on there was only gray water around them.

A bit aside of the busy crew and the other passengers stood the Duke of Shrevenport, his wife and son. Their gaze still in the direction of the French coast. They did not yet exchange words, still savored the memories of the land they left behind.

After what looked like hours, Marguerite opened the leather purse she held in the palm of her hand. For a last time she stared at the magnificent string of diamonds it contained.

"Are you completely sure?" her husband inquired.

She nodded her head. "Yes. We have discussed it over and over again. I honestly believe this is the best thing to do."

Quickly, before she could feel even the faintest pang of regret, she closed the purse and held her hand over the railing. With a splash the Medici diamonds disappeared into the deep. The water ruffled up a bit but soon nothing could be seen anymore. From now on the diamonds would rest on the bottom of the sea, where they could cause no more harm.

Marguerite let go of a deep sigh and caught the arm of her husband in a tight grip. She felt relieved of a heavy burden. She had not only parted with the necklace, but also with all the bad memories of the past. Now a new leaf could be filled with only happy memories. "Let's go to our cabin," she urged Anthony. "I want to check if the nurse has looked after the baby. Besides, I want to hold her in my arms and cuddle her before she goes to sleep again."

"I don't understand how people can be so fond of little babies!" the eleven-year-old John remarked with a grin. "She only bites my fingers!"

Of course, he was just as fond of the now six-month-old baby, Anne. She had rapidly captured his heart and already she managed to push through her own will. Since the day she was born, her parents and older brother had become her devoted slaves.

While they mounted the stairs to the rear deck, the boy looked down at the sea for a moment. Between his teeth he hissed: "Good riddance! Those damned diamonds have caused enough trouble for us."

Epilogue
Somewhere in Brittany, eight years later

The little girl was playing between the rocks in the cove. An older woman, dressed in black and wearing the white bonnet of the Breton women, kept a discrete eye on her.

"Not too far, *chérie*!" she warned the girl, before closing her eyes again.

"I won't, Dame Rozenn!"

The child, apparently not afraid to get wet, splashed happily around, digging up shellfish and other creatures from the sea. Some time passed away. It was a quiet afternoon in June.

The nurse had settled on a flat rock and was almost lulled to sleep by the monotonous breaking of the waves and the tedious shrieks of seagulls. She did not hear the girl's happy laughter as the tiny fingers felt something heavy buried in the moist sand.

Using both her hands, the girl dug the package out of its hiding place and undid it of the seaweed and dirt which clung to it. Then, finding it difficult to untie the cords holding the leather purse together, she hurried to the woman and pulled at her sleeve. Her excited voice woke up her guardian. "*Régardez!*"

The wet purse was dropped into Rozenn's lap. The nurse was urged to try her best in revealing the contents by the impatient child.

With a lot of patience and the use of a sharp stick found on the beach, she finally managed it.

Even under their layer of dirt and other remains of the sea, the string of diamonds sparkled as never before...

"Where did you find these, sweetheart?" she asked, not too urgently. She did not want to alarm the girl.

"I wanted to pick up this stick, and something was tied to it. I had to dig a hole in the sand to get it out!"

"This must be worth a fortune," murmured Dame Rozenn.

"What does that mean?"

The nurse finally regained her composure. "It means you will have a very nice dowry when you are old enough to marry, my dear. We will keep this safe for you. In the meantime, I will contact Père Dupuis and he can lock it away somewhere in the church."

"And I can have it when I'm old enough?"

"You will, sweetheart."

The Medici necklace was locked away. It rested patiently in its new hiding place, biding its time.

About the Author

Nickie Fleming was born and raised in the historical town of Dendermonde, Belgium, home of the legendary Horse Bayard. Now she spends her time between Dendermonde and her family's flat on the North Sea Coast.

She Studied English and Dutch literature and grammar at the University of Ghent, where she received her Master's Degree. She started working as a high school teacher, a job she loves as it brings her into contact with a variety of people and keeps her young.

VISIT OUR WEBSITE
FOR THE FULL INVENTORY
OF QUALITY BOOKS:

http://www.roguephoenixpress.com

Rogue Phoenix Press
Representing Excellence in Publishing

Quality trade paperbacks and downloads
in multiple formats,
in genres ranging from historical
to contemporary romance,
mystery and science fiction.
Visit the website then bookmark it.
We add new titles each month!

www.ingramcontent.com/pod-product-compliance
Lightning Source LLC
Chambersburg PA
CBHW051416170626
46809CB00006B/2186